A Studio On Bleecker Street

A Novel of the Gilded Age

Joseph P. Garland

DermodyHouse.com

Copyright © 2020 Joseph P. Garland
All rights reserved.

The characters and events portrayed in this book are fictitious. Any similarity to real persons, living or dead, is coincidental and not intended by the author.

No part of this book may be reproduced, stored in a retrieval system, or transmitted in any form or by any means, electronic, mechanical, photocopying, recording, or otherwise without the express written permission of the author.

ISBN:
978-1-7355923-6-7 (ebook)
978-1-7355923-5-0 (paperback)
9798432851048 (hardcover (KDP))

The cover image is a self-portrait by Ukrainian artist Marie Bashkirtseff. She would have been in Paris when Clara Bowman visited. She died of tuberculosis when she was twenty-five. The painting is entitled *Self-Portrait with a Pallette*.

For Bernice (always)

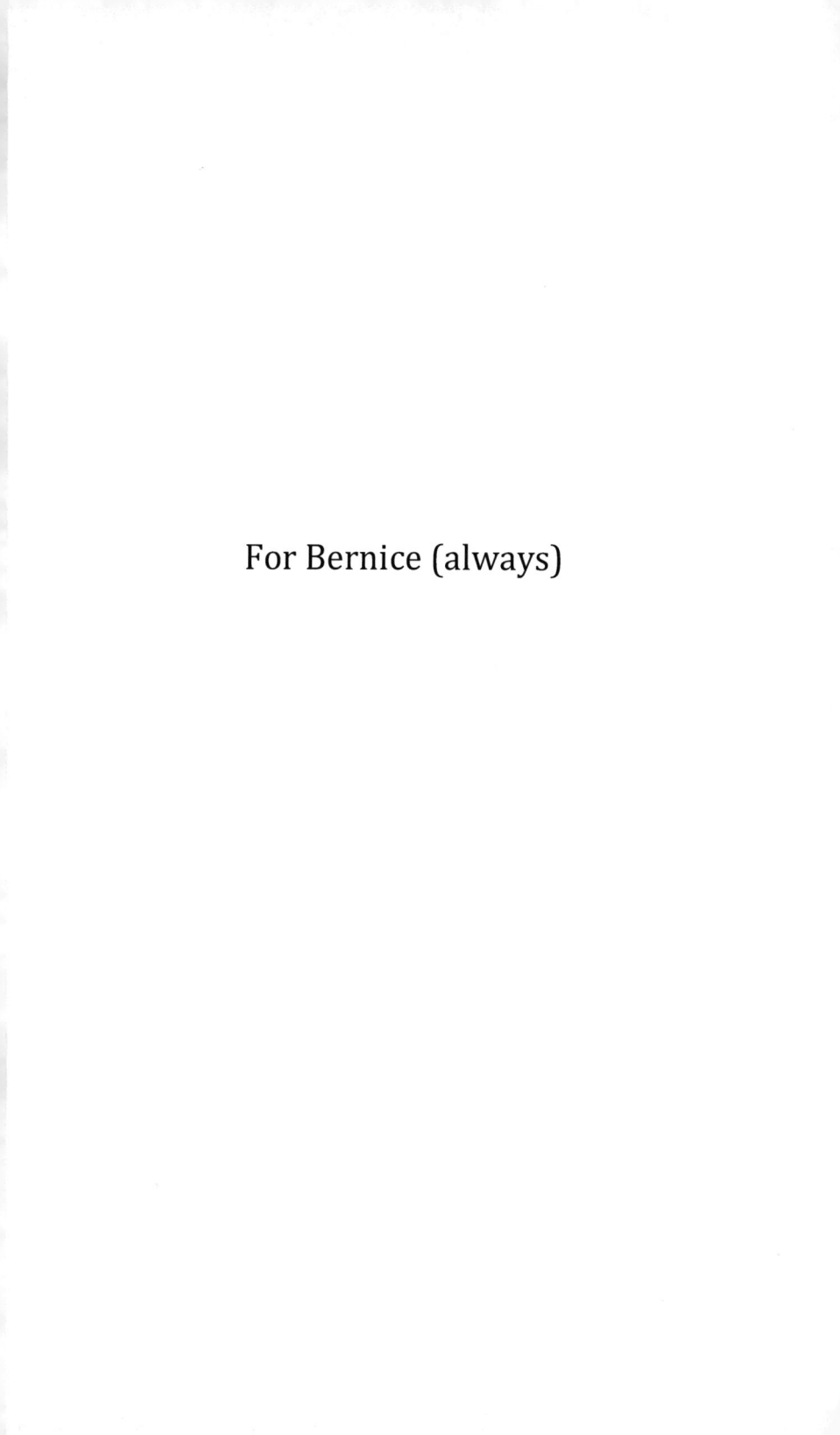

Introduction

Although this book tells the story of Clara Bowman and events that occur in her life, many of its characters appear in *Róisín Campbell: An Irishwoman in New York*. Indeed, in that novel, it is noted that in early 1874, Emily Connor, who you will meet, "decamped to Greenwich Village, moving in with an unmarried friend who had artistic aspirations." That unmarried friend was Clara Bowman. This story begins nearly two y ears earlier, and the denouement of Róisín Campbell is spoken of here.

This novel continues past the final scene of that book and provides updates on some of the characters in that earlier one. While I do not think it necessary to have read the earlier book to enjoy this one, it will provide some insight into the story of some of the characters here.

"Harry," said Basil Hallward, looking him straight in the face, "every portrait that is painted with feeling is a portrait of the artist, not of the sitter. The sitter is merely the accident, the occasion. It is not he who is revealed by the painter; it is rather the painter who, on the coloured canvas, reveals himself. The reason I will not exhibit this picture is that I am afraid that I have shown in it the secret of my own soul."

The Picture of Dorian Gray

1.

May 12, 1872 was a typical, if rainy, spring Sunday in New York City. Clara Bowman spent it as she always spent her Sundays in town. She was the largely spoiled second daughter (and second and last child) of a respected and wealthy family. She celebrated her eighteenth birthday six months earlier, and her long-anticipated coming out in society was in March. She lived with her parents in their large house on East Thirty-Second Street in Manhattan. It was between Fifth and Madison Avenues.

As a rule, Clara's Sunday began with church services at Madison and Thirty-Fourth in which the readings were familiar and the sermon was forgettable. That done, she and her mother and sister, born Grace Bowman but now Mrs. Richard Lawford, strolled with similarly spoiled and rich women until they reached their respective houses. They could have taken their carriage on this particularly unpleasant Sunday but that would mean waiting until who knew how many other carriages would have to be loaded and would depart before theirs was ready, so as it was only a few blocks they walked beneath their umbrellas and dodged puddles and manure that others would have to clean up. They were home well before they would have been had they opted to take their carriage.

Ashley Davis, Clara's closest friend, was normally among the women with whom she walked, and Ashley's only brother, Thomas, sometimes accompanied them. It was universally understood that Thomas would marry Clara and the engagement was expected to follow Thomas mounting the courage to ask her father's permission—which would surely be given—and to ask Clara for her hand—which would even more surely be given.

The Davises lived two doors to the west, and the girls grew up together, sharing governesses and nurses. For several years they attended an all-girls academy on Twenty-Third Street.

Clara was a little taller and lankier than her contemporaries, and she was somewhat awkward. Ashley was a little shorter than average with flowing blonde hair in contrast to Clara's, which was flat and nearly jet black.

Thomas looked much like his sister, and he shared her sparkling blue eyes. His features were quite pleasant. Especially to a girl looking to fall in love. He was two years older than Clara and knew Clara for nearly as long as his sister did. He studied at Columbia College and was heir to his father's estate, though Clara did not need to marry for money.

On May 12, Ashley and Thomas were visiting an ailing aunt on Long Island, and the best that could be hoped for was that they would appear at the Bowmans' shortly before dinner was over.

Not long after the parade of umbrellas of the Bowmans and the Lawfords reached the former's house, and after the three women spent some time with Grace's two girls, the five were seated in the dining room for dinner. As they were finishing, their coffees and desserts before them, the bell rang. Clara was glad her friends were finally stopping by, and two empty chairs awaited them. She heard Haskins, their butler, open the front door and expected the pair to be with them in a moment. But they did not rush in and they were not there. Instead, Haskins entered with an envelope on a silver plate, which he brought to Mr. Bowman, who ripped it open.

"Oh, my God." He stared at the paper. "It is your friends, the Davises. They are…dead."

Surely it was a poor joke. Surely.

Her father looked at her, the note from Mr. Davis shaking. "A train accident in Queens is what it says."

Ashley and Thomas were killed in Hollis, Queens, as they returned from their visit when a freight train derailed and the engineer on their passenger train waited too long to hit the brakes on the wet rails and the engine and several cars on that train derailed. Four people were killed, including both Davises.

The Bowmans would learn this later, but when her father was finished, Clara had to be helped upstairs by her sister and her mother. As they sat with her in her room, the continuing rain clicking against its windows and a lone candle providing light, she told them that she realized finally what love was and that now it was too late. She would never know it again. Mother and sister sat with her until she fell asleep, and Grace remained throughout the night, though she, too, fell into a troubled sleep on an uncomfortable chair near the bed.

Clara Bowman remained like this through the week and into the next. By then, Mrs. Bowman was tired of her daughter's grief. Clara was not getting younger, and Thomas Davis was gone.

"Give her time," Grace said whenever her mother brought this up though she agreed that her sister's conduct, however sincere, was bordering on the self-indulgent. Mr. Bowman was resigned to allow the ladies to handle his youngest daughter and preferred not to be troubled by it in the interim.

Clara's loss was an agony. She had seen Ashley just on the Saturday and Thomas two days before that. Now they were gone forever. She kept to her room, her meals brought to her, passionless in her hopeless despair, as Browning observed. She often stared out her window, and her mother decreed that she not be disturbed.

She left the house once in that first week, to attend the funeral. It was a large, elaborate event. Clara was asked if she wished to sit among the Davises, in which case space would be saved for her, but she could not bring herself to do that, and found a spot near the rear and on a side aisle and mixed in with her mother, her sister, and other ladies in black. She remained towards the back at the quay later as the two coffins were placed on a boat to be buried in Queens, but their uncle saw her and insisted she travel with them to the cemetery.

She went and stood by the graves. Then she returned home to her room.

2.

Clara reacted badly to the collapse of her life and of her dreams and expectations. By week three, though, she ventured downstairs and ate with the family and joined them in the drawing room after dinner. But she suddenly resented her happily-married sister and the slightest affection displayed between her parents. She hated herself for avoiding Mr. and Mrs. Davis when she saw them at services two Sundays later and was glad when they left for an extended stay in Saratoga in mid-June. Clara did not realize until he was dead how deeply in love she was with Thomas and was determined to suffer for it and to have others suffer with her.

Her ennui was noted by family and the few friends she was willing to see when they tried to visit, and "What are we to do about Clara?" was frequently asked when she was not in a room. Finally, her father said "enough." Clara did not hear him say it, and fortunately Mrs. Bowman convinced him not to broach it himself. She would do it. She sat Clara down in the corner of the drawing room on another of Clara's "bad days."

"This cannot go on."

"I know, mama. But I do not know what else I can do. Grace has Richard, and you have papa. I have nothing. Not even a friend in the world."

"You have me and Grace and the rest of us."

Mrs. Bowman hesitated, and the pause caused Clara to look at her mother.

"Most of all, my dear, you have you. You need to understand and accept that. Your sister, father, and I have spoken, and we agree that a change in scenery could not but help."

Clara's countenance narrowed at the conspiracy being unfolded before her.

"We will make arrangements for us, just you and I, to travel to London for a month. You will be free of the memories while—"

"I will never be free of the mem—"

"I spoke too loosely. We realize that. You will, though, be free of the sights and sounds and smells that will, that have, triggered unpleasant thoughts about what you have been through and who you have lost."

"If you think it is what I must do."

"Clara. You must understand now or I fear you never will. You are old enough to know that you must make your own decisions. All we can do is facilitate them." Her voice rose slightly. "If you wish to remain here, cloistered, that is your prerogative. But I say I am tired of it. You are a woman, and it is time you acted like one."

Both were shocked by the explosion. Mrs. Bowman was to be the gentle touch but sounded like her husband. Clara turned to rush to her room to be done with this unpleasantness. As she reached the door, though, she turned.

"Have I been so awful, mama?" her question clouded by tears.

Her mother stood and walked slowly to her, with her arms outstretched. She pulled her daughter, and Clara bent slightly so her chin was on her mama's shoulder. It lasted but a moment, and Clara pushed away, using the back of her hand to wipe some tears away.

"You are all right, of course."

And with that, Clara found her attention wonderfully diverted to what she and her mother could do and see in England. Time was spent assembling and supervising the packing of the appropriate dresses and shoes and hats and the countless other things required for such a journey. Quite fine accommodations were arranged aboard one of the newer steamships.

So over two months after the young Davises were laid to rest, and a few hours after their trunks were brought to a pier that jutted out into the Hudson, the Bowman women, accompanied by George Bowman, Richard Lawford and the Lawford girls, and various other friends who watched the tugs position the ship in the river and accompany it south, were headed to the Old World.

It was a pleasant crossing, but the Bowmans kept to themselves. They finally disembarked in Southampton, where they and their luggage took a train to London and a carriage, their trunks on its roof, carried them to the Langham Hotel about midway between Hyde and Regent's Parks. It was a hotel popular with Americans and as it was new it was laden with all the modern conveniences.

They were treated like royalty as their cab arrived and both were amused and impressed that the doormen and others wore livery from the eighteenth century, long out of fashion in New York. The hotel had a narrow lobby with a cathedral ceiling from which several chandeliers dangled. There was a large restaurant to the right and a small, more intimate tearoom to the left. It was to the latter that the pair went after checking in, and they found a small table at which they had their first proper English tea and from which they could observe the comings and goings through the lobby as they waited for their suite to be made ready for them.

After several nervous moments as they ascended in the elevator, they were led to their rooms. There was a small sitting-room and their bedrooms were on either side of it with a bathroom on one side and a large closet to the other. Their dresses were hung and their other clothing and necessities were placed in dressers in their rooms with the trunks presumably taken to wherever it was that the Langham kept guests' trunks.

They were glad that the room was more feminine than not, with neither the smell nor the feel of cigar smoke. Instead, the wallpaper was a light color, tan in the sitting room, a soft blue in Mrs. Bowman's bedroom, and a rosy pink in Clara's. In New York, they often found hostesses overwhelmed their houses, but here the roses and lilies and other freshly-cut flowers were tastefully arranged about each of the rooms and added a barely detectable but extremely pleasant aroma. The windows were open, but the suite faced the side and the traffic on Portland Place, where the hotel's imposing portico faced, barely intruded.

"I think I could die a happy woman in this room," Clara said as she lowered herself to one of two small sofas that faced one another.

Mrs. Bowman found this a peculiar moment, seeing Clara more girl-like and more alive than she had been since receiving the news in that horrible note months earlier.

"Do not get too comfortable, my dear," her mother warned, "for you must bathe and get out of those clothes so we might see the city."

Clara, her eyes tracing the dental molding that went around the ceiling, happily replied, "Soon enough, mama, soon enough," and continued her lounging until she mustered the strength and the will to lift herself so that she could begin her stay in London.

It was late July, and the timing was not advantageous since society would be fleeing to its various country estates in two weeks' time, and the Bowmans would be left in the doldrum period of the capital. Hot and with few to see and little to do. But it was a change.

They knew three or four members of English society, and they quickly ran through the roster in a series of afternoon visits and dinners. Some hinted that an invitation to a country estate would be forthcoming, but none actually arrived. It was just as well. Clara's despondency was reduced but too often made an appearance, and it was enough that she was able to walk with her mother and plan what they would do when they returned home come September.

Some days after they settled in, they were on Oxford Street among stores that sold ready-made women's clothing, and one window caught Mrs. Bowman's eye and she tugged her daughter to it. There were three day-dresses displayed, and the older woman noticed their colors.

"What do you think of the red one?" she asked Clara, meaning the one on the left. It had an open collar and its sleeves did not float as much as was normal and the bustle did not seem to protrude dramatically. It was sleeker than customary, but that was not what caught Mrs. Bowman's eye. The red did. She was hoping for the opportunity to get something less mournful for her daughter and this might do it.

"The red one?" said daughter responded. "It would suit someone going to an afternoon party, I suppose, but would be entirely inappropriate for me."

"Why?"

Clara looked from the dress to her mother. "Because I am in mourning."

"Clara," Mrs. Bowman said, "we are in London and we are in London because you need to break free. It will not be disrespectful of Ashley or Thomas if you enjoy yourself in some small way while we are here. We will go in, we will see if it suits you, and if it does, we shall buy it. I think it would suit you quite well, and I do not believe I have seen one like it in New York."

Clara reluctantly followed her mother in. She would never buy such a pre-made dress for anything important but for a stylish yet comfortable one, she would humor her mother. The owner of the store was a large woman who rushed to them from the rear with a tape measure draped about her neck. It was a quiet time for the bespoke dressmakers as society women were out of town for the season, but her clientele were the wives and daughters of wealthy tradesman, bankers, and lawyers and so her shop enjoyed a steady flow even in August.

But it was empty when the two women came through the door and the owner, Mrs. Trolley, immediately recognized what they wore as high-quality and American. They likely wanted some dresses they could get quickly for their stay, and Mrs. Trolley was sure she could accommodate them. She also appreciated the black armbands they wore, which would require some delicacy if they were to buy one of the brighter dresses of which she was particularly proud.

"Good morning, ladies," she said in her practiced but not cynical way. "What may I help you with?"

"The red dress. Might there be one my daughter could try?"

Mrs. Trolley turned to Clara and assessed her. She was taller than the cut of the dress accommodated and the shopkeeper thought on it. As she did, Clara told her mother, "This is a bad idea, mama. Let us just go."

"Hush, Clara. We are here now. Let us see what Mrs.—"

"Trolley. Mrs. Trolley. A widow, ma'am."

"Oh, I am sorry." She turned to Clara. "We are here, and we will see what Mrs. Trolley can do."

Clara huffed in her well-practiced way, but Mrs. Trolley did not let her go far. "You are a tall girl. That red dress will not do. And you are in mourning, yes? I am sorry."

"Yes. Two people she was very close to."

"I am sorry, my dear. But you are in London now, and I hope that helps you with your loss."

Where they stood was not large but large enough for the dressmaker to circle Clara and with a touch here and a touch there to get the measure of the girl, with several "yes"s and "very nice"s as she did.

"I believe I have just the thing," she said as she disappeared to the rear. She presently returned with something maroon draped across her left arm. She lifted it and held it against Clara's front and looked to Mrs. Bowman for confirmation. It had a square collar trimmed by a rectangle in a cream lace. The sleeves hung easily down, and a belt made of the same maroon material as the dress itself allowed the dress to fit comfortably about Clara's midsection and below it the material was allowed to flow. The latter would have to be trimmed lest the wearer trip on it, but Mrs. Trolley saw that that was one of the few things she needed to do to make it fit the American.

"Perfect," Mrs. Bowman smiled, and Mrs. Trolley echoed, "'Tis, isn't it? The color suits her so well. It is an artistic dress, far more practical than the day dress."

There was a tall mirror to the side, and Clara held the dress against her front and looked.

"It is somber enough, Clara, to be respectful, and its color is perfect for you," Mrs. Bowman said and then turned to the dressmaker. "What will it take, how long, for her to have it?"

Clara, who was silent and allowed herself to be poked and prodded through all this, spoke. "It is a beautiful dress and I believe it would look very well on me," she said. She turned to her mother and Mrs. Trolley, still clinging the dress to herself. "But, mama. I feel it is too early."

Mrs. Trolley moved away, and Mrs. Bowman stepped closer, only the dress separating them. She ran her right hand across her daughter's left cheek.

"Clara. We will only do what you wish to do, and you must not think otherwise." She paused, unsure of the tack to take, never having experienced the loss her daughter had.

"It must be you who decides. I can only support you. We are here to begin anew. We both know you need not wear mourning clothes to confirm your respect for the Davises. But...but when you look at that dress," and she moved to the side to allow them both to admire it in the mirror, "does it not convince you how beautiful and full of life you are?"

Clara remained conflicted by the norms of society but she was in London. She was beginning to feel she was herself and the mirror suggested who she could be. It truly was a wonderful dress. It was not nearly so large as the tailored things she had in New York and it would be more comfortable than what she brought with her. At the least she knew she must see how it looked on her body and not just being placed against it.

"Mama. Mrs. Trolley has gone to so much bother. It is the least I can do to try it on, don't you think?"

Mrs. Trolley was near enough to catch her name and was quickly leading Clara to a room beside her worktable in the back.

"Miss, I believe you may put it on so we can see, and I will then attempt to perform my magic to make it worthy of you."

Clara smiled at how this was said, so different from the gruffness of the men who were the dressmakers at home. The fitting room was large enough for her mother to join her and assist in removing the suddenly drab thing that she had on, the product of one of those gruff men, as well as the crinoline on which it draped itself, and replacing it with Mrs. Trolley's somewhat ill-fitting dress.

Mrs. Bowman brushed aside the curtain to the room and led her daughter out.

"Yes," Mrs. Trolley said as she approached Clara. She put her hands against Clara's waist, strong but not brutal hands. "This will fit nicely on you." She rotated Clara so the three could look at the dress in the mirror. The dressmaker pulled its waist, which revealed Clara's slight curves. She turned to Mrs. Bowman, on Clara's other side. "I do hate when pretty girls on becoming beautiful women do so much to hide the fact from the world, do you not agree Mrs.—"

"Bowman. Muriel Bowman and my daughter Clara. We are visiting from New York."

Clara was embarrassed by the nonsense being spoken as she looked in the mirror. She was just as plain a woman as she had been a girl. Yet the image offered a glimpse, not of beauty—of that she was sure—but of something…pleasant.

With one hand gripping the dress's waist, Mrs. Trolley used the other to pull back on its top, allowing it to frame Clara's bosom. She had seen this before. The wave that washes over a young woman when she sees who she is. There was an element of cynicism in it since it helped her sell dresses, but that did not alter the affection she had for those who came through. She took particular satisfaction attending to the well-off but not wealthy who were her usual clients.

Clara hoped the others did not notice her smile, though they both did, and decided she liked what looked back at her. "How long would it take, Mrs. Trolley?"

The older women exchanged smiles in the mirror, though Clara did not notice them, and Mrs. Trolley said, "If I measure you out now, I will prepare it immediately and you can return in two days for it. Would that be satisfactory?"

It was and when they returned it was ready for Clara. Mrs. Bowman was happy to pay for it and for two others—the cost was less than for just one bought in New York. Without a bustle, there was no need for crinoline and the weight and discomfort that came along with one. On those days when she and her mother went for long walks, Clara wore one of those dresses instead of the more formal things for shopping and the occasional visiting. She always dressed formally for dinner.

Their days passed well enough. As they strolled with their parasols and intertwined arms, they spoke of the sights they saw and the people they passed. Shopping and sitting on a bench with a bit of refreshment in a park. The one thing they did not talk about during the day was the reason for their trip, though it was uppermost in both their minds. With each evening, sometimes while they ate in the Langham's or a nearby restaurant recommended by the concierge, but more often when they retired to their sitting room, Clara spoke more and more of her loss. Mrs. Bowman took to measuring her daughter's revival by the tone as well as what she said. While she still spoke of her times with Thomas, it was far more often about Ashley.

More and more Clara smiled as she began a sentence with "Do you remember...?" Memories of happy days, the simpler the happier it seemed with the caveat that nothing compared to the night they came out into society together and the giggles and swooning they shared between the dances they so laboriously practiced for with the boys who were even more uncomfortably dressed and more awkward than they were.

"Mama, have I ever told you about...?" Clara would say, and she had of course told her mother about this or that boy dozens of times and how much she was in love with him and he with her until the next partner and the next waltz. "Oh how Ash and I were cruel about some of them but, mama, you could not blame us, they were so ridiculous."

Some of these sessions would end in tears, as they reminded Clara of how much she missed Ashley. Mrs. Bowman would then sit on the side of Clara's bed holding her daughter's hand until she fell asleep. But about two weeks after their arrival, Clara said, "I know she is gone. And I miss her so much. I am glad that we had time to share such nonsense," and she insisted that she was perfectly capable of putting herself to sleep and managed to do that.

So their days were spent having breakfast in the hotel's dining room adjoining the lobby and taking in the sights of the comings and goings there. They changed after they ate and walked north or south, east or west, as the mood dictated and weather permitted, enjoying the winding paths in the two large parks nearby. Often, they shopped and were able to supplement what they brought with some of the newer fashions, including some with hints of Paris, such as they saw in Mrs. Trolley's shop.

A return to the hotel for lunch and then generally they sat together in their suite or on the hotel's terrace writing letters home or reading or doing needlepoint. Dinner in the dining room, sometimes with people of their acquaintance from New York, and if the weather was kind a short walk nearby. It was a pleasant routine and it and simply being away helped Clara begin to forget.

About a week after nearly everyone fled town in mid-August, she and her mother entered what had become a familiar section of Regent's Park. It was to the southern end, and they sat in one of a series of benches arrayed among a number of rose bushes. Not far from them a young woman stood before an easel, painting a watercolor of one of those bushes.

"I must see," Clara told her mother, and she jumped up. Upon arriving, the artist ignored Clara looking over her shoulder, the American's glance alternating between the painting and its subject. The artist, a fair-skinned woman named (Clara would learn) Felicity Adams, lifted her brush from the paper and without looking away she said in an uppercrust accent, "You must tell me what you think."

Clara had little idea what to "think" about a painting. The art of her world was the portraits in the Bowmans' and other similar houses and the occasional broad landscape of the country. She attended her share of exhibitions of newly-rich men eager to show off their artistic tastes and, more, their financial acumen, and she and Ashley had visited the new Metropolitan Museum on Fourteenth Street several times.

What she saw as she looked over Felicity's left shoulder was, for want of a better term, alive. Somehow the still-damp watercolors brought out a depth Clara had not noticed in looking at the petals and the stems and the leaves and the thorns themselves.

She was silent, and Felicity said, "It's not very good, is it?" which shook Clara from her stupor.

"It is the most beautiful, most magical thing I have ever seen."

Felicity looked over, hearing and seeing her admirer for the first time.

Clara continued staring at the paper. Felicity had never known someone to respond so viscerally to her simple bit of water coloring. She was, like Clara, a woman with much time on her hands. Thanks to the persistence of several governesses, she was adept at any number of things at which a wealthy city woman of society must be adept. She found art, though, something beyond a mere lure for a husband. She often received compliments on the things she painted or drew but had never seen the expression on this American's face.

"You must have it."

"No, surely not," Clara said.

Felicity laughed. "It is but a quick study. I wish you to have it."

By this point, Mrs. Bowman was beside Clara. She chastised her daughter for interrupting the artist, but Felicity insisted it was far from a bother.

She turned back to the watercolor of the rose bushes.

"Please give me a moment, and I shall be done."

As the others watched, she dabbed her brush in the paint and lightly drew it across, creating more texture in one of the roses, and then she pronounced that it was finished and that it would be dry presently and that she would present it to, "I am sorry, I do not know your names," and when told she continued that she would present it to Miss Bowman as a souvenir of her visit to Regent's Park and would then take the two women to tea "or whatever it is you Americans currently enjoy."

For most of their tea, Clara was quiet, allowing her mother to carry their end of the conversation. Mrs. Bowman made the nature of Clara's situation generally known straight off, especially the horrible deaths of the Davises and the need to flee America so she could breathe again. And then the lonely weeks in London.

Clara paid little attention. She had heard it often on the crossing and on visits and had no interest in becoming engaged in it. During a lull, she asked, "May we see your studio?"

The others turned to her.

"Do not be presumptuous, Clara."

Felicity ignored this.

"There is nothing I would rather do," she said, and so after the bill was paid (by Felicity after a battle with Mrs. Bowman) and Felicity collected her easel and supplies from the café's corner where she left them, the three went to the street. Three or four blocks later, they came upon Felicity's small building. It was like its neighbors, built in the Georgian period, with their three steps leading to a black door. Felicity said they were in the Primrose Hill neighborhood, just to the east of the hill whence its name derived and just north of Regent's Park itself. The flat was on the third floor (to the Americans) and faced the rear, overlooking the neatly-tended gardens in the backs of the houses beside and across from it.

It was bright, as its back looked south, and the gardens were abloom with a panoply of colors not unlike those recently seen in the park. The flat itself was square and felt larger than it was with a calming pattern to its wallpaper. It had a small and tidy kitchen. A bed was lengthwise against the left wall and several very fine but well-worn pieces of furniture dotted the place. More than anything, the room was an artist's studio and smelled like one. There was an easel on which an incomplete landscape lay, and drawings and paintings leaned in columns along the wall to the right.

Mrs. Bowman was fatigued, though, and so the Americans left soon after the tour ended, but not until she insisted that she and Clara take Felicity to dinner. Felicity suggested a restaurant not far from the Langham, and the three were seated shortly after seven-thirty. Within minutes, a lady and a gentleman stopped by their table. When the former had Felicity's attention, she asked, "Are these your latest protégés, my dear Felicity?" She was a bit stout and wore a fine emerald dress that did well to complement her chestnut hair.

Felicity smiled. "No. They are from America. I have just met them. Allow me to introduce Mrs. and Miss Bowman of New York. Miss Bowman admired one of the watercolors I was doing in the park, and I thought that warranted my payment with dinner. So here we are."

Turning to Mrs. Bowman and Clara, she said, "Ladies, this is my dear friend Alice Jones and her husband Michael Jones."

At this, the latter, a fine-looking Englishman in a well-tailored suit, stepped around his wife and reached for the hand of Mrs. Bowman. He kissed it lightly, and with a practiced bow said, "It is a true delight to meet you, Mrs. Bowman." He looked at Clara and said with the hint of a second bow, "And you, of course, Miss Bowman."

With that, the couple began to move away. Alice turned back to Felicity and said, "We must get together sometime but for now my husband is beckoning me," and with that, she followed her husband to their table.

When they were out of earshot, Felicity turned to her guests and lowered her voice. "We were once great friends. But when she married and I moved to London, she did not seem to know me anymore. We see each other sometimes when she is in town."

Mrs. Bowman asked Felicity about her plans for marriage.

"Perhaps someday, but I'm too much enjoying my freedom. My father lives for his horses and hunts and he allowed me to take this time in London when I convinced him that doing so would be like exhausting a horse and breaking her to become a compliant mare. I told him at that point, when I was well and truly 'broken,' I would gladly enter his and my mother's world and, for that matter, Alice Jones's. It's been just over one year now, and I am afraid I shall never become the compliant mare he hopes I will."

At this, Clara asked, "What would you do then? Of course you must have a husband."

Felicity laughed. "Of course I *must* unless I *do not*. I am too young." She whispered conspiratorially, "I am twenty-one, you know," and then looked at Clara. "Much too young to worry about how much I am enjoying my life here. I do have a few friends in my world, and each day is far from the days and the friends of the world of my parents and Mr. and Mrs. Jones."

Looking back and forth between the other two, she added, "And it allows me to meet people like you, sitting in Regent's Park."

Felicity said that while the family had a house in the city, she convinced her father to allow her to rent her own flat using the significant savings he enjoyed as a result of him not having to buy her dresses to go to event on event.

"Fortunately, we are well enough off that my father need not worry about auctioning me off to some rich American industrialist or his son, so I have the small flat and enough to live on and enough to take people I like to dinner."

Clara interrupted, "So you like us."

"Indeed I do and I will be sad when you leave us forever to go home."

At this point dinner was nearly over and the summer sun over London had not yet faded. They decided to forgo dessert or coffee or tea and walked two blocks to Regent's Park where they strolled around the lake, a pond really, in the southern end.

Felicity was between the two Bowmans, her arms through theirs. She was happy to agree to meet Clara again, at the rose bushes the next morning.

When Clara arrived around ten in the morning, the early mist was burnt off though the grass was wet. Felicity was already set up, and she had brought a folding stool for her new friend in the small wagon she sometimes used to transport her supplies. After a quick "hello," she returned to her work, and Clara sat beside her, shortly saying, "I would like to be able to do something like that."

"There is no reason you cannot." She turned from her easel and smiled. "And I shall teach you."

When the watercolor was finished and drying, Clara helped Felicity put her things in her little wagon except for the painting itself, which was carefully placed in a folio that Felicity carried. Then, Felicity rifled through some things and produced a sketchbook, which she handed to Clara with a pencil.

"Sketch me," she said. Clara protested that she could do no such thing and Felicity insisted that she at least try. The Englishwoman turned her head slightly and held the pose. Clara hesitated until she put the pencil to the paper. Finally, she let the former touch the latter and hoped what she drew would bear some resemblance to her new friend's forehead.

When it was done, Felicity took it and studied it. She then folded it and placed it carefully among the things in the wagon.

"Will you not tell me what you think?"

The pair had started walking to Felicity's flat, and as they left the park, Felicity ended her silence.

"It is not good. But I do not think it bad, either." As they waited to cross the road that ran along the park's eastern border, she turned to her new friend. "It is not bad, Miss Bowman, and I believe we might just be able to make something of you. I truly do."

There was an opening in the traffic, and they raced across, with Clara pulling the little wagon like the girl she sometimes still was, and Felicity's last words made her feel like one, too.

As they resumed a walking pace, Felicity commented, "Wherever I go, I carry a sketch pad. I often dine alone so I am not deterred by conversation in sketching the others at the restaurant. They all know me, and people let me sketch them because I give them the product of my efforts."

She said she often went to the park with her easel and watercolors to paint the trees and bushes. After Clara helped carry the supplies to the flat, they arranged to meet again at the Langham.

3.

Felicity Adams took to her self-appointed role of tour guide with great spirit, and her two new friends discovered more in three days than they had in the prior weeks. After several days, Felicity took them to Piccadilly and along a street lined with mansions. At the third one on the left, she turned.

"The family left for the country a few weeks ago but there will be a few members of staff."

Felicity simply opened the door and called out "Jones" as she entered the foyer. A moment later the butler appeared.

"Good morning, miss. I had no idea you would be stopping by. Your brother is expected tomorrow so we have prepared the house. Do you intend to stay?"

"No, Jones, I merely wish to show my new friends the house."

Felicity told him to resume whatever he was doing to prepare things for her brother, and he bowed and went on his way. The Americans had seen many a fine house in New York but nothing as elegant as this.

"Why would you leave all this?" Clara asked as she twirled around in Felicity's bedroom, which had a large four poster bed, and walls covered in a blue paper sprinkled with yellow flowers on green stems.

"'Tis a cage. My papa tolerates my acts of independence." She threw herself on her bed and lay looking up. "He is sure I will tire of them and settle down with one of the appropriate men he has chosen for me." She raised herself to look at the others, who were studying each nook of the room. "Perhaps I will.

Perhaps he will break me like one of his horses." She flopped back down. "We shall see."

She was surprised when she felt Clara fall beside her, the mattress vibrating for several seconds.

"I don't know if I shall ever marry since the man I love is gone."

Her mother was frozen, holding her breath as she looked down on the two girls. In all their talks, Clara had not told Felicity this part of why she was in London. Only that she suffered some horrible loss with the death of friends.

"What do you mean 'gone'?"

Clara adjusted her body and rolled on her side so she could look at her friend, who was looking at the ceiling. She ran her left hand mindlessly across the other's stomach.

"I was in love with someone who died in a stupid train crash." She again flopped down and also stared up at the ceiling. "A train crash in Queens! Killed with my best friend."

Felicity mimicked Clara's actions, rising and turning so she could study the American's face.

"Tell me."

Which is how on the plush bed in a lavish bedroom decorated in an incredibly tasteful manner with the sound of passing carriages slipping through the window Clara Bowman released the hold the ghost of Thomas Davis had over her heart, by the simple act of telling a friend—a stranger, really—of how she loved him and how his death nearly destroyed her.

All three were quieter after leaving the house than they were entering, but Felicity lightened things by insisting that they have lunch at a small café some blocks away. It was a refuge she frequented when she was at the house before she got her flat. They sat at a small, round table near the front window and enjoyed the view of the few passersby while they ate. Clara's revelations were not forgotten but placed to the backs of their minds while they spoke of less important things.

From that day, as a rule, Felicity arrived at the Langham at ten and took the Bowmans out. Sometimes they took a cab to a row of West End stores on or near Oxford Street where Felicity was recognized and catered to. On other days she insisted that they wear shoes and dresses that were as comfortable as possible and even convinced Mrs. Bowman to forgo a corset to take a long stroll. They either ate at or near the stores when that is where they went or returned to the hotel to lunch in their suite, after which Mrs. Bowman would bid the younger women continue their explorations.

After lunch nearly a week after they met and after Mrs. Bowman was deposited at the hotel, Felicity insisted that Clara accompany her to her flat. There, Felicity grabbed her folding easel and a couple of stools as well as a satchel of supplies and the two carried them to the ground floor. Felicity opened a door in the hall and extracted her wagon. The two loaded it with the materials and together carried it to the sidewalk. Clara volunteered to pull it as the pair walked to the northern reaches of Regent's Park.

They found a small garden beyond which the traffic flowed. It was defined by a series of ornamental shrubs divided by flower beds. The path around it was wide enough to set up their stools without obstructing others. After they were placed, Felicity positioned the easel in front of Clara's stool. She told Clara to "simply draw what you see." Clara would not, saying that insofar as drawing was drilled into her as a girl, she shed any interest in it as soon as she could. She had done that slight thing where Felicity posed and did not like the result.

Felicity insisted. With much hesitation, Clara made a primitive drawing of an innocent flower bed in Regent's Park. It was pronounced "not terrible for a debut effort." After several more attempts dissolved into fits of laughter, the girls reversed their procession, going back to Felicity's, with the host now pulling the wagon as they chatted.

It rained the next morning, which put Clara in a foul mood, but Felicity relieved her by taking her and her mother to a department store in Knightsbridge. The three had lunch in the store's restaurant. It was close enough to the Langham to walk there after the rain let up. The girls dropped Mrs. Bowman off and continued to Felicity's. Clara said she wanted to watch Felicity at work and sat on the side of the bed as the Englishwoman resumed the detailing on the landscape that was her current work-in-progress, tidying up a small oil of a bridge over the Thames.

Minutes later, Clara rose and after a nod from Felicity began to go through the drawings and paintings strewn against the walls. They were there for perhaps twenty or thirty minutes when there was a knock on the door. Felicity stopped her work and opened it. Standing there was her brother, John. He passed her and was inside.

"Jones has advised me, my dear sister, that you are entertaining visitors from America. Assuming this is one of them," looking at and bowing to Clara, "and seeing as this is one of them, I am now particularly perturbed at your failure to tell me."

Felicity looked from her brother to her friend, still wandering through some of Felicity's oils, and to the latter said, "This is my older brother, John, but do not take him seriously. He is spoken for."

"Ah," he said. "Spoken for, perhaps. But not as yet *taken*."

Felicity waited a moment. "This is Clara Bowman. She and her mother are visiting us from New York."

He nodded and with that dropped himself onto his sister's bed while Clara resumed her browsing. He became quickly bored by being ignored.

"Felicity. I have come all this way to see you and your friend, and it is the least you can do to keep me entertained."

Clara looked at her friend, who shook her head.

"I can assure you, dear brother, looking at one of my sketches is infinitely more entertaining than conversing with you."

Clara hid a smile, then said, "No. While I am certain speaking with you would be far more enjoyable, I am endeavoring to learn from what your sister has done."

John raised himself. He looked at the American.

"What my sister has 'done'? She puts squiggles on paper and passes them off as something significant." John flopped back down. "Ah, but I see you have been ensnared in her web and I shall burden the two of you no more."

With this, and after being at the flat for less than ten minutes, he rose.

"But I do not surrender. I insist that I be allowed to take you and your mother to dinner this evening. It may well be the highlight of my stay in town. I shall pick you both up, and your dear mother, Miss Bowman, at the…Where is it that you are staying?"

"The Langham."

"The Langham. Of course. I will pick you and your mother up there at seven o'clock. Felicity, dear, you must be there too, of course. We shall adjourn to its fine dining room and I will learn about you and you will learn more than you ever care to know about me."

With that, he bowed to Clara and to his sister, restored his hat, and was gone.

"He is not so pompous as he likes people to believe, and on his good days he can be quite kind. He is to be married in the fall to the daughter of someone in my father's horsey set with no money and a heavily mortgaged estate. The alliance of the families is considered an act of *noblesse oblige* by my parents, and Diana does make John happy enough, I suppose.

"You will learn further of him and my family at dinner this evening. But he is practiced at the art of flirting, and do not allow it."

* * * *

FELICITY WAS RIGHT. Clara discovered John Adams's charm and she was taken aback when the maître d' referred to him as "Sir John."

When the four were seated, Clara asked about it, and Felicity said, "Oh that. Our father is a baron and so he is sometimes referred to as 'Sir.' Please pay it no mind, much as he likes others to."

Of course, Clara and Mrs. Bowman could not help but pay it mind. They did not know what a baron was and what this particular baron or an ancestor may have done to gather the title, but it was more than enough to set aflutter their Yankee inferiority. As to Sir John's charm, he displayed it chiefly to Mrs. Bowman, as Michael Jones had done when they had their encounter days before.

It was a fine dinner, and Sir John held the floor for most of it. But by the time the coffees were drunk and the dessert cart sampled, it was late and the room was still warm, and the two Adamses bid the two Bowmans good night.

Mrs. Bowman promptly ran a bath, and Clara sat with her.

"Mother. I should like to stay longer in London."

"I must say that Miss Adams is a pleasure. But please tell me you do not wish to stay longer because of that brother of hers."

"I am not such a fool, mama. It is Felicity. I like her. I do not know why. She has opened me to a new world, and I would like to explore it. It will not be too much trouble to stay here for another month, will it?"

"I expect not. I am sure they can accommodate us here."

Clara rose and kissed her mother on the forehead and sat down again, and her mother rose as she did. Her daughter handed her a towel and left to prepare for bed. Mrs. Bowman came to her room and asked about Felicity.

"I do not want you to attach yourself to that girl. Nothing can come of it, with you leaving."

"I only wish to be her friend, mama, much as I do like her. But I want her to teach me."

4.

It was a simple matter to extend the Bowmans' London stay, and Mrs. Bowman was pleased with how the prospect lifted Clara's spirits. The trip, after all, was intended to allow her daughter to move on. And the days continued, with a stroll in the mornings and the two girls spending afternoons together. They followed it with dinner, usually in the Langham's dining room. Felicity accepted Mrs. Bowman's kindness of paying for their dinners and repaid it slightly with a sketch she did of the older woman near her favorite rose bushes.

The weather was at times awful, but that did not matter. Clara enjoyed spending rainy days in Felicity's studio, either looking over her work or doing exercises under her tutelage. She advanced to watercolors, and Felicity refused to confirm Clara's opinion that she had no talent for it and that none of her things would be worthwhile.

At lunch on one such inclement afternoon, Felicity told Clara that they were going somewhere special and that she had to be on her best behavior. This time Mrs. Bowman agreed to accompany them. The three took a Hansom cab to Trafalgar Square and walked into the National Gallery.

To Clara, it was superior to the Metropolitan Museum in New York, perhaps because some of Felicity's excitement about art had virus-like found its way into Clara's blood. Again and again while Mrs. Bowman kept her distance to take in a painting as a whole, the girls approached it to study how that whole was created and accomplished.

At some point, Mrs. Bowman tired. The three went to a small café on the premises for tea to sustain them for the rest of their visit. But it was still too much for Mrs. Bowman, and she found a pleasant bench across from a more-than-pleasant painting of the English countryside and allowed the girls to wander off while she rested and chatted now and then with others who shared her admiration for the clouds above the Lake District.

As they wandered from gallery to gallery, though, Clara found herself increasingly disturbed. She saw the beauty in work after work, especially those of more recent vintage. Broad landscapes. Intimate portraits. Street scenes of London and Paris. Each one convinced her that she could never create anything that would represent what the artist saw or move the viewer as she was moved and so all the explanations from Felicity about technique and how it created the magic would be wasted on her.

Shortly before they returned to the gallery to rejoin a happy and rested Mrs. Bowman, Felicity noticed that Clara's step had slowed and her enthusiasm had waned. Seeing a bench across from a large Renaissance painting of some saint or another, Felicity told Clara to sit.

"I do not know why I should bother. Nothing I will do will amount to anything. It was a foolish thought all along."

"Clara, you fool. You'll probably never paint something that will hang in the National Gallery. Nor will I. But I think you can do a very fine job. That's all you can be expected to do. You paint in a way that you enjoy doing it. If that's not why you paint or draw, don't bother."

Felicity got up. Clara had a legitimate point, but they were in the National Gallery and of course everything—or most everything—was a masterpiece. Neither she nor Clara would know whether she would create a work that others found worthwhile unless she tried, and Felicity sensed that Clara was displaying a bit of the selfishness and lack of confidence too often found in society girls in London and, she dared say, in New York.

Watching Felicity storm away, Clara did feel the fool. Felicity was trying to fan an interest that Clara had, and she threw it back at her. At least she would stick with it and do her best while she was in London. When they were on board their ship returning them to America, she could reassess things in the solitude of the crossing.

She got up and rushed to catch her friend, which she did shortly before they came upon her mother chatting with a well-dressed society lady who vanished with a nod and a smile when they arrived.

Mrs. Bowman was largely recovered. It was only a mile back to the Langham, so the three elected to walk. As they did, Felicity reminded Clara that it took time to master painting, especially watercolors, a medium more difficult to excel at than oils. If Clara could feel for the touch necessary to bring life to the foliage or St. Paul's and the other parts of London the pair looked over while sitting on Primrose Hill, Felicity promised she could become accomplished, even if not enough to have them hung for the public's consumption. Clara promised she would not give up, and the three had a pleasant dinner in the Bowmans' suite.

* * *

SEVERAL DAYS AFTER her visit to the National Gallery, Clara heard, "Miss Bowman?" as she was leaving Felicity's in the late afternoon for her walk to the Langham. She turned. Sir John was rushing to catch her.

"I thought that might be you." He was slightly out of breath. "I sometimes take a walk in this area before getting ready for dinner and I was passing near Fel's on the off chance that I might run into you and here you are."

Clara smiled. "'On the off chance'?"

He stepped slightly back and bowed. "You have caught me out. I wanted to walk and thought it likely that you would be here and heading to the hotel about now, so I confess to having waited for you to come out. Can you ever forgive me?"

The two began to walk south and soon Clara found her arm through his. Having company, and of a handsome male member of the aristocracy, was quite a pleasing break.

"If you think I will be taken in by your English charm, you are in for a surprise."

"I only seek to take you to your hotel, Miss Bowman. It is a pleasant afternoon, and frankly I was hoping to enjoy this little stroll with you. I know too few Americans and those I do are loud and unsettling."

"I cannot object, Sir John, to you thinking me an exception, so let us walk and enjoy this little stroll together," and Clara was more charmed with each

step until he bid her "good afternoon" upon reaching the Langham.
 He took three or four steps when he heard, "Sir John," and it caused him to turn.
 "I did enjoy that. Perhaps we can do it again."
 "Miss Bowman. It would be my pleasure."
 "I leave your sister's at about the same time each afternoon."
 With that he doffed his hat and bowed, punctuating it with, "I look forward to it," and after he stepped closer, he suggested that they keep their rendezvous *entre nous*, lest her mother or his sister object to their innocent strolling. She entered the Langham strangely excited about another walk with Sir John Adams, the future baron.
 For all her claims of being immune to his charms, as with the Adams house and how for some reason she could not articulate it was superior to the grand ones with which she was familiar in New York, there was something about Sir John that was a cut above the gentlemen with whom she had been in contact at home. His Saville Row suit was slightly better tailored. His laugh the slightest degree more amusing. And even his face and his moustache were the slightest degree handsomer than even the most well-regarded young man who attended the balls and operas that Clara enjoyed before that horrible day in May. For all his protests of being pleased to be in her company, she felt the pleasure was on balance more hers.
 Sheltered as she may have been in her mother's eyes, Clara picked up a fair amount about…men in her conversations with Ashley and others in her circle and in the pulp novels they shared with one another.

Meeting and then walking with Sir John removed a veil over everything that she did not realize she put in place with Thomas's death. She suddenly felt deep inside her the *physical* loss from Thomas's death. They had never had intimate contact, nothing beyond a brotherly kiss. But that was the point. They had never had physical contact. Now they never would.

An ocean from home and a charming, titled man. Clara dared to think about him as a man and herself as a woman. So, yes, she would keep it *entre nous*.

She began to anticipate his appearance on the street when she prepared to leave Felicity's flat over the next days, but he failed to come. Until he did. It was quite a nice afternoon, and Felicity offered to accompany her guest to the Langham, but Clara declined, and when she stepped onto the sidewalk, she was thrilled that she had.

The stroll was much as it was that first time a week earlier. Yet Clara felt it was worlds apart. She walked slightly closer to him and held his arm slightly tighter and they did not speak quite so much. By the time they reached the Langham, she felt a desire to lie with him. She knew he was opportunistic. She knew he was shallow. She knew he was engaged.

She also knew that she would soon be gone, and they would never cross paths again so when he suggested they share a walk the next afternoon, when he said Felicity had an obligation with the family barrister to review and sign some papers, she agreed. Felicity had mentioned this appointment to the Bowmans.

The next afternoon, Clara told her mother she wished to take a walk alone for a change, and her mother was pleased Clara seemed excited about doing so. After a morning together and lunch at the Langham, Mrs. Bowman went to the suite, and Clara accompanied Felicity to the street. When they parted, Clara said she was planning to take her own stroll to Regent's Park. Which she did. It was where she met Sir John.

She quickly was lost to him. His modesty and kindness so at odds with how he was with his sister. Felicity warned Clara about him, yes, but she was perhaps jealous that Clara would spend time with him and not with her.

She lost track of the time, but it was warm and she was tired. John asked if she would like some refreshment, and when they left the park near its southern end, they were in Piccadilly, not far from the family house, and they soon were in its foyer.

Jones appeared, and John directed that refreshments be brought to the drawing-room to the left of the top of the grand stairway. Jones brought lemonade and small sandwiches and left the couple to it. Clara was on the sofa, and John was beside her.

"You look awfully warm." He reached for her neck, and she allowed his fingers to graze against her skin. Far from rejecting his touch, as she knew she should, she embraced it with a moan. She inhaled his smell, a masculinity she never before knew, and it filled her like some strain of opium and fueled her excitement. He stood and reached out his hand and she followed him up each step of the flight that brought the pair to his bedroom. It was infinitely more masculine than his sister's. The shades were lowered but not so much that the room was dark. The window was open and let in the slight sounds of the street. Even the air had a musky, manly smell.

Clara let him lower her gently to his bed and lift her dress and petticoat. Her moans had grown to panting, and she felt the sweat on his neck as she pulled him down for their—her—first lover's kiss. She allowed him to make love to her. It was in some respects painful but in others glorious, until he was done. He stood and cleaned himself as well as he could before pulling up his trousers, leaving her unfulfilled and alone on his bed.

"I shall be waiting in the drawing-room when you are decent," and Sir John was gone.

Clara knew every moment what she was doing and she did it. Her mother had spoken to her shortly before she came out about relations with men, and her friends had spoken in general and sometimes very specific terms about it. They at times circulated particular passages from books purloined from beneath a brother's bed and half-laughed at what they read. While there were times Clara was tempted to explore matters with Thomas, she never did, and he never insisted, much as she knew he wanted to. Now Thomas was gone and it was never done and it never would be done. She would not let that happen again. She knew what she was doing and insisted to herself that she did not regret it.

Until the moment she heard the door of Sir John's bedroom close behind him. It took her some minutes to make herself presentable, though she feared the bloodstains would be noticed before she could destroy her soiled undergarments. She could do nothing about the bedsheets. She slowly went through the door and down the stairs to the drawing-room. She was able, with some difficulty, to compose herself.

He was at a window, looking out. He had a glass of lemonade in his right hand and a half-eaten sandwich in his left. He turned when he heard her.

"That was very pleasant. But I must get you back now."

Without waiting, he put what he held on a nearby tray and passed her on his way to the door, his steps then bounding down the stairs. When he saw her at the top of the broad stairway, he called out, "Thank you, Jones. We shall be off now. I shall be back to dress for dinner in an hour or so."

He waited, and Jones appeared. When Clara's foot hit the floor of the foyer, the door was opened for them, and she followed Sir John to the street where he hailed a cab to return her, alone, to the Langham, kissing her hand before she left.

When she was deposited at the hotel, she told her mother that she felt under the weather—"Perhaps it is something I had at lunch." She took a bath, alone, and remained in her room when she was done. Mrs. Bowman sent a note to Felicity regretting that they could not meet for dinner and that she hoped Clara would be better disposed in the morning.

At breakfast, Clara told her mother that she was feeling better and that she would be happy to walk with Felicity. When their friend appeared, she said her brother, sadly, sent her a note. "Whatever has delayed his departure has been resolved and so he is heading to the country. He said he regrets not being able to see you again or even wish you a proper farewell, but he is in quite a hurry to reunite with my parents."

Clara's stomach rattled, not helped by Felicity adding, "More likely he completed some conquest, but he is gone and so we need not worry about him further, though I do admit he can be entertaining at times."

With that, the three left the hotel and found a cab to take them to Piccadilly.

Over the next days, Clara told no one what happened with Sir John Adams. She managed to sufficiently bury it in her mind so she could continue to enjoy London and especially Felicity, who, in fairness, had warned her. She knew enough to be relieved when two weeks after the event she had her normal monthly pain and blood.

So, things continued as they had been until four days before the Bowmans were to depart.

"Why did you not tell me?"

Felicity had bided her time in the morning until she was alone with Clara, walking north to the spot in Regent's Park they considered their own, one with several benches that overlooked a small pond alive with birds.

"How did you find out?" Clara asked.

"Jones, of course. There are limits to what a servant will keep discreet. And me, saying those horrible things about him and his conquest before leaving town. I should have known it was you."

"It was me, but he did not force me. I wanted to lie with him. I did not want to lose the opportunity as I had done once before."

They agreed not to spend their remaining time dwelling on what had been done. Though it was but slightly below the surface, the two enjoyed the final days of the Bowmans' adventure in London. Felicity was as sad at their leaving as they were to be going, it being unlikely they would see each other again. Several of her sketches, including a brilliant color portrait of Clara Bowman with three roses—representing the little group that spent time so pleasantly together—in the background that Mrs. Bowman knew would look superb in the house on Thirty-Second Street, were carefully wrapped and safely stowed for the journey. Felicity made sure to keep several of Clara's early efforts. They were good for all their faults and as the visitors' train disappeared from view, she wondered whether Clara would keep at it and follow her, bolting from her paddock before she could be broken.

5.

On the return crossing, mother and daughter replayed their visit (excepting perhaps the most significant part). Clara assured her mother that the trip did wonders for her depression. As they neared home, on an evening cool enough that they sat on the deck with blankets, Clara said she might, just might, like to explore becoming an artist. Since it was something Clara had never shown the slightest interest in before meeting Felicity, her mother humored her and said they would speak of it with Mr. Bowman when they reached home.

Tired as she was on her first night back, Clara brought it up at dinner with her parents as well as her sister and brother-in-law, hoping Grace and Richard would be allies.

"I do not understand you, Clara," her father said. "You went to England to clear your head. To allow yourself to return to us and your life here, and now you say you are still not ready? I am sorry, Clara, this sounds self-indulgent to me. We, your mother and I," and Mrs. Bowman, who had mentioned what Clara said on the boat to her husband, avoided her daughter's glare, "believe that you must move forward, and this sounds very much like an effort on your part to, well, move to the side, to delay your recovery from that awful thing that happened earlier this year."

"But papa," Clara said.

"Do not 'but' me. You have never had the slightest interest in art. Or, frankly, anything else for that matter. You are just a normal young woman and always wanted to do what normal young women, like your sister here, do. I am sorry. It is out of the question."

He gave a nod, and Haskins immediately removed his plate, and the other servants were just as quick in removing everyone else's.

"I think I shall retire with Richard now."

Before Clara could say another word, her father and her brother-in-law were gone, and her mother and sister were heading to the sitting room. Clara followed.

"This is not some passing fancy, I promise you. What did you tell him? Did you say you thought it was a way of avoiding becoming a responsible woman?"

"I told him what you said on the boat. Clara, I must be honest. I think it is just a passing fancy. You must get back into society or you will be too old and passed over. I think you are just afraid to search for love again."

"Is that all my life is to you? A 'search for love again'?"

Mrs. Bowman expected this.

"Please, Clara, you know she didn't mean it like that," said Grace.

"Do I? That's all you and she ever talk about as to me. 'When will she find her Richard?' I had my Thomas. But he is gone."

"That is the point. He is gone but there is someone else for you. As Richard is for me. He will not simply appear. You must get back."

"Don't you understand? I do not know if I *want* a new Thomas. I do not know what I want except I want the chance to find out, to do something different. Not for the sake of doing something different. But to know myself. I love you both and I see how happy you both are.

"I allowed Thomas and Ashley to go without truly knowing them and what I could have been with them. I am not saying I will not end up back in society. I am saying that I feel something about art. I do not wish to go without truly knowing whether I have a calling."

Mrs. Bowman and Grace sat watching Clara pace back and forth while she gave her speech, occasionally exchanging glances with each other. If either wondered whether there was something they would have liked to have done before marrying, they would not admit it. Neither doubted that having fleshed it out so, Clara always would regret not doing it and that it was best to have her explore it since it was unlikely that it would lead to anything. She was young and foolish with traces of impetuousness. It was best to let her have a brief period to put the notion to rest.

"I will speak to your father," Mrs. Bowman promised when Clara sat in a wing chair after exhausting herself. Soon, the Bowmans went to their beds and Grace collected her husband and went to hers.

6.

Two days after that dinner and the conversation with her mother and sister, Clara stepped from a trolley on Broadway and Houston Street. Greenwich Village was the place for artists. She walked. Broadway. Lafayette. Bleecker to the Bowery. Some women wore fashionable dresses in all their discomfort. Most did not, electing the more comfortable (and coincidentally named) artistic dresses of the type Clara discovered in Mrs. Trolley's shop. The several art-supply stores she passed were crowded, and she entered the third or fourth. She wandered up and down the aisles with their papers and paints and brushes and pencils. Along one wall were the larger items. The easels and the stools. A pile of small wagons like the one Felicity pulled.

Clara was startled when a voice behind her asked if she needed help. She turned. It was a young man in an ill-disciplined beard, and she said that perhaps some basic supplies, please.

"Pencils, water, or oils?"

"Good God, not oils. I have been told I am far from them."

The clerk laughed. "You'd be surprised how many newly to this world insist on canvas and oils when they come in. I fear they give up because that's not the place to start."

Clara left with an easel and a stool, three sketchbooks, and a collection of pencils. It was a good starting point, the clerk assured her, and she promised to return for paper and paints and brushes so she could start on watercolors.

He hailed a cab for her on Broadway and helped her load her purchases. On the way to Thirty-Second Street, she wondered whether she could find a place for herself in the strange world through which she just passed. (The clerk wondered whether any of those supplies would be touched; if not, it would not be the first time.)

At home, Clara put her new things in her room and could not help but pace and pace, waiting to hear her father's return from work and watching for it from her window. When she saw him make the turn to the house, she rushed down, reaching him just as Haskins shut the door behind him and quite short of breath.

"Papa. I must speak to you."

Mr. Bowman looked at his daughter.

"Very well. Give me fifteen minutes and we will sit in my library."

After more pacing, a quarter hour passed by the foyer clock, and Clara hurried into her father's space. He sat in an armchair and not behind his desk, with a whisky and the afternoon *New York Herald*. He was changed from the suit he wore when he was at his office, and there was a second glass on the desk with whisky, which he passed to his daughter when she sat. It was rare of her to drink hard liquor, but he suspected things would turn momentous and thought drinks were appropriate.

"Okay, my dear. Say what it is you wish to say."

"Oh, papa. I truly want to do it. I truly do. I went there and—"

Clara proceeded to detail her day and her purchases. Her whisky was left untouched though she twirled it in the tumbler, at times watching it lap up and down against the side.

Mr. Bowman took three or four sips of his drink. After one, he held the glass in his lap and leaned towards his youngest daughter.

"I will make you a proposal. I can see you are still adjusting to things and need more time to do so. I will give you six months. Your mother will go with you to where it is you want to go, and you and she shall report to me on what you find. We will calculate an appropriate allowance, but I will pay the landlord directly. You will need money for food and supplies and such, and that I will give to you."

He leaned back again and took a long sip of his Scotch. She cradled her still-untasted drink in her hands.

"You will have six months. I expect by that time you will have exhausted your enthusiasm—"

"But papa, that will not be time enough and my enthusiasm will not flag."

"If what you say is true, we will revisit the matter at the end of the six months. But you are not to disappear. You will be here for dinner regularly and you will spend Sundays with us, including Sunday services. Is that understood?"

"Yes, papa."

He paused.

"I hope this is what you want. I do not know that it is. Your mother does not know that it is. But you have suffered, and I...we will allow you this little adventure. I expect that when it is over, you will settle down and again be happy."

She would be fully back in society by spring. This was the consensus of everyone. Except Clara Bowman.

Clara was to exchange one day of obligations—to which she did not object—for six of exploration.

7.

Clara knew not the first thing about being or becoming an "artist." She saw plenty of art but other than boring classes with a governess and the thrill of sitting with Felicity Adams and wandering the halls of the National Gallery with her and watching the bustle of men and women in Greenwich Village, she was utterly ignorant.

Still, she and her mother found a one-bedroom apartment on Bleecker Street. Its bedroom was large with an unfortunately dark wallpaper in some sort of green, and the sitting room was large as well, painted in a mustard yellow with light green wainscoting. It was loud and smelly and Clara thought it perfect. Both rooms looked south onto Bleecker Street from the third floor, so the light was good. It had a small kitchen, and its ceilings were high, with cracks and peeling paint. Her parents insisted she have proper furnishings, and Clara did not object to the bed, tables, and chairs they bought for her. They doubted they would need to do anything about the wallpaper since Clara would be home within the six-month term of the lease and in any case it sufficed that a large Persian carpet added color to the place.

It was not large enough for an artist's studio—or what she hoped would be her artist's studio—so she rented other space, again for six months, on Third Street, just off Broadway. It had a tall ceiling and large windows at an angle to allow the light to come through. Those windows looked out to the south, and the space was bathed in the sun unless clouds wandered in the way. There were five or six other artists renting portions of the studio, and two of them were also women. All were older than Clara. Some were, like Clara, from society likely doing the same as she.

Once settled in with her supplies, Clara spent hour after hour on her first day in that space staring at a blank sheet of paper placed on her easel with enthusiasm and optimism. Others in the space offered to help her, but she declined. She must do it.

What would Felicity say? *Draw.*

She walked around. A variety of things were in the others' spaces. She saw various still lifes and portraits and landscapes scattered among the finished works. Since she had no model and she was cloistered in a building in Manhattan, her options were limited. She left her pristine cubbyhole and its paint-dabbled floor (none of it from her) and walked to the street. At a grocers around the corner, she found apples that would do for her purpose.

Thirty minutes later, three apples sat on a plate. They were red with hints of green and brown stems and they were the first portrait that Clara Bowman completed.

It was an awful portrait, and no one would see it. But it was the first and Clara did several more before the apples turned and after a few attempts at recording their rotting on paper, Clara threw them away and replaced them with other fruits until she felt confident enough to take a photograph from the house after she spent Sunday with her family. It was a photograph of her sister, and she spent the next several days and several sheets of paper attempting to capture the essence of Grace Lawford with her various colored pencils. Or at the least to draw something that could be recognized as being Grace Lawford.

And so began Clara Bowman's experimenting in the world of art and its mixture of elation and frustration, honesty and illusion.

8.

About six weeks after the trial period began, Clara stood on Bleecker waiting for traffic to clear so she could cross Lafayette. She felt a hard push to her back, though not so hard as to push her to the ground or into the street. She turned to see who shoved her, and there was a young woman, several inches shorter than her, in a simple dress and hat, beneath which was very dark amber hair put up in some sort of improvised braid, and looking shocked.

"Oh my goodness," said the shover to the shovee, "I am sorry. I was hurrying and not paying enough attention and—"

Clara said she was little bothered by the contact and turned to again await a break in the traffic.

"Do I not know you?" she heard.

Clara turned to the other, now standing beside her.

"I am Emily Connor. Perhaps our paths have crossed?"

Clara still could not place her. Emily Connor was slightly older, making it unlikely that they had met until Emily reminded her that it was at a small charitable event over the prior Christmas.

"Ah, yes. Miss Connor. I do recall. How do you do?"

"And you are Clara Bowman. I heard of what happened with your friends. I am sorry." After a brusque "thank you" from Clara, Emily sought to lighten things.

"I must pay you for my awful negligence in hitting you. May we have coffee or tea?"

After a more pleasant "thank you" from Clara, the two sat at a small table in a café that Emily frequented when she was in the neighborhood. Each had coffee and a Danish, it being not yet eleven on a Tuesday morning.

They chatted about mutual friends and other things they had in common. Emily said her indulgent parents gave her leave to wander about now and then when she made it clear that sometimes she could not tolerate the boredom she was expected to endure. As they stood to leave, Clara asked Emily if she could draw her.

"You have an…an interesting face. I think I would like to draw it, though I am not at all competent, and if possible use you as my model so I can see what progress I make as an artist."

Emily was flattered and since she took a liking to Miss Bowman and enjoyed every opportunity to avoid doing the mundane things she was at times supposed to be doing, she agreed and within the hour she sat on a stool in Clara's studio space while the artist attempted to draw her.

And this led to their routine. On Tuesdays and Thursdays, the two met at the café at ten and when they were finished with their coffee and gossip, they adjourned to the studio space Clara rented.

Emily became accustomed to Clara's humming while she drew and the regularity of her ripping a half-completed sketch to shreds, usually punctuated by words no decent woman should hear, let alone utter. Clara became accustomed to Emily's frequent interruptions. Emily would disagree with Clara's conclusion that she had no talent—"none at all"—as an artist and that her life would be better spent being what it was supposed to be. Then they headed out in the early afternoon for a sandwich at a little place on Broadway where the main topic of conversation among the artists was which of them was the most hopeless.

9.

The Saturday after Clara met Emily, she went to her parents' house for dinner, where she would stay overnight. Her mother was in her favorite corner of the drawing room, and when Clara went to her, Mrs. Bowman handed her a letter received at the house which, she noted, was from England.

1 November 1872

My Dearest Clara,

The deed is done. My dear, sweet brother has vowed to the world that he will love, honour, and obey the sweetest creature, who I have come to admire greatly. (Though not as greatly as I do my American friend.) It was a large ceremony with much pomp, and the two are off to honeymoon in Rome and Venice and Berlin and they may venture to Paris if conditions allow. I do fear for my new sister—Diana by name—and am determined to provide her with comfort in the (likely) event that her expectations for married life, and more particularly married life with my dear, sweet brother, are left unsatisfied.

I should like for you to have been here if only to meet my parents. When I spoke of you to them, I found that my brother would crawl away were he in the room, and I was glad of that. I do not know if he knows what I know, but this lack of knowledge makes him uncomfortable around me.

While my parents say there is much to admire in you and your mother based upon my stories about you, they dismiss it all as you are Americans and, as I told you, since they have enough money for at least some years they need not wander hat-in-hand for some industrialist's daughter to refill the family's coffers.

I am sending you separately a book I acquired concerning certain artists that have recently invaded all of the parlors of the West End. The people who see their work are enthusiastic about it but too many cannot recognize what they see since few of the works have pictures of horses or fields or passable relations. I do hope you have continued your drawing. I believe you can be quite adept at it if you set your mind to it.

You may have heard of some of these painters in New York but do not chastise me for presuming that you have not. Instead, I hope you take what you see and make it your own, as I have endeavoured to do.

I miss you very, very much, my dear Clara, and hope you miss me at least slightly after all that you have been through. More, I hope you are finding oils manageable. Be glad, as am I, that you have parents who have sufficient funds to keep you in canvas and paint.

I know it is too soon, but I do hope you decide to embark upon another tour of Europe so we can meet again. With your mother or your husband, I will be most pleased to take you to dinner at the Langham.

> *With love and the suggestion that you burn this letter should you deem portions of it impolitic, Felicity Adams (whose father is some kind of baron)*

Clara began to exchange letters with Felicity. By Christmas, she knew art would never leave her system and she was tempting fate by dabbling in oils. She thanked her distant friend for the news about her brother and wished his bride the best and that was the last either of them had to say about the subject.

More was her updating Felicity on what she was doing on the artistic front since returning to America: "I think it might work out, and I am forever in your debt for the path to which you directed me."

10.

John Evans was some ten years older than Clara. He held a junior staff position in Washington during the War and became known for his pencil portraits of others in the War Department. He was selected when the rebellion was put down to paint portraits of several of the more senior staff members. He tired of the rigors (and heat) of Washington, though, and in early 1866 he returned to his native New York, where his father was a clerk for a shipping company.

In New York, he was quickly introduced to members of society as a formidable talent and found himself in demand from those hoping he would do justice to their strength and wisdom and to their wives' beauty and intelligence. In this manner, by 1870 he was among the most sought-after portraitists in town. He had his own large studio on Houston Street and a Greek-revival house on the northern side of Washington Square, which itself had a studio on the third floor.

Evans was well-learned in the art of self-promotion, and he regularly held court at a table in the left back corner of the Moving Hand, a tavern on the corner of Bleecker and Broadway. He was famously a bachelor and enjoyed the company of artists male and female, the quality of their work and the degree of their promise being the main criteria for being among that company.

More and more men and women were flooding into New York aspiring to become artists. This included a significant number of children of middle-class families seeking an alternative career from the limited options otherwise available to them. For women, being an artist was suddenly viewed as a means of filling a societal need concerning culture. Groups began to form with students, and thoughts were given to the formation of formal art schools along the lines of some in Europe.

John Evans was one of the somewhat established artists who took to the idea of teaching. Clara, aware of her need, was among those who went to his studio on Houston with samples of her work, chiefly some of her *Emily*s, and she was among the six he invited to attend informal classes there, to his *atelier*, as the French called such schools. Three were women. Three were men. Several were, like Clara, from rich homes, but the others had more modest backgrounds, not unlike Evans's. He charged nominal tuition to the former and none to the latter, though each had to provide their own supplies, with the nearby shops affording the students of Mr. Evans a significant discount.

When Evans asked Clara to join, the two went to the Bowmans. Evans told them how naturally gifted their daughter was and how genuinely enthusiastic she was to develop as an artist. He used all the charm he fine-tuned in his years as a society portraitist, and the Bowmans agreed to extend Clara's freedom to a full year.

Clara decided she needed more space than she had in the carved-up spots on Third Street so she could have own studio. With Grace she explored alternatives, and they found an apartment in the front of the third floor of a building on Bleecker Street several doors west of her first flat that met her criteria. It had a large central room with a large bedroom off it. Most important, there was plenty of room for her to work and to store what she was doing. The front window faced south, across the street, so there was light. She enjoyed hearing the noisiness of the street below, which thankfully (though never entirely) quieted somewhat late at night so she could sleep.

With Grace's endorsement, her father agreed to the move and to the new space, and Clara had six more months to prove that she was an artist.

Evans had little formal training, but he knew of the emphasis on mastering form as the basis for artists to be able to express themselves. To understand and appreciate the symmetry of the human face and body necessary to bring life to a portrait. Balance and perspective. He knew there would soon be formal schools for this, as there already were in Europe, but for now it was up to generous artists such as John Evans himself.

For the first months, Clara and the others did little actual painting. Each day, though, she improved in drafting the curve of a woman's upper arm or the curl of a man's lip. Her ability to do eyes is what first brought her to Evans's attention, and she did not disappoint him in this regard as she drew eye after eye.

The class met three mornings a week, but Evans was strict and required his students to practice, practice, practice what they learned on their own time and bring the results to him when they next met. Each student, whose innate talents were what brought them to the *atelier* in the first place, improved week by week, and on a temperate Wednesday in April, Evans took them to an exhibition further west on Houston Street. The oils on display were portraits painted by one of Evans's friends. Some subjects were immediately recognizable. Most were not.

When they entered, an older gentleman approached.

"Ah, so these are John Evans's famous protégés. Come, come."

The man waving was Arthur Fisher, another of the renowned New York portraitists who was most famous for his large battle scenes from the War, particularly Gettysburg. Afterward, he foreswore such large works and devoted himself to portraits. While those of industrialists and their wives made him his money, those of the working class, often Irish or German immigrants, provided him fame among the artist class.

He gave the students a tour of his work, generous in answering questions. When they completed their circling, Evans said each student was to sit and draw what Fisher painted.

"I want you to imagine the subject is posing for you and you have nothing but a sketchbook and some pencils. As Fisher has brought them to life, so must you. You are not to copy what he did. You are to view the image as being a live model posing for you."

With that he let the students choose and said they would return, and he and Fisher left.

Clara was too slow, and the portrait of a servant girl was selected by another student. Then a nurse caught her eye. She quickly moved to her. She was not a girl, and the things the nurse saw over her years appeared in each of Fisher's brush strokes. She sat in her uniform, a blue frock and white apron with a white cap, like the uniform of a domestic servant. An infant lay in her arms. She looked down at the baby, but the angle allowed one to catch a glimpse of her right eye, enough to make the viewer believe she has a slight view into the woman's soul.

The nurse's lips were open slightly. Perhaps she was humming a lullaby. When following her glance, though, one could not be sure that the child was alive. Was she holding it from a distraught or even dead mother? Or was the mother in the room, recovering on a bed and looking over at her child and its protectress?

The nurse was very proper, but there were enough stray hairs on her head and wrinkles in her collar and perhaps even blood on her apron to show her image was captured when she was at work. For a moment she seemed a Madonna and Child, but its reality was blunter. Brutal even.

Clara lifted her fingers inches from the canvas, tracing them from the nurse's cap and down before circling the infant. The murmurings of her fellow students as they made their selections had stopped. Each had pulled up a stool and was beginning to sketch their subjects. She found her own stool and positioned it near the nurse and child and stared at it for several minutes before opening her sketchbook. After moving her pencil in small circles above the paper, she leaned down and drew the outline of the left side of the nurse's face.

When they returned, Evans and Fisher were pleased with the students' work, and Clara found in the endorsement something to include in her next correspondence with her English friend.

June 1, 1873

My Lady F,

You must excuse your serf's delay in writing as I have been deep in my own "New World." As I told you, my dear papa granted me six months to determine whether I had any artistic talent worth cultivating. He agreed to extend that to a full year because it appears that I may.

A well-known artist in New York, Mr. John Evans, has taken me under his tutelage. Do not fear that his motives are unkind. I am one of several in his group, men and women, and I have no fear of a repeat of the episode.

He is confident in my talent, however rough it is, and has included me among his students. There is a debate here in America, as I daresay there is in Europe and England, about the merits of formal education in arts. Many of the older gentlemen are of the view that they did not require schooling and that one's greatness is given by God and not developed in study. Study, they say, is for those doing mechanical arts, the drafting of drawings and illustrations in magazines.

Mr. Evans is the son of a clerk and learned his craft on his own while he was in Washington during our recent war. He is now welcomed in some of the great houses of New York and realizes astronomical prices for the portraits he does.

He has included me in his little group. "You have a special way with eyes," he says. I cannot say that this is true but perhaps you will give me your opinion. I am sending you a drawing in pencil that I did of Emily, a good friend of mine—though I must add not as great a friend as you would be were you here, My Lady—and you must tell me if I have captured her soul. And you must promise to be honest with me.

For now, though, dear Mr. Evans is having us draw, draw, draw. We should be banished were we to use the word "oil" even in conversation. "That will be for later, my dears," he tells us again and again. "And when you get there, you each will be glorious, not be producing the turgid gobs that pass for 'fine arts' in some places."

I have put aside the oils with which I confess to have experimented and instead draw, draw, draw. He promises that we will see a nude model someday and I hope he is not taunting us. He is a great man—a sworn bachelor—and I believe he shall make me into what I can be as an artist.

I am sorry to go on like this and you must surely by now be wondering whether there will be anything of interest in this missive. My dear mama has not surrendered her desire to see me married. She has long since surrendered a requirement that I marry "well" and it seems it is enough that I simply marry someone and give her a grandchild, at which point I daresay she will permit me to disappear into my New World so that she can properly tend to the child.

So, I meet men again and again at her house on Sundays. Each is perfectly fine, I suppose, but it is clear that their interest in me, beyond my father's money, is identical to that of my mama. To bear their child. "Yes, yes," they will say. "You can have your little studio to keep yourself entertained if you provide me with an heir."

Well, I can assure you, I shall not "know" any of them. Indeed, I find many, though not all, of the men who I meet in Greenwich Village to be uniquely non-possessive about women. We are too young to be competitive for the crumbs of commissions we might get and for now (at least) we are supportive of one another without regard to whether we are men or women. I assure you, though, that there are more than a few men who might pique my interest should I be so inclined! I have deferred such ambitions so that I might concentrate on my art. But I assure you that, as the Baron might say, the fields are ripe with game and I intend to bag me one. Simply not as yet.

There is also an unspoken rule among Mr. Evans's students. Romantic involvement will not be permitted. I am sure each of us could easily fall in love with others in our little group—I know I could—but we are on our happy journey together and we share the goal of reaching our destination together and, well, hope to become life-long friends, even after the brutality of having people buy our works.

On this, though, I confess to some ambivalence. I have plenty of resources from my family to long remain but several of the others, some the children of clerks as Mr. Evans is, find it difficult to manage. Mr. Evans charges no fees to them, and I am glad of it. As of now, they can remain by making little bits of money on side projects and by living cluttered up in small apartments on the top floors of the buildings here. Having made it thus far, I hope they will remain.

    I again apologize for my delay in writing. To an extent, I admit to suffering on the anniversary of the deaths that remain so painful to me. But I continue, as I did when I had the joy of meeting you. I know you will understand and forgive me and write back and make sure to tell me about my drawing of Emily. It was done quickly, but I am quite fond of it.

> I am
> Forever your
> devoted servant,
> Miss Clara Bowman

* * * *

FELICITY RECEIVED THE SKETCH of Emily some days after the letter arrived. It was a rainy morning in Primrose Hill so she brought it close to the window.

    Clara had come far since the primitive scratches she made when she was with Felicity. *Emily* was lacking in many of the skills that Clara was working on, but it was beautiful. The woman was pretty, no more, and the lines that defined her were a little off so that it seemed unbalanced. There were evident erasure-marks, and Felicity suspected that Clara hurried to get what she saw down on paper. She would learn that being deliberate would not sacrifice spontaneity and that technical skill would translate into having the image she drew reflect the image she saw.

Clara surely knew of the defects, but they were not why she sent it. The eyes. She wrote that Mr. Evans said, "'You have a special way with eyes,'" and she wanted Felicity's opinion of whether that was the case.

29 June 1873

My Most Precious C,

I shall be honest, as you demanded. You must take your Mr Evans's instructions about the technical aspects of drawing. You show great promise, especially in contrast to the glimmers I saw in London.

But you ask about "eyes." You have captured your Emily's spirit remarkably well. I am quite jealous. I shall never allow you to draw me as in so doing you will expose the dark secrets of my soul, of which I fear there are many. Evans was right in his judgement of you. I think you have the artist's temperament and will soon have the artist's skill and one day we shall hold a joint exhibition in Covent Garden and you will be the toast of London and we shall both be forced to decline far more commissions than we can possibly fulfill.

I am pleased with your Emily and am confident that you shall improve by leaps and bounds. Now you must congratulate me in turn. For I am in love. He has no title, not even a minor one, and I do not know how The Baron and The Baroness will respond when I tell them. I have been afraid to do so, and you are one of the few who know, though perhaps I will have told them by the time you read this.

He is a clerk at a law office at Lincoln's Inn though he is also a Cambridge man. I met him, much as I did you, when he admired my drawing of some flowers in the Park.

His name is Edward Wilson and I wish you could draw him so that I can see into his soul. For now, it must suffice that he is almost intolerably handsome and the kindest of creatures. We happen to run into each other at the same time each Saturday afternoon not distant from the pond where you and I so often sat. He lives with his parents in Camden Town—which is close to the Park and not far from my flat. I have yet to meet them but am hopeful of having done so by the time you read this.

I do swear that I never knew what love was until I met my Mr Wilson and am now hopeful that I can do justice to the idea in my painting.

Please, please tell me you approve and pray that my parents will as well. I have not told the Future Baron for he would laugh at me and at him and I should not wish to have yet another reason to loathe him, as I have more than enough as it is.

I am sending you a sketch that I have done of my dear Mr Wilson, being confident that you are too far away to steal him from me.

Clara. I have never even thought this before, but I would very much like to have his children. I know this is silly of me. But it is what I truly feel, and it is why I know I am truly in love with him and I think he surely must have some feelings for me. So please tell me I am the luckiest woman in the Old World when you have seen my picture of him and know he is infinitely better than I could ever portray him to be.

I am, and shall always be,
Your dear friend
F

Clara received the sketch about a week after she received the letter. Felicity was right. Enhanced, perhaps, by her undeniable skill, it showed a man with a round face and smallish nose. His hair was well-trimmed, with a part to the right, and he had a mustache but no other facial hair. Felicity was too modest about her own skill with eyes, and those that looked out at Clara were soft and sparkling.

She wished that she could have her Mr. Wilson. Her liaison with Sir John had pushed her deep into herself when it came to men. Perhaps her wish to live in Greenwich Village was a wish to be free of the pressures of her parents and their obsession over time for her prospects and long-delayed settling down with a man.

Since that London disaster, she often, too often, thought of that train ride that took the lives of her Ashley and Thomas. *Why that train? That car? Those seats?* She would have been happy living in a house with Thomas and their three children, Sunday dinners at the Davis house or the Bowmans'. Godmother to Ashley's firstborn as Ashley would be to hers.

She would not have lain with Sir John Adams. She would be happy, and when she saw Felicity's note, dear Felicity whom she also would have not met but for the idiocy of that train engineer in Queens, she knew her Mr. Wilson was long dead and always would be.

She needed air and walked to Broadway. It was early summer, but damp. It was not long before she was sweating, not quite sure of where she was going or why. She had not eaten yet that day and came upon a tavern some distance from her flat. The restaurant was dark inside, which suited her, and a barmaid, a short older woman with wrinkled skin and a pleasant brogue, showed her to a small table to the side and brought her an ale. She ordered a cheese sandwich.

As she often did since London, she carried a sketchbook, and she opened it on the table. She began to lightly draw lines, but with no thought. When she moved it aside to make room for her sandwich, the barmaid complimented her, and to Clara's puzzled look she nodded to the pad and with a smile she left.

The drawing was sparse, but it was clearly a face. A man's face shrouded in streaks of slanting lines that could be rain or could just be a failure on the artist's part of seeing him. She lay the sketch above the plate and stein while she ate the sandwich and drank the ale.

Even she did not know what it was at first. *Was it her Mr. Wilson? Was he some fictional character searching for her, and her for him, in the rain?*

When she finished the sandwich and ale and paid the barmaid, she headed north, going up a side street to avoid the Broadway crowd. With the nourishment, she did not feel as tired, and her pace was faster, and the route was more direct than the meandering one she took earlier.

Back at her flat, she took a photograph from the top of her bureau. She did not need it. Clara adjusted her small easel and placed a paper on it. She so wished she had the skill to do it justice, but she did not and could only do what she could do.

In a trance, she quickly drew the outlines of a face. It had smooth contours and was a bit narrow. She stepped back and recognized it as one of two people. She would only know which when she continued and she honestly did not know which until she drew the lines of a nose, and then things flowed as if she already had the talent she hoped to acquire one day. She only stopped when she was satisfied and when the image had leaped from her soul to the paper.

August 8, 1873

My Lady F,

You should be happy that I may not simply magically appear at your door to take your Mr. Wilson away or I should surely attempt it. Alas, I must find my own.

I am sending to you a sketch that I fear you will find inadequate, but which is full of meaning to me. When we met, we spoke of the tragedy that led to my visit, and your drawing of Mr. Wilson—surely it is more than a mere "sketch"—has caused me to revisit the events that took my best friends from me. Do not chide yourself for expressing your own happiness to me, I pray you. I am overjoyed.

But I am also reminded of what is absent from my own life. I believed myself beyond the weight of the memories of my dearest Thomas Davis but your Mr. Wilson, through your words, reminded me that I am not. I pray, though, that this revelation itself will aid me in moving forward.

I hope that by sending it to you, you will understand me. I cannot now, nor I daresay will I ever be able to, do him justice. Nor of his sweet sister. I feel that I have somehow become an "artist." I have, however inadequately, used my creation to express my loss (and perhaps my guilt). And surely my feelings.

I do not know that this is what "artists" do, to use the paper or canvas to receive their thoughts. But it is all that I know how to do. I know you will understand me. I hope you will not let my ache cause you to doubt the unabridged joy I feel for you and the hope for you and Mr. Edward Wilson.

I am, of course, jealous of your good fortune, for which I assure you is your entitlement and can only hope that I shall soon meet my own Mr. Wilson and that I can be half so happy as you plainly are.

Your friend,
C

Felicity found the drawing itself raw, but that was part of its essence. Clara was right in her letter. There was a debate in London as there was in New York and she assumed elsewhere about artistic talent and whether it needed to be enhanced by systematic training in the basics.

Her drawing proved that deep emotional art could be created in the absence of technical skill. Clara was vastly improved even since her earlier sketch of Emily. But Felicity understood she still had much to learn and master. Yet the image of Thomas Davis had a visceral core that made it an extension of Clara's, the artist's, self.

By that point, any doubts Felicity may have had about herself and her Mr. Wilson were gone. She wrote her thoughts to Clara, a letter bounding in encouragement as to both Clara's improvement as an artist and the reality that she was, in fact, an "artist." She also hoped Clara would find her Mr. Wilson and told of her own confirmation that she had found hers.

11.

It remained for neither woman that her life was entirely her own. Each depended upon the largess of her father. Felicity spent many hours speaking to Edward about how to approach the baron and many restless nights concerned about it. It was clear by the time her parents last returned from their estate in Derbyshire that she wished to marry Edward and Edward wished to marry her and that not only was it best that they get the baron's permission for the union but that it was necessary.

Edward met the baron and baroness but once. They were in town before departing for the country house, and Felicity brought him round one Saturday for tea—one on which she knew the future baron was not in—and introduced Edward to them.

All was civil. Edward confessed never to have been on a hunt or on a horse and that he scarcely had left London other than to go to the seaside sometimes when he was a lad and for his period up in Cambridge for his study. He complimented the baroness on her Piccadilly house and the baron on one of the several paintings of the Derbyshire house and grounds. He opined how he would relish the opportunity to explore them "someday."

He bowed properly and thanked them profusely before he left, alone, for his parents' flat. Before the door was shut, the baron turned and walked towards his library, and the baroness and the daughter watched before following him.

He stepped to the table on which he kept his whisky. It was still early, and dinner would not be for some hours, but he poured himself a dram and added some water before turning to the women in his world.

"He seems a nice enough fellow, to be sure. Tell me, Felicity, what are his intentions?"

She and her mother sat on either side of a large leather couch while her father sank into a matching leather chair across from them, his tumbler safely in his grasp.

Felicity had long pondered what she would say to this question.

"My intention, father," and she turned to the baroness, "mother" and then back to her father, "is to have his children."

The baron nearly choked on the impudence of his child, reaching his wrist to wipe some errant drops of whisky from his mouth.

"Have his children? Are you—?"

Felicity smiled and jumped to her father.

"Oh, father, you are so cute," which caused him to try to shake her from her hug.

She stepped back and returned to the couch, allowing her mother time to recover as well.

"He is the most wonderful man I could imagine, and I want to marry him. 'Tis as simple as that. I want to have his children and your grandchildren, and I want him to learn to ride and go on hunts with you when he can afford to spend time away—"

"That is another thing, my dear. 'When he can afford to spend time away.' This man…he works. He will not have enough time to take care of you. If he thinks he will get a settlement that will do away with his having to earn your keep he is very much mistaken."

"Father, do not think him a fortune hunter. We have spoken and, yes, he expects some settlement from you for taking me off your hands. But it will be not nearly what you would forfeit should I marry one in your circle, capable as he might be on a stallion. No. Only enough so that we can be set up in a decent home in a decent neighborhood. No more.

"He is a proud man, papa. He will not take anything more."

"But, Felicity, surely there are others," the baroness said.

"No, mama. Surely you see that, given the line of 'gentlemen' you have forced me to converse with over the years. Edward has neither money nor title, and I truly believe he wants neither from me. Mama." Felicity put her hands to her stomach. "Mama, you must understand. I feel it here," and she nodded down. She took one of those hands and reached for her mother. "Surely you understand that."

The baroness blushed before looking at her husband. The two knew that neither felt it "there" before they wed and neither expected that they would. It was not required and there were those of their class who thought it an actual impediment. It threatened both the man's world and the woman's and their well-defined roles.

Felicity's father was not a baron when her parents wed. Her grandfather was alive and well but succumbed to consumption when Felicity was only ten (and her brother was twelve). She had an uncle who resented the distinction between the first- and the second-born male but he grew satisfied with a living he had near the Derbyshire estate. Plus her two aunts, who Felicity's grandfather managed to marry off with large settlements to lesser families.

Her father was young when he acceded to the title. He and the baroness were to complement each other and no more. But they had become more than fond of each other over the years and could fairly be considered to be in love, though they would never be so foolish as to say so. Felicity knew so, and it was what she hoped would allow her to get her father's consent to marry Mr. Edward Wilson when the time came.

Edward had no inkling of who Felicity was when they met, and she revealed her lineage only some weeks later, well after she ensnared him. She liked him from the start, from his compliments of her work in the park and even more when she showed him around her flat, and he could see the other things she had done. He had a liking for paintings and frequented the National Gallery during quiet times during his rare quiet hours at Lincoln's Inn. He was of average size and well-built but more than anything, to Felicity, was his easy smile.

12.

The happenings in Piccadilly were unknown to Clara between letters from Felicity. She was dealing with her own explorations. At a coffee shop, on a sweltering afternoon, Clara was sharing with Emily the excitement she often felt after a class with Evans. On that day, she was going on and on about the beautiful nude, posed like a Grecian statue, she drew. She saw ancient sculptures in books, but to see it alive, the gorgeous muscles defining the man's form, was a wonder.

She knew she did not do justice to the form in her drawing, but Evans said it was "surely an excellent effort." Seeing the model and her attempt at capturing him taught Clara that she had far to go. She was telling Emily about this revelation when suddenly Kyle Smith appeared by their small table.

"Won't you introduce me to your friend?" he asked.

Clara vaguely knew Kyle as an artist with more enthusiasm than talent. He had one of the small spaces in the studio that Clara rented before she had enough room in her new flat. Kyle Smith was of the inspirational school, believing that one's own talent was enough to transform a canvas into an artist's vision. While he showed glimpses of insight, he was too sloppy and undisciplined to make it a consistent part of his work.

For all his limitations as an artist, Kyle found it easy to charm women and had gathered the reputation for being something of a Lothario. He had a quick and sometimes cutting wit that too often turned sarcastic, but he was given leeway by his boyish smile. Though not conventionally handsome, his imperfect parts came together to make a pleasing whole. His older brother died in the War, and most who knew Kyle thought his family treated him unfairly because of that. He shrugged this off, though it ate at him. He was expected to take his brother's place as the oldest boy—he had two older sisters—but fought against it, and much like Clara had wrested a promise from his parents to be allowed to uncover his artistic talents.

But, as noted, while endowed with some God-given talent, he refused to apply himself as Mr. Evans's students did. He did good work, yes. It would never be great, and there were scores of others who could be similarly described within ten blocks of the coffee shop where Clara introduced him to Emily.

Emily was not concerned about art. She enjoyed it but was not discerning beyond appreciating Clara's creativity. She allowed her friend to draw her and hoped that perhaps she would someday paint her. She enjoyed the time they spent together. It was an oasis for Emily. She was flattered by what Felicity said about Clara's drawing of her when she was shown the letter from England.

On that day at the coffee shop, Emily thought it might be interesting to get to know the engaging Kyle Smith. When he offered to join her in getting a cab, she readily agreed, and Clara let the two disappear without her.

Clara realized she was being unfair. To both Emily and Kyle. She knew enough to know he was not as talented an artist as she was herself and never would be, even if he were to work on the basics. She disliked that she diminished him for that and for his stubbornness and that it reflected her increasing arrogance about her art, being sufficiently self-aware to recognize it.

And she was jealous that shortly thereafter Emily seemed to prefer spending time with Kyle, visiting in his portion of the Third Street studio and sometimes agreeing to sit for him instead of for her.

But whatever happened between Emily and Kyle would only be learned over time. Clara would only watch and hope she did not lose her friend to him.

13.

Clara was hinting to her parents each week that she was committed to her new life. In time, she assured them, she would find a man to love. What happened then she could not say. But she could say that she had no intention of stopping what she came to love.

By understanding her progress, as her year neared its end, after another afternoon tea with John Evans, Clara's parents were satisfied it was not a temporary diversion, and Mr. Bowman gave Clara his blessing to remain in her studio on Bleecker Street.

14.

"They will be their own ruination. It serves them right."

Sundays were not always pleasant at the Bowmans' and September 21, 1873 was one of those days. Clara had just sat down at the table, with the Lawfords there too, and her father could no longer control himself. Everyone at the table knew of the just-revealed financial collapse involving a railway in the northwest into which some Philadelphia banker had thrown clients' money only to see it evaporate although, it was widely believed, not before the main villains had gotten their own money out. It was spoken of in pockets of those at that morning's services and the usual thoughts of dinner were replaced in many a congregant's mind by who could still afford to be in town by Christmas.

Mr. Bowman's outburst was not unexpected.

"People like the father of that great friend of yours," he said to Clara.

She thought for a moment, a bit of salad midway between her plate and her mouth.

"Emily? Emily Connor?" Clara had brought her to Sunday dinners two or three times.

"The very one. I did not like her because I thought her father was a scoundrel and now it is proved. I do not want you to have anything to do with her. Is that understood?"

Clara looked from her mother—who appeared shocked by the threat—back to her father. She slowly returned the fork to her plate.

"Are you saying, papa, that unless I terminate my relationship with Emily Connor you will terminate my allowance?"

"You cannot mean that George," said his wife.

George Bowman's certainty flagged. He realized he overstepped. Surely Emily was free of guilt for her father's folly. He looked from his wife to his youngest daughter and back. The Lawfords were ready to intervene on Clara's behalf but hoped it would prove unnecessary and were holding their fire.

"No, I suppose not." George Bowman eased in his chair, still holding his own salad fork. "I am sure he is honest enough. Without our advantages, he has done well enough. I can only say, Clara, that you need to be careful with that girl. That is all I can say."

With that, the topic was ended—though not forgotten by Clara—and the family finished their salads.

Some days later, Emily did report that her family was badly hurt in the Panic, as it became known. It was while Clara was lightly sketching her. Emily's father confessed this to her, and she told Clara (only after she extracted a vow of silence) that her family was in deep financial trouble and hoped to make things right with a South American investment that sounded promising.

"What am I to do if it doesn't work?"

Clara did a final line, of one of Emily's eyebrows, before putting her pad and pencil down.

"If you have no money?"

"Yes. I should be married by now, but I could not bear the thought without finding a man I wanted to be with. Have I been a romantic fool?"

Clara stepped up to her friend and ran a hand across the cheek she had studied and drawn countless times. She seemed shrunken, fearful.

"What about Kyle?"

Emily pulled her head back from the pose she was trying to hold.

"Kyle? I do like him. Quite a bit, in fact. He is not as some people see him. He is not as staid as so many I meet elsewhere. He pays attention to me and it is exciting. Isn't that what we are supposed to do when we're young?"

Clara was not so sure and let the question go.

"But I could not imagine marrying him," Emily continued, "growing old with him. He is a bit full of himself, and he has not even had me visit his family. Even his sisters. There is fondness. Yes. But I cannot foresee that there ever will be love."

Clara went back to her seat and resumed her drawing. She continued it even when she announced, "I once lay with someone."

Emily was shocked at the turn of the conversation. Clara stopped mid-line and rose from her stool and sat in one of her armchairs, and Emily was soon in the one beside it.

Clara confessed to that unsatisfying afternoon, minutes really, with Sir John Adams. How no one knew but Felicity. How it hurt her to keep her secret and that she felt she could no longer do so. She did not provide details. She did not even use his name. Simply "an English gentleman," the last word causing Emily to chortle. Beyond that, Clara merely said she wanted to make love with him but discovered during the act that he merely wanted to use her for his personal enjoyment. "If enjoyment it even was."

Clara feared it colored her view of all men.

"Is that why you seem so tentative around them?"

The question broke Clara's reverie.

"I think it is. Not the men with whom I draw. We are all friends and no more. And those who make advances to me I quickly disabuse of the idea. I have become quite adept at it. I am sure some think I may be otherwise inclined, but I am not."

"So, I am safe?" Emily asked, regretting it until she saw Clara's smile.

"Yes, Emily. I will always love you, but you are safe in that regard."

It was Emily's turn to approach her friend. She sat on the arm of Clara's chair and grasped the artist's shoulders, giving her a slight peck on the top of her head.

"What are we to do when I have no money?"

"Well, I cannot get any for you from my father, I can assure you."

Clara told Emily of the Sunday confrontation, and how her father backed down when he realized that Clara might abandon him before abandoning Emily. But that was small solace for the financial difficulties in which the Connors might find themselves. If this South American thing did not work, her father warned her of dire consequences, saying that perhaps they could remain in the country house in Berkshire County in western Massachusetts.

"No," she said. "I shall be fine in the end. But I think to be independent I must find something to do that will pay me something so I am not the spinster people whisper about at church or at parties, assuming I can afford to go to parties or that anyone would invite me to one."

Emily did well to hide the concerns she had about what was happening, financially, with her family. Her father was as morose as she ever saw him and more often than not her mother warned her against interrupting him while he sat drinking in his library after dinner. She took refuge with Clara, again working on her portrait.

That particular session with Clara soon ended. Neither was in a mood to do art. But things were better when they next met. By then, Clara was regularly drawing live models—not yet oils—with Mr. Evans's class. While the models, men and women, were nude, she did not dare take such a step with Emily.

She was due to send a new portrait of Emily to England. Clara knew she was not the master of the form but hoped her facial portrait would satisfy her English friend.

For this sitting, Emily brought a blouse with a broad, open neck. It was far too revealing to be worn in public. Clara selected a necklace with large stones among the jewelry Emily also brought. She decided to use chalk on white paper.

Clara often experimented with Emily's hair, and this time she put it up to expose the neck on which she draped the necklace. The blouse was very light. It would appear as a series of vertical lines cascading from the shoulders. The hair itself was a wonderful brown, neither dark nor light. Light vibrated about the curls that rose above Emily's face. Her ears were exposed, and her nose was prominent as she leaned slightly to her right. Wisps of her hair fell from what was otherwise well ordered and reached to the nape of Emily's long neck.

Her lips were painted, but not much, and were a tone between a peach and a rose.

Clara had, of course, promised Felicity that the eyes would stand out, and she succeeded. Emily looked to Clara's left, and one of her eyes was only partly in view. The other was clearly defined beneath a long, curved eyebrow. Blue. It was a magical blue. Azure perhaps, like the sea. And one could not help but wonder what thoughts flowed through the woman as she was observed and recorded by the artist.

Clara knew Felicity would be pleased.

15.

In early December, Clara saw in the *New York Sun* that a huge investment in a Bolivian railway was a fraud and that, as it said, "a wave of destruction crashed over Wall and Broad Streets from which many are sure to have drowned." Her fear that the Connors were among them was confirmed soon thereafter when Emily appeared at Evans's studio and interrupted a class.

Evans permitted Clara to meet with her openly-distraught friend, and the two went to a small café on Mercer Street where Emily confirmed her family's downfall.

"Some think my father among the ringleaders, though he is not, and we will be leaving in the next day or so to escape from the mob. I do not know when I shall see you again," and with that, she rushed away, and Clara wondered too at her question.

She was surprised how Emily's departure affected her. Her model, perhaps her muse, suffering and much as she enjoyed the Christmas holiday with her family, Clara regretted Emily's absence. But the two exchanged frequent correspondence, with Emily assuring her friend of her and her family's survival. As 1874 began, her spirits were lifted sufficiently that she regularly bemoaned the boredom of Stockbridge, Massachusetts. The only saving grace, she said, was being able to socialize with similarly unmarried refugees from New York society.

Clara assured Emily she could stay at her flat as long as she liked since, as she said, "I will find my own boredom improved immensely by the presence of one Miss Emily Connor."

Clara also said that Kyle Smith was regularly pestering her about Emily. *When is she returning? Has she said anything about me?* Emily said she missed him at times and would enjoy herself more were he around, but when Clara responded that he asked for the Connors' address Emily was glad she did not give it to him. The thought of him being with her was far more pleasing than his actually being in Massachusetts.

During a warm spell in early February 1874, Emily took the carriage the Connors managed to keep to a train that took her to the Grand Central Depot. She found a cab and presented herself at Clara's flat, promising that she would be followed by only the minimal clothing that she would need for her new life as a woman who needed to find a job.

Accordingly, the next order of business was finding employment. Although Clara was happy to take no money for the rent, Emily insisted that if she were to be independent, she could no longer rely on the financial kindness of others. Finding a way to earn her keep became her priority.

Opportunities were limited to a woman of Emily's background. Perhaps a good man would come her way eventually. For the moment, she needed an alternative. She was far too independent to fall into the role of a governess. After inquiries in the neighborhood, she decided she would enjoy working at a restaurant, interacting with people, and that is what she ended up doing. It was work far more strenuous than she anticipated, but she came to enjoy it.

16.

Shortly after Emily's arrival, Clara received news from London.

22 February 1874

My precious C,

As feared, I have lost myself to my Edward Wilson, but in exchange, I have received his name. For, yes, I am now Mrs Edward Wilson.

The Baron finally came around though Edward does not hunt or ride and did not pretend to do so when he visited with me in Derbyshire. It was the Baroness who did the trick I think. Over many conversations, she probed and satisfied herself that not only did I love Edward with all my heart, but I had never and would never care for the attentions of anyone else.

So this is what love is, and I hope you envy me to the bottom of your bones.

Edward's parents are lovely, if a bit intimidated by the Baron. They, too, joined us in Derbyshire but they are city folk, real city folk, and I was pleased with how they comported themselves in the face of the Baron's assault.

I do believe that by the end, he had a slight change of heart, and this was proved by his agreeing to attend a small party at the Wilson house in Camden Town. It is a small house, but very tidy, and it was clear that Mrs Wilson—by which I mean the elder Mrs Wilson since there are now two of us—had worked for days to make it so. She could not change the furniture or the wallpaper, which I assure you was not to the liking of my father or my mother, but the Baron seemed content enough with the expensive whisky Mr Wilson bought for the occasion, even if he frowned at the glass from which he drank it.

The Baroness was won over first by the other Mrs Wilson and even offered to assist in the kitchen, an offer that was graciously declined, which compelled my mother to speak with me and Mr Wilson—by whom I mean my Mr Wilson—while his father tried to converse with the Baron.

I go on too long, as ever. These events must serve as my excuse for not writing to you earlier. I have been overwhelmed with joy, and I hope you will share some of it.

I fear that I neglected my art but am now comfortable in the small house some doors from my in-laws in which I now pleasantly live. Edward has allowed me one room entirely for my work, and it is as comforting as the flat in which you and I spent so many enjoyable hours.

Oh, I do wish you were here and that you were here for the wedding. Please promise me that at some point you will visit us. And by "us" I hope there is more than just Mr and Mrs Wilson. (By which I mean the younger pair.)

Your English friend,
Mrs Edward Wilson

It was not unexpected news. Felicity sprinkled her letters with references to Edward Wilson and to their engagement though this knowledge did not lessen Clara's enthusiasm for the consummation.

April 18, 1874

Mrs. Wilson,

I am overjoyed for you, and my only request is that you tell me where I might find the Edward Wilson of the New World. Now that you are his wife and have returned to your work, you must send me another portrait of him so I might see the blanket of happiness you have placed over him by marrying him. I know you too well to doubt that he is a lucky man, perhaps even as lucky as you so clearly are in your choice of a spouse.

(I do wonder as I write this whether you are already along the way of welcoming a third member of your family, and I pray that it is true.)

Alas, my search for someone like him, or half like him which should suffice to a commoner like me, has failed. Though I admit to not being as enthusiastic as I might be. I told my Emily what happened on my London visit. She is the only one but you who knows, and I trust her as I do you. It may affect how I view matters of the heart though in the end, no one else's heart has anything to do with it.

I am also committed to my studies. I am sending you my most recent effort of my Emily. I think it vastly superior to the scratches I sent to you before, although you were too kind to call them so.

Please, please tell me what you think. Send me a portrait of the (I know it is true) fortunate Mr. Wilson. And send me news as soon as there be news of any potential additions to your household.

Tell Mr. Wilson that I love him with all my heart and that someday I hope to visit him, you, and the rest of your new family—I should not be able to survive meeting your old one—and tell him so in person.

> *Your most jealous and now second dearest friend,*
> *Clara Bowman*

About two week after she sent her letter to London, Clara was anxious for a response. She did not need to wait long.

> *1 May 1874*

My Precious C,

Thank you for your kind note and warning with respect to my beloved E. As to your beloved(?) E, I think it is beyond a first-class effort. You capture her, or I assume you have captured her as I have never met the good woman. I beg you to continue your work which will help to inspire me.

Why, you will ask, do I need inspiration? As we both prayed, I am nearly fulfilled as our little child is growing within me. I did not know, nor did I hope, to feel this but I realize how important our child—God willing—will be to us.

> *Mrs Edward Wilson*

Felicity's letter bolstered Clara and especially news that she was with child, for which Clara indeed prayed each morning and each evening. She had long since abandoned thoughts of an active God even as she sat through services with her parents at the Church of the Incarnation on Madison Avenue each Sunday. She sometimes gazed across the congregation as the reverend gave his sermon and knew that few of those in the pews gave any attention to what was being said, focusing instead on appearing attentive while thinking of the dinner they would have when it was all over.

She knew her father was among that group, but her mother was not. After Felicity's letter, which Clara did not at first mention to Mrs. Bowman, Clara made a point of often reaching for her mother's hand during services, and she felt an intimacy she could not recall having with her before. She did not tell her mother of Felicity's condition initially for fear of raising expectations as to her own prospects. It was only some weeks later that she mentioned it as they walked home after a service.

She was right. Her mother did speak to her of her own prospects.

"This little venture of yours. Surely there will come a time when it will stop and you will find someone. You are getting old, too old already for some men."

"Mama. I would not wish to be with any such man. Let them all take younger brides."

Since Felicity's last letter, indeed since her first reference to the desire she had to carry Edward's child, Clara often thought of her choices. Without question, she could have one or two children by now, tended to by others but still hers. She understood that she deprived her mother of the pleasures of more grandchildren to spoil. It was what was expected of her, and it was what became of most of the girls with whom she came out. She saw many on Sundays at the Church of the Incarnation, and watched their nurses push carriages with their charges or hold the hands of those charges as they headed up Madison Avenue while those mothers strolled together.

Perhaps that would be the case had Thomas Davis lived. That it would be her and her dear sister-in-law Ashley who strode arm-in-arm while their children—surely Ashley would be a wonderful mother—lagged as they headed to Clara's or Ashley's family for dinner. But as thoughts of Thomas had led her to the bed of Sir John for fear of never experiencing something, so, too, they led her to refrain from a connection with anyone whom she did not love as she loved Thomas.

She was now in a place completely apart from her Old World. She could marry any number of men she knew, even if she was already past twenty. Perhaps had she thought of falling in love with one of them she could or would have. But her days with Felicity in London redirected her. Now Felicity was forcing her to reconsider herself, and she needed to speak about it with her mother.

"I know you too well to allow that you would just take any man. I only wish that you would open yourself to the suggestion, much as Lady Felicity has done."

There was a bit of a chill in the spring air, and it proved a useful excuse for Clara to pull herself closer to her mother.

"I promise you, mama. I am open to it. I promise you that you will have your grandchild. I cannot promise when."

Mrs. Bowman reached her free arm to touch her daughter's hand. "I know you will."

The thought was never far from Clara's mind, particularly as she received a drawing of Mr. Wilson with a note dated three weeks after the prior one in which Felicity assured her that her pregnancy was advancing without complications.

17.

John Evans made it a practice to bring a student with him for his portrait commissions, not only to assist him but to learn the art and politics of portraiture.

"Those who are willing to pay for a large portrait are delicate creatures and must be handled delicately," he often said. "You must not only paint them well but treat them in a manner that they believe themselves worthy of being treated. Some obsequiousness, yes, but always reminding them that you are not a tradesman but an artist revealing their inner beauty, real or imagined."

When Evans was hired to do portraits of Mr. and Mrs. Peter McNabb, it was Clara's turn to join him. Teacher and student met with the couple, both in their twenties, in their sitting room. Evans asked them each to hold various poses briefly so he and Clara could do quick sketches. After finishing several, he suggested a single portrait of the couple, done in the sitting room with him seated and her with her arms draped around his shoulders, but Mrs. McNabb demurred. She was happy about using the sitting room, or perhaps the library, for her husband but insisted that her own portrait be of her alone, done in her study. She suggested that Mr. McNabb's be done first.

For several spring days, Peter McNabb sat stiffly in a high-backed leather chair in the sitting room. The fireplace was over his right shoulder with a landscape horizontally above the mantel. Though there was no fire, Evans intended to include one to create some brightness in what would otherwise be a dark work. McNabb wore a simple suit. The jacket had a wide lapel, and his neck scarf was maroon with yellow stripes beneath the winged tips of his collar. The table to his right had a simple blue vase atop it, and a seemingly randomly arranged group of yellow roses jutted up from it.

Mrs. McNabb was often out, but when she returned, she invariably stopped in the sitting room to assess the progress being made on her husband's portrait. She also made a point of looking at Clara's smaller effort. This was Evans's practice with his students and if the student's product justified it, it would be included with his portrait's unveiling.

Mrs. McNabb had nothing but praise for the master's work but only criticism for the student's. "Too much" this and "too little" that were repeated again and again, and Clara thanked Mrs. McNabb for the assistance and would pretend to alter a hand or a lapel as she suggested so she would leave them be.

By assuring Mary McNabb of Clara's competence notwithstanding the criticisms heaped upon her while Mr. McNabb's portrait was being done—it would be finalized in Evans's studio—Mrs. McNabb consented to "the girl's" presence with her portrait.

Her study was bright. It was not unlike Grace's study, and Clara felt a twinge of regret that she would never likely have one of her own. This one was decorated as Grace's was, though the colors were different. Mrs. McNabb's walls had peach-colored wallpaper with veins of green stems on which varieties of blue flowers were strewn. The room smelt of the recently-cut lilacs distributed precisely but (seemingly) randomly in vases throughout, and it was a pleasant feminine aroma. The desk was moved to one side and a low-backed chair with rounded arms and dense with a floral pattern was positioned so the light hit it at the proper angle. Evans had seen to the arrangement, and Mrs. McNabb was satisfied with his decision.

A small table was placed to the left of the chair—Mrs. McNabb's right—and there was a photograph of Mr. McNabb in a silver frame beside three books piled (seemingly) haphazardly atop one another. Evans selected the books, and Mrs. McNabb approved, though she had opened none of them.

> *Sense and Sensibility*
> *Little Women*
> *The Scarlet Letter*

Mrs. McNabb herself selected a dark blue dress with a low neck. It was not formal. It was the type of dress a woman alone and contented in her thoughts might wear on a fall afternoon with her household instructed to advise visitors that she was indisposed.

"Do you believe it formidable enough, Mr. Evans?" she asked the artist, and he confirmed that it was. Satisfied with his answer, she sat, stiff with her hands folded in lap and looking towards the door, to Evans's left.

When she rose after sitting for about an hour, she walked towards Evans and attempted to see what he had done.

"I'm sorry, Mrs. McNabb, but my subject may not see a work until it is finished."

She huffed slightly and turned towards Clara. Before she got there, Evans said it applied to Clara's work as well, and after a pause, she left.

Several days after they started, Evans and Clara took their works to the studio to finalize them. When the artists were confident in them, Evans sent a note to Mr. and Mrs. McNabb and told them the portraits were ready for unveiling. He soon received a response.

May 26, 1874

My Dear Mr. Evans,

Thank you for your note. We should like to set June 1 for a formal reception to reveal them. Would that be agreeable to you?

With Warmest Regards,
Mrs. Peter McNabb

Evans sent word that it would be. In the late morning of the day, he and Clara unveiled their four works to the rest of the class. Evans was as secretive to them—except for the one chosen to participate—as he was to the subject. Approval was unanimous, and Clara relaxed and went in the early afternoon with Evans to the McNabb mansion followed by a carriage with the four canvases, two large, two small.

18.

Upon arrival at the large house, John Evans and Clara Bowman were directed by Bradley, the butler, to the large drawing room on the second floor. Furniture was moved so that the two large portraits could be shown side by side, with the imposing windows with their extravagant treatments as their backdrop. Noting the slight, Evans directed one of the footmen to make room to the left of Mr. McNabb's portrait and the right of Mrs. McNabb's for Clara's pair. They would complement Evans's portraits. He thought them of the first order and was proud to have them displayed.

When all was set up, Evans and Clara were given refreshments in the garden. It was a large space with tables and chairs arranged orderly and a trellis through which plum-colored roses climbed. A fine day.

"You see, my dear," Evans said as they sat on either side of a small table on which an assortment of sandwiches with ales and lemonade had been placed. "Tradesmen would eat in the kitchen. We may not be of their class, although I know you abandoned it, but they treat us with respect and that is something in this town. Very much something."

The birds were loud and varying in their songs as the two spoke. One reason Evans insisted on bringing a student with him on his commissions was the chance to know them. He learned much from their art, and the day-to-day contact and idle conversation aided him in filling in their unique colors. He liked Clara, but not markedly more or less than he did his other students.

They, in turn, all adored him. They all knew he never crossed a line with any of them and that he never would.

Evans sometimes enjoyed unveilings and sometimes he did not, but he knew it was an important part of getting additional commissions and, too, for his students to speak with people, perhaps not people who would commission them but who might have children who would. The business was seeing a sea change, with formal art schools opening in New York and elsewhere, and Evans knew those who went through his lessons had the skills and the heart to be amongst the forefront of the next generation of men and women painters.

It was generally the case that each student had a natural facility for one or two things. For Clara, she seemed able to bring out the subject's eyes, perhaps the choicest skill an artist could have. It came naturally to her.

Lowering his voice and leaning across the table as the afternoon drew late while they waited to be called in to prepare for the unveiling, Evans asked whether she had ever been in this house before. Clara did not recall but doubted it. It was more likely that Grace might have been there although it was a Catholic family.

"We may appear to be one large family, but we are actually just a collection of small ones that little know or care about those outside our little worlds, except when it comes to gossip, in which case we are all ears until the next scandal appears over the horizon."

"And the McNabbs? Any hint of scandal?"

"I believe Mrs. McNabbs' parents were seriously hurt in last year's financial disturbances and her older brother died from some type of drug thing after the money was lost. Also, her younger sister, I heard, had it out with Mrs. McNabb and ran away to do something on her own, but I do not know what that was. My friend Emily—who is my most frequent model and who, you will recall, once interrupted your class to see me—became friends with the younger sister, but they lost touch when Emily moved back to town."

"So," Evans laughed, "not particularly more or less of a scandal than the norm."

Before getting further into this, Bradley appeared to advise that the formal proceedings would commence in about half an hour and that they should prepare. Evans and Clara brought a change of clothes. The event would be formal, and Evans wore the black formal suit with a white shirt and black tie he had for such occasions and Clara donned a somewhat-out-of-fashion maroon gown that she collected from her parents' house the Sunday before for the event.

"You cannot wear that old thing," her mother warned, but Clara insisted. She would hardly be seen, and it would suffice even if it were a bit loose on her.

At precisely twenty-five minutes past six, Clara joined Evans in the drawing room. The two large and two small easels were in place with cloth covers. A footman offered them drinks from a tray. A few minutes later, the first guests arrived, and the room was soon crowded. Evans and Clara were for the most part ignored as people broke in and out of groups offering greetings and small talk. The two artists kept themselves engaged beneath the din by offering insights, not malicious, on the guests.

At ten to seven, Bradley lifted his voice.

"Ladies and gentlemen. Mr. and Mrs. Peter McNabb."

The two walked in arm-in-arm. When they reached the center of room the guests formed a circle around them, except for Evans and Clara, who remained by their works, and an older couple who stood to one side cradling their drinks. Peter spoke first.

"Thank you all for coming. It has been some time in the making, but we are finally able to include our portraits in the house. They are by the eminent artist John Evans, who is standing by them with his assistant," and the guests turned to see him and he gave a slight nod, "and I confess to being somewhat nervous in that I have not seen the result. I should like to thank my parents for coming as well as my charming in-laws"—the couple to the side, who raised their glasses—"and my brother-in-law and his charming wife, Michael and Katherine. My sister-in-law, alas, cannot be with us but we must make do. Thank you."

There was a spattering of applause, which stopped when Mrs. McNabb began.

"I, too, thank you for coming. I am nervous as well, not having seen what Mr. Evans has made of me. We shall discover it together."

With that, she and her husband walked towards the artist, a path opening for them. Evans leaned to say something to Mr. McNabb who said something to his wife, who nodded and said, "We shall see Peter's first."

She reached to the cloth covering it and pulled it up and away. After a flight of applause, Mr. McNabb said it was his wife's turn. Hers received a slightly louder reaction.

Both portraits were flattering to their subjects and the happy couple wallowed in the compliments made. Evans knew the crowd would be curious about the other two, smaller paintings. For some of his students, he did not put them beside his own lest they pale in comparison. Those would be left inconspicuously to the side. Not Clara's.

He spoke, thanking the McNabbs for their support and the guests for their applause.

"You wonder, I daresay, about these other two covered paintings. I teach a small group of gifted artists, and it is a vigorous course of study. When I deem them ready to fly, although perhaps not yet ready to soar, I have them paint the subjects that I am painting. Mr. and Mrs. McNabb kindly permitted Clara Bowman"—there was a slight small hush of recognition at the "Bowman"—"to assist me.

"Mrs. McNabb, will you again do the honors as to your husband's portrait by Miss Bowman?" and she hesitated a moment before complying.

"And now, Mr. McNabb, it is your turn," and he stepped up and unveiled Clara's portrait of Mary. There was applause, though not nearly so enthusiastic as was afforded Evans's portraits.

The paintings were very alike. The subjects were identical, and only the perspective was slightly different between what Evans did and Clara's work. They both showed Mr. McNabb as a jovial sort, kind if not particularly insightful.

For much of the two pictures of Mary McNabb, there was little difference beyond the greater technical skill of John Evans. The faces were of the same shape and the small noses blended well. The backgrounds were closely matched. But Clara, perhaps because she was herself a woman, displayed more of Mrs. McNabb's shoulders than did Evans and the gentleness of the woman's slight bosom. Clara offered it in a mildly seductive light.

More interesting were the eyes. To Evans, Mrs. McNabb's had an insouciance of a bored society lady. He was well accustomed to painting such eyes in his society portraits and if there was any criticism of his work it was that his own boredom was reflected in the eyes of his bored subjects.

To Clara, Mrs. McNabb's eyes were at once vacant and sad. Perhaps her work was influenced by what she knew of the woman. The mouth still had its well-known smirk—how could it not?—but the contrast was remarkable. To a person, with one exception, all thought Clara's portrait truer to its subject than was Evans's and that, if anything, Clara made her more attractive than she was.

The exception was the woman herself. Her life was built on the display of her supposed strength and hardness. This false image from Miss Clara Bowman suggested she was weak and vulnerable. Her friends would laugh at it, so she decided they would never see it again. She would not take it even were it offered to her.

The crowd exhausted its reaction to the four paintings, and Mrs. McNabb thanked Mr. Evans "and your assistant" for their work. She said that the former's portraits would be hung in a place of honor in the house and the latter's could be done with as he pleased. "They are nice enough, I think, and I hope you find an appropriate place for them."

As she finished, Bradley announced that dinner was served, and the guests went down to the dining room. Excepting Evans and Clara, who guided the packing-up of Clara's paintings and the movement of Evans's and journeyed south. They were both pleased, Clara exceptionally so.

Several days later, Evans handed a letter to Clara.

June 2, 1874

My Dear Mr. Evans,

I must again thank you for the wonderful portraits you have done of my husband and me. We shall treasure them always.

I must ask a favor. My parents live in our house. You may have met them at the unveiling. I believe it would be appropriate for portraits to be made of them. They will not be displayed in a significant part of the house and thus we do not require an artist of your renown. Your assistant, however, showed that she is capable of making a passable portrait and I assume would be far cheaper to commission.

My favor, thus, is that you arrange for your assistant to come to my house on Thursday next at eleven to meet with my parents so that she can arrange to do their portraits, for which I will pay.

With Warmest Regards,
Mrs. Peter McNabb

19.

Clara arrived at the appointed time, and Bradley led her into the sitting room where Mr. and Mrs. Geherty awaited her. Coffee, tea, and pastries were on a mahogany server beneath a landscape. With a coffee cup in hand, Clara sat across from the couple.

"Are you, by any chance, George and Muriel's daughter?" asked Mrs. Geherty.

"I see my secret is out," Clara said. "Indeed I am. How do you know them?"

"Oh, we do not know them well," Mr. Geherty said. "We have seen them now and then, but we never quite ran in their circle. We just remember hearing about you. You are the one to whom Emily Connor fled, are you not?"

"You know more about me than I could have imagined. Yes, that is me."

"Emily got to know our daughter Elizabeth quite well when we were in exile in Stockbridge after the financial difficulties both our families encountered," Mrs. Geherty said. "How is she?"

"Emily is Emily and doing quite well. She remains with me and has become my chief model, not to mention a good friend. She is happily working as a waitress."

She declined to get into further details about the life of that friend. If she was to be an artist, she needed to distance herself from the society in which she was reared so she turned to the matter at hand. Clara would paint them. Evans had told her what Mrs. McNabb would pay for the commission and seeing as it was Clara's first—though she received ten percent of the fee Evans received for the McNabb portraits—she was thrilled notwithstanding how small it was. Even better, she took an instant liking to the Gehertys and hoped to do them justice.

The three discussed how the couple wanted the portrait done. "Together," Mrs. Geherty said, and Mr. Geherty nodded.

"Any particular place?"

"We should like to have it be where we once lived, but that was a lifetime ago. Can we do it in the garden in the back?" After Clara walked out with them to survey it, she agreed it would be ideal and said she assumed Mrs. McNabb would have no objection.

She had her pad and did a quick sketch of the yard for use in deciding how she would arrange things. She then asked if she could do a quick sketch of the two subjects, and they agreed. Within two hours of arriving, Clara was returning to her studio.

Over the next week, weather permitting, Clara did the portrait. The Gehertys were dressed simply, as if they were sharing a morning meal. They sat near one another at a small table with the background dominated by the trellis adorned by roses. The couple immediately put Clara at ease with how relaxed they were with one another, worlds apart from their stiffness during the unveiling of the portraits of their daughter and son-in-law and, for that matter, of the McNabbs themselves during their sittings. Clara knew of their financial circumstances and their dependence on that son-in-law—though it was not mentioned—and found their clear affection for one another almost inspirational. She hoped that if she succeeded at anything in painting them it would be displaying this love.

She adopted Evans's practice of denying her subjects the chance to see her work in progress.

"You must be patient," she chided them whenever they tried to steal a glance. She made them promise that neither they nor anyone else in the house would look at it while she was away. Mary McNabb, she expected, would ignore this injunction but she did not care.

20.

In the days between the McNabb unveiling and the Geherty meeting, Clara received a note at Evans's studio.

June 6, 1874

Miss Bowman,

I did not have the opportunity to introduce myself at the McNabbs'. You will, I am sure, not recall me, but I have confirmed that you are, in fact, the Clara Bowman with whom I had the good fortune of spending a pleasant weekend at your parents' house in Lenox several years ago. I was one of several "gentlemen" from Princeton who were invited by one of your houseguests.

If you do recall me, it is as the fool who fell from a horse in an ungainly manner—how could a fall from a horse not be ungainly?—while we were seeking to impress you and the other girls as you sat on your porch.

I was reignited in this memory by seeing you again, and I should very much like the opportunity of seeing you yet a third time. Perhaps a dinner?

I work long hours at my father's financial firm but am sure I can accommodate whatever openings you have in your own schedule in the next week. Or anytime, really.

I look forward to your response and pray that if you have only one memory of me it is not of my sprawling on the ground while my fellows laughed at me for my clumsiness.

Regards,
Reginald Turner

Clara did not remember Reginald Turner. She vaguely recalled, oh, some years earlier, some fool fell from his horse while making an ass of himself and that when it was clear that he was bruised but not battered she joined the others in laughing at him. He must have slipped away or at least into the background as she recalled nothing else about him in the day or so that the Princeton boys remained before heading back to town.

Nor could she picture who he might have been at the McNabbs' among any number of interchangeable men near her age mingling about. Or whether he was known as "Reggie" or some other appellation that Princetonians were likely to call each other.

Reginald Turner was, in fact, known as "Duckie" at Princeton. It was ironic since he did not know how to swim and his fall from the horse established that he was not particularly adept at doing that either. He was tall, over six feet, and slim with a narrow face and neatly trimmed beard caressing his chin. His hair was very black.

Still, Clara did not recall him but she had no reason to doubt his representation. While she often thought of men, since London she had difficulty thinking of a *man*. She engaged in self-satisfaction and though erotic materials were made illegal in 1873, they could be found in the liberal precinct where Clara lived, and she took advantage to read such stories.

Given that she almost knew him but also did not, she decided to chance venturing out with him, and they agreed to meet at one of the finer taverns on Houston Street on the Saturday night. She arrived first and waited near the door. She had no difficulty recognizing him when he entered, her memory having been jogged from both the unveiling and the infamous equestrian mishap in Lenox.

He disarmed her, and she enjoyed his company. It was as magical an evening as she recalled spending since the Davises were killed. They walked for some time in the early summer heat afterward until they said their goodbyes in front of Clara's building.

Two weeks later, after the Geherty sittings were over and after another enjoyable date, she brought him to meet her parents. They knew of his family but did not recall him. His father was a partner in a well-regarded financial firm, the type that was not overly aggressive as some of the firms were with their clients' money. The firm provided a slight but steady return but was mocked in some circles as being too timid. But its clients were surviving the Panic that began in September 1873 and other calamities that had brought many families to their knees, including, of course, the Gehertys and the Connors.

Reginald was of similar conservative stock, both in the management of others' money and in his own deportment. He was gentle and self-effacing. Clara's brother-in-law Richard Lawford was comfortable with him from the start, knowing the father's reputation though not Reginald's.

Reginald was two or three years older than Clara and was among the few unmarried men in that group of Princetonians that sometimes partied too hard in the country. The others had moved on from him. They were married, and he was not. He had matured and, as a rule, they had not. His former friends were types who Clara disdained, even were she to open to the thoughts of a man.

From that first dinner, she knew he was different, and five or six weeks later, after their renewed acquaintance, she asked to draw him, and he obliged. He was built much as she was, tall and lanky, though larger. She would draw his upper body naked above the waist. She imagined how it would look and was not disappointed when he showed her. His was the torso of a man of leisure. Some would think it soft, but Clara found it beautiful, almost feminine, and she spent longer doing her art than was necessary and spent more time positioning him than was required.

Perhaps it was wrong, but she was electrified as the tips of her fingers adjusted how he stood. She thought that he might have felt something as well. More, she feared she was falling in love with him notwithstanding their short acquaintance. She did not dare think what he thought of her.

After she made the final touches on the drawing, knowing she would do an oil of him, she put her pencil down and walked to him. In the small space of her studio, she smelt him, a muskiness she never encountered before. It drew her to him. He did not move, unsure of whether he was supposed to still be posing, until Clara ran her hand across his cheek and leaned in to kiss him.

She read about this enough in the pulp romances she devoured. But she had never done it. Her moments with Sir John were fleeting. Animalistic. This was tender, and their lips opened and their tongues met and she could taste him with hers. She felt as she dreamed she would feel if she could ever fall in love again. When she pulled away, it was only to tell him she loved him. And in the gasps they shared, he told her he loved her. Perhaps it was true.

She fought to control herself and bit her lower lip but the act was futile. She was well past the point of being able to stop, and she felt his hands running down her arms and then leap to her waist as he rose to stand with her, towering over her but pulling her up slightly so he could reach her lips again with his own. She felt a passion she had not known. She made that horrible, horrible mistake with Sir John but that, she knew, was because he did not love her.

Reginald, her Reggie, loved her, and she let him pull her towards him.

She was breathless but had enough awareness to know she had to tell him. He would find out soon enough, she hoped, so he must be told that she was not a virgin. The smell of his sweat was clear as was the sound of his labored breathing. She mustered her strength to push away, and his eyes jolted open at the interruption.

"I must tell you something," she said, and those eyes became confused. "I have been with another man. I think you must—"

Even before she could continue, he, her Reggie, pushed her away with such force as to send her to the floor. As she fell, she knocked the drawing she made of her lover with his wonderful face and perfect eyes across the room.

Those eyes, so kind and gentle a minute before, turned. She looked up at him, and he quickly turned away.

"Reggie, please let me—"

But he would not let her explain. He grabbed his shirt and threw it on, buttoning it quickly without looking at her. With a last, hard glance, he spat "whore" at her and he was through her door, which he left open in his haste to escape, and his steps rushed down first one and then the second flight to Bleecker Street.

When she heard the outer door slam, she released the arm that was holding her up, collapsed, and cried herself to sleep.

21.

It was dark when Emily got home from her restaurant, and she was afraid when she saw the open door. She turned up the gaslight and closed the door and only then saw Clara on the floor. She did not appear injured in any way. She sat staring at the door, not registering Emily's appearance. Her legs were crossed and her hands folded neatly in her lap. She was well spent of tears.

"He left me. Forever."

Emily dropped down and put an arm around her friend.

"We need to get you up," she said, but her attempts to lift Clara were in vain.

"I loved him and I thought he loved me."

Emily tapped Clara's shoulder several times, and Clara began to rise.

"I must clean myself," and she went to the bathroom down the hall.

Emily made a sandwich from some chicken in the icebox and placed it on the table beside a glass of ale. When Clara returned, she dropped into a chair and noisily began to eat. She said nothing. Nor did Emily, who sat opposite, waiting and watching. After several large bites and two or three gulps of the ale, Clara began.

"I could not deceive him. I started to tell him about London." She lightly restored the stein to the table and lifted the sandwich from the plate but no farther.

"He thrust me from his arms and left me as you found me. I could hear him go down the stairs. My only other regret is that a man I loved, or thought I did, would cast me off for it."

She lifted the sandwich and took another bite and replaced it on the plate.

"Will you say nothing?"

"About Reginald?"

Clara nodded.

"What would you have me say? You tested a man you loved, or thought you did, and he failed. What more can I say? Do I blame you for...being a woman? What kind of a friend would that make me? Have I lain with a man? I have not, I will tell you. But I will never look askance at you for having done so. That is all I can say except that any man who thinks differently is not worthy of your love."

"What do I do if he comes back?"

Emily looked straight at her friend.

"It is your heart. I can only promise you that whatever it decides I will support it. And you." She reached her left hand across the table, and Clara extended her right to take it. "I always will. Tell me you know that."

Clara nodded, but Emily insisted, and after a pause Clara said it aloud.

"Good. Now finish your sandwich and ale and we will see if you can get some sleep."

* * *

CLARA SAID REGGIE was the first man she even looked at since London. She said she loved him, and he said he loved her. *He said he loved her.* She could not help herself, she was so desirous. They were in love and would be married, she knew it, so she would do with him what she would forever regret not doing with Thomas Davis. It would consummate their love. She had not thought of it but knew she had to tell Reggie of that afternoon with Sir John and before she could say anything beyond that she was "not a virgin" he was gone, calling her a whore and rushing away from her as fast as he possibly could.

When the plate was cleared and the glass was empty, Emily picked them up and put them in the sink. It was late, so she led Clara to bed and watched her drift into a sleep she did not envy.

When Emily arose the next morning, Clara was gone. She left a scribbled note for her friend.

E,
I must think.
C

Frightened as this made Emily, there was nothing to be done except wait. She had no notion of a secret spot where Clara went when under stress. She ventured to the market to get things for a meal for Clara's return. As she approached the building with her bags, she saw someone sitting on its steps whom she did not recognize. When she turned to enter the building, he stood.

"Excuse me, do you know Clara Bowman?"

Now she knew.

"Are you Reginald Turner?" and to his nod, she said, "She has gone out to clear her head. After what you did to her last night. I do not know when she will return."

"Please. I must see her. I said something to her that I should not have said and I regret it."

Keeping her voice down from the passersby and still holding her bags, Emily tried to control her temper. "You called her a 'whore' and did not give her the chance to explain what happened."

"So she told you."

"Of course she told me. She was on the floor when I got in. Right where you left her." She paused again, letting her steam lessen.

"I know it was wrong of me and I need to speak to her to explain, to make it up to her." His voice, too, was low.

"Make it up to her? How do you propose to do that?"

"I cannot say and I do not know. But I must try."

Much as Emily wished this man to go and never return, it was not for her to decide.

"I do not know when she will be back. When she does, I will tell her what you said and that you would like to speak to her." She pointed to the corner. "There's a tavern. Go there. If she wants to speak to you, she will find you there."

"Will you tell her to come? Please, tell her to come."

The man who called her friend a "whore" did not look so imposing. He was almost pitiful, and Emily doubted that he had even gotten the sleep that Clara managed.

"I cannot and will not tell her anything other than that you will be waiting at the tavern. Now I must go in."

Reginald watched her enter the building and stood before it for several minutes before walking to the White Hart.

When Clara returned to the flat, she was hot and tired and hungry. She came through the door, and Emily led her to the sofa to sit and told her she would make her some tea. While she did, and after several false starts, she told her that Reginald wanted to speak to her.

Clara barely moved at the news.

"I suppose I must see him if you think I should."

Emily brought over the tea.

"I cannot tell you what to do."

"But you must."

They looked at each other.

"You're right. It's for me to decide, and I think I must see him."

She sipped her tea.

"He is at the White Hart. It was hours ago. I assume he is still there."

He was still there. It took Clara a moment to adjust her eyes to the dim interior, but she saw Reginald sitting alone at a small table in the corner. There was a stein in front of him, and she did not want to think how many ales he had while he sat staring at the door.

Now his stare was locked on her as she wound her way towards him. He jumped up and pulled out a chair across from his.

"Thank you for coming," he began. "I cannot tell you how sorry I am for what happened. I was surprised, is all."

A barmaid who knew Clara asked what she wanted, and she nodded and said her normal ale, and the two were again alone. They said nothing until Clara's ale was in front of her. She gripped the handle of the stein and tasted the drink. Looking into it she asked him whether he was a virgin.

He stuttered before saying, "I am not."

She slowly lifted her head to look at him.

"Then why is my not being one so offensive to you? I had a single episode years ago but it is enough, without you knowing more, to label me a 'whore' and rush from me as fast as humanly possible."

While she spoke, she put her stein on the table and when she finished speaking, she stood and began to leave. She had not prepared what she said even in the hours she walked. It was simply said.

And she left him sitting there, slightly drunk and completely devastated. As she walked the half-block to her flat, Clara did not know how she felt. She meant to forgive him. She loved him, or at least thought she did, less than twenty-four hours before. And yet...

She understood it was in part the time in which they lived, with its double standards. Or more than double with respect to all of the different treatments people were afforded based on their sex or race or where they came from. She knew she was not above it, with her own privileged upbringing and her father's money allowing her to do what she loved.

But this was between her and him. Woman and man. If he could say what he said, call her what he called her, for doing something that he himself did— and she doubted it was the once that was the case for her—in the end, she would be nothing more than the wife, and his promises about her being able to continue with her art or anything else would be as shallow as he revealed himself to be.

Emily sat on the steps to their building and jumped up, surprised at how brief Clara's encounter was. Clara put up her hand, and Emily was silent as she followed her friend up the two flights of stairs.

"It is over." The first words, said by Clara, when they were settled. "I wish not to speak of it again. He may be better in some respects than most men. In the end, though, he is not good enough, and I will not settle."

For the next weeks, Reginald sent letters to Clara, but they were thrown out without being opened until finally they no longer came. Clara's father was furious, though Clara did not tell him or her mother or even Grace the reason for the termination, and after several visits, her parents stopped mentioning him and the Bowmans' Sundays reverted to what they had been before the flurry of attention that arose when Clara met Reginald.

22.

It was her first real commission and Clara was proud of it. Plus it did much to ease the pain from what ended so unpleasantly with Reggie. Emily was the first to see it. She knew Mr. and Mrs. Geherty from when they were all in Stockbridge. She very much liked them, and they were one reason she visited Elizabeth in the Berkshires as often as she did. She thought Clara's effort was excellent and true to life and, more, that it conveyed their affection for one another, which was Clara's goal.

It was not a dreamy-eyed picture, something Clara found abhorrent in the young let alone this long-married couple. She posed them as equals. Mr. Geherty wore a dark gray jacket over blue trousers with broad stripes. His shirt had a high collar framing a red tie, which was neatly tucked into a mustard vest. He looked slightly out of place and uncomfortable in the garden, with a folded copy of *The New-York Tribune* in his left hand, at which he looked. There was a half-full cup of black coffee on the table beside a plate with a half-eaten pastry.

Mrs. Geherty sat on the opposite side. She wore a comfortable cream-colored robe with bits of embroidery, and the upper portion of a nightgown of a slightly darker cream reached to her neck. Her feet were clad in plain slippers and her hair fell in a manner few but her husband ever saw. On her lap was a bit of needlepoint, revealing the start of a rose pattern. Her right hand was holding a needle with a thread of yarn stretched behind it, but her attention was elsewhere. In contrast to the frown on her husband—something in *The Tribune*?—she could not conceal her slight smile as she looked across at him.

The true roses, those intertwined in and out of the bars of the trellis, were bright on one side and dark on the other, reflecting an early-morning sun. On the table were the two hats the Gehertys would soon put on as the sun rose.

Emily thought it very good. Evans and several students assessed it, and they agreed. Later that day, Clara went alone to the McNabbs' for the unveiling. It would be nothing like as happened when the portraits of Mr. and Mrs. McNabb themselves were revealed to the world. Clara's great regret was that Emily could not be there because of work.

Bradley got two footmen to aid Clara in setting up. The unveiling would not be in the large drawing room upstairs but in the sitting room on the ground floor. The room was dominated by the two portraits by Evans, side by side over the mantel. Furniture was cleared so that the backdrop was the large window that looked out to Twenty-Fourth Street, framed by mustard-colored drapes.

Things were arranged to Clara's satisfaction, and as it was late afternoon, Bradley led the artist to the kitchen where a plate of food and some ale were set out for her while preparations for dinner proceeded nearby.

Clara was well used to the preparation of dinner in a fashionable house and occasionally ventured into the kitchen of her own, but she never before ate in one. She smiled at the pettiness of Mary McNabb, appreciating its reinforcement of her pre-existing view of the woman.

It did not matter. Soon after eating and handing the plate and glass to a scullery maid, Clara returned upstairs. She went directly into the sitting room. Mrs. Geherty was already there, pacing hither and yon, and she proudly admitted to resisting the temptation to peek beneath the cloth covering the portrait.

"I hope you like it, Mrs. Geherty. I hope you will like...you."

As the two walked to chairs arranged on the other side of the room, Mr. Geherty joined them. He shook Clara's hand. He said he was sorry Elizabeth could not be with them. Since neither he nor Mrs. Geherty volunteered the reason, Clara remained quiet.

Soon, Bradley announced the appearance of the first attendees, George and Muriel Bowman themselves. Clara formally introduced them to the Gehertys, and the couples spoke, though awkwardly at first given the Gehertys' financial condition, but it slowly faded as more guests appeared, chiefly those with whom the Gehertys remained friendly after their bankruptcy. After some time, all who were expected to come had come. Bradley said he would get his mistress, and the others were quiet, awaiting the sound of her coming down the stairs. Everyone stood when they heard it and turned to await her entrance, made with a practiced flourish and bow to the respectful response of her parents' friends.

She walked next to the painting and to Clara and without a word to the artist said that she was happy the guests could come to share in the pleasure of the portrait that was done of her parents.

"My parents have long been living with me, and I am glad to have had the opportunity to enlist an artist to paint them. I have not seen it except in its earliest days, so we will discover its merits together. Does it have a name?"

This last was directed at Clara.

"It is *A Couple*."

"Ladies and gentlemen. *A Couple*."

Without further ado, she threw the cloth over the horizontal painting and stepped to the side to allow her parents to see it clearly. They were surprised. This Clara Bowman, whose parents they were acquainted with, created a single portrait of the couple. There was no mistaking it. Mr. Geherty was to the left, and Mrs. Geherty to the right. But you could not look at one without seeing the other.

Had Clara accomplished what she set out to do? Her subjects had no doubt she did, and Mrs. Geherty hugged her as did her husband and Mrs. Bowman.

A buffet was set up on the far side of the room, and Clara and her parents sat.

At some point, George Bowman took his youngest daughter aside. "My dear. What you have done is quite nice. Better. I am prouder of you than you can imagine. If you are ready to return to society, your mother and I will be there for you. But if you decide otherwise, you will always have our love and support."

He lifted her hands and lightly kissed them, and the two separated, Clara stunned by the unexpected endorsement, and resumed their mingling among the guests who stayed after the unveiling, mixing conversation about her painting and her work with tidbits about her parents. Mary McNabb was not among those who remained.

23.

"Finley!"

The shout echoed through the office on Broad Street, and all who were not Finley were thankful for the fact. The man himself was readily identified as the one hastening to Richard Lawford's office.

"Did you see this report?" Lawford asked when Finley arrived, the report he meant being the one being shaken violently in the employer's fist.

"I have, sir."

"And?"

"And we need to speak. I was waiting for an opportune time."

"'Waiting for an opportune time'? Finley, I do not pay you to 'wait for an opportune time.' Why I pay you at all is sometimes a mystery to me."

He calmed a bit. He knew his temper sometimes got the better of him. Too often it slowed the communication of unhappy news in the office. Finley was a good man. Lawford would let it pass.

"So what do we do?"

The report was about a shipment of bolts from Baltimore. They were poorly manufactured and cracked or even broke when tightened.

"I think we must see Mr. Porter about it."

"I think you are right."

And after confirming that Mr. Porter was available that very day, the two, Messrs. Lawford and Finley, sat in Theodore Porter's office on Pine Street to discuss what could be done about it. The office was dark, thanks to walnut paneling and a row of bookcases containing legal volumes and treatises. Porter's desk, too, was dark. His father had long been the attorney for Lawford's father but when Richard assumed the day-to-day reins of the firm, he decided younger blood was best for how cut-throat the world of importing and reselling product in New York City had become since the War.

Ted Porter was not from society. He was tall and wore thick spectacles. He kept his beard and mustache neat, and their light brown matched his hair, which he kept slightly longer than would be acceptable in the leisure class. It identified him as a professional. He lived in one of the newer apartment buildings on East Thirty-Fourth Street.

The report established that the dealer meant to cheat Lawford & Son, plain and simple. There was no way around it, and Ted Porter agreed. Breach of contract without doubt. Angus Donald, Inc. agreed to sell crates of bolts and Lawford & Son paid for them upon delivery at the New York docks. They looked like bolts but did not act like bolts and, more to the point, were not of the quality expressly provided for in the contract. Breach of contract.

The difficulty, he reminded his client, was in the recovery for the breach. It was always a risk doing business with a new supplier. This one, though, had a decent enough reputation. It contracted to provide the agreed-upon product quickly and at a good price. Lawford hated being taken advantage of. Perhaps he should have gotten a personal guarantee in the event, as now appeared likely, that the corporate seller would evaporate into bankruptcy.

While he had the law on his side, as Ted Porter confirmed, the practicalities might be another thing entirely. Richard Lawford agreed he would think on what to do over the weekend. As he and Finley were nearly through the door, he turned to his lawyer.

"Tell me, Porter, I have not asked. Are you married?"

It was a peculiar question from a client, but Ted Porter said that he was not.

"Good. You must come to my in-laws' house this Sunday for dinner. Twelve or twelve-thirty would be good."

To Porter's stare, Richard said, "Do not worry. I am sure nothing will come of it, but my wife is desperately seeking a husband for her younger sister. She's I think a few years younger than you. She has not taken to any of the scores who've been displayed for her before and I daresay she will not take to you—a reflection more on her than you, I assure you—but I will have done my duty in having you come, and you shall have a good meal and some fine wine out of the bargain."

With that and the address in hand, Richard Lawford left, and his bachelor lawyer wondered just how fine Lawford's father-in-law's wine would be.

24.

As cynical as her husband was, Grace Lawford was undeterred by the unvaried failure to arouse Clara's interest in any of the eligible men who enjoyed her father's wine at a Sunday dinner. She and her mother agreed. All they needed was the one right man who would steal Clara's heart. Clara's dealings with Reggie Turner ended badly, and abruptly, but they never knew why. And each passing week added another week to Clara's age.

On the first Sunday in September, Emily had the day off, and as she sometimes did on such days, she tidied herself and joined Clara at the Bowmans' for dinner. George Bowman's initial hostility to the idea of Emily faded rapidly when he met the reality of Emily.

This Sunday was the one for which Richard extended the invitation to his lawyer, so it was Ted Porter's turn to be the chosen bachelor. Before he got there, Grace sounded his virtues to both girls, based on what she could extract from her husband.

Ted Porter was quiet at dinner and as he left in the early afternoon, he feared he threw away an opportunity. As he chided himself walking to his apartment for his timidity, his "faint heart," he was unsure which of the women he most regretted as to his failure. He liked them both. While both were older than he expected, they were younger than him.

The two women were impressed, and they spoke kindly of him when they went for a walk after he was gone. Both doubted they would again see or hear from Theodore Porter, Esq.

They were half wrong. On the succeeding Wednesday, Emily returned to the flat, and Clara showed her an envelope with Emily's name and address carefully scrolled.

Dear Miss Connor,

It was an honor and a pleasure to meet you and Miss Bowman on Sunday. Should you be inclined, I should very much like to invite you to dinner with me at your convenience.

I am,
Your faithful servant, &c.,
Theodore Porter, Esq.

She asked Clara about it.

"Could he mean both of us?"

"He could. But I am sure he does not. Do you see a letter to me?"

She shook her head.

"He must have obtained your address from my brother-in-law."

After a moment, Emily asked, "What shall I do?"

"Do? You shall answer it of course."

"But what shall I...say?"

Clara sat Emily down on the sofa. "You found him to be a pleasant, handsome man without airs of the sort we both abhor."

"But he was there to meet you."

"He met us both. And he wrote only to you. He is interested in you. More, I daresay, than in me. I think you must say 'yes.'"

Emily said "yes." She and Ted met for dinner on the ensuing Monday. Things went well during the meal, and loosened by some ale and then some wine, Ted became talkative. As happened that Sunday with his taciturn alter ego, he now chided himself for its opposite, speaking too much. He could never, he thought, find a happy medium between his two parts. Emily, though, found his loquaciousness a fascinating glimpse into him, and she thoroughly enjoyed it. In particular, his not being a member of society and being a lawyer meant he was sympathetic to the Connors' fall from grace. "I have seen many a good man," he said when Emily apprised him of how her parents came to flee New York, "make an error in judgment and it does not leave him less a good man."

It was light out when they left the restaurant, and they continued their discussion as they walked to Emily and Clara's apartment. At some point, their arms found themselves intertwined. Just as they crossed Broadway, Kyle Smith was walking in the opposite direction. Emily did not notice her friend, and Kyle thought he was being ignored. He turned and quickly caught the couple as they reached the other side of Broadway.

"Who is this?" he demanded of a surprised Emily.

She took a moment.

"Oh, Kyle. This is a friend I met at Clara's parents' house, Theodore Porter. A lawyer."

Ted extended a hand, but Kyle ignored it. He looked the lawyer up and down before turning and heading north on Broadway.

Emily was speechless. "That was Kyle Smith. He is a friend, but he must be late for wherever it is he is going."

Ted was disturbed by what happened but shrugged it off as he and Emily resumed their walk. When they reached her building, he said he enjoyed himself, a sentiment she echoed, and they agreed to try to meet a week later, on Emily's night off.

In the apartment, Emily promptly dropped onto the sofa and when Clara joined her, she replayed her dinner. Then she mentioned the incident with Kyle. Since her return from Stockbridge, she did not see him as often as she had. She still enjoyed being with him, but not as much as she once did. When they did meet, he was anxious about her. *Where had she been? What was she doing?* Now this.

"It was as strange a thing as I think I ever saw."

"You are sometimes cruel to him."

"Kyle?"

"You know you have been cruel to him, and I have told you so. You will never love him, but he is like a puppy dog to you. So you are surprised when he reacts as he did when he sees you with another man? Emily, you must speak to him. If not Ted Porter, there will be someone else. It will never be Kyle Smith."

Emily stood and after some steps she turned back at Clara. "I like Kyle, in his way."

"You like having someone adore you as he does. You must end it with him."

"You just do not think he is much of an artist."

She said it more sharply than she intended, and Clara responded in kind. "I have made no secret of that, but that has nothing to do with you. I know you and I know you will not love him and I know you must end it."

Emily sat back down on the sofa but said no more on the subject. Clara thought she may have said too much. The point was made.

Because of her work schedule, Emily thought she would have time to do what she did know she had to do about Kyle. She was not prepared when he appeared at her restaurant the next night. It was early, and things were not busy. Her boss allowed her to step to the sidewalk with Kyle when he demanded to speak to her.

At the wall by the entrance, all the words Kyle intended to use vanished and instead he berated her unfaithfulness.

"How could you? You do not care for me."

"I do care for you. Just not the way…the way you care for me."

"You must give me time to prove myself, and my love. Emily, please. Just give me more time. Tell me what I have to do."

She did like him quite a bit, but he was doing her a favor by forcing the issue of *love* with her. She reached a hand to his cheek.

"I am sorry, Kyle. I truly am."

He pulled his head away, turned, and was gone. She returned to work.

It was late when she got to the flat, but Clara was up.

"Something strange happened with Kyle. He appeared at the restaurant, and, well, he forced me to do what you have been telling me to do, I did it, and he just walked away and I feel horrible."

"You would feel horrible no matter what you did. You like him, but he must move on."

"I suppose," and with that Emily prepared for bed and after replaying her encounter several times she fell into a shallow sleep.

In the morning, she feared what would happen when they inevitably ran into one another on the street. She had no idea of how she would respond and, more concerning, she had no idea how he would approach her. She thought they were good friends. Now she feared they no longer were and no longer would, or could, be.

Over the ensuing weeks, Emily became a stranger to Kyle, ignored by him when they passed on the street. It hurt Emily each time. She saw Ted at night on her off-days. Although it would be a stretch for her to pay for dinner, she offered but he insisted. Once or twice, Clara went with them, but she felt out of place and demurred going again.

Which was just as well as Emily came to more than like the lawyer. She knew it was far too forward, but she asked if he would join her at her parents' house in Massachusetts after Christmas—she would spend the holiday itself with the Bowman clan—and into the new year, when things would be quiet for him at work. She was committed to going, and it would be nice to have company on the way up and back and in the quiet time she would have to endure in the Berkshires.

She met his parents about a month after meeting him, and they liked each other, and Emily recovered some of the smart tongue that came out when she was comfortable with someone.

25.

Ted Porter was the first of the parade of bachelors at her parents' Sunday dinners in whom Clara might have an interest, yet he preferred Emily. She hated the jealousy that bubbled up for her friend's happiness.

In light of her perceived loss of the lawyer, Clara reverted to the shell she entered after Reggie. She sometimes thought of offering him another chance. When she suggested this to Emily, her friend made her examine what led to the separation in the first place, and the result was that she knew there could be no future with him. She wondered whether there ever could be with another man.

So she threw herself even more into her work.

She picked up small commissions from the recommendation of John Evans. He was generous in suggesting one or another of his students when he was approached about a "portrait by someone not quite as...expensive as you." In October, Clara was anxious about finishing a portrait of one such son in time for it to be unveiled a week later. It was late when she finished for the night and since it was a clear, pleasant evening, she took a walk to clear her head before Emily got home from the restaurant. The streets had lost their earlier chaos and quieted down. She enjoyed the sense of the relative calm and the freedom to pick her route almost randomly as she had walked it countless times. She was nearly home, crossing Elizabeth Street, when a man jumped in front of her from the shadows. His trousers and shirt were dark as was the hat he wore. He had a scarf around his lower face. His eyes were deeply set and crowned by thick black eyebrows. He carried a stick in his right hand and was enveloped by a haze of cheap spirits.

She had no money, not even a purse, and she began to tell him this when he raised his hand and thrust the stick against her. But not at her face. At her left arm, which she was moving to shelter herself. Again and again, he struck her upper arm and her lower arm and the hand she held up to shield herself as her screams were caught in her throat. She would never know how many times she was hit before she collapsed to the sidewalk and all she heard were the stick bouncing on the sidewalk and the feet running away.

Moments later she felt hands upon her. A man was shouting after the attacker and another was tending to her.

"Stay calm," he insisted again and again. "We will get help."

It was late, but a crowd was gathering. Many were artists, and they recognized Clara Bowman. There was a clinic over on the Bowery, and while it was closed, the doctor lived above it, so it was there to which several of the men gently carried her, with another running ahead to get the doctor.

At this moment, Emily was returning to the flat after her shift ended. She noticed the crowd half-a-block away. She approached, thinking she might have seen someone standing across the street watching the goings-on. As she neared, she was recognized by a mutual friend who rushed up to her and held her arms.

"'Tis Clara. She's been attacked."

All stopped in Emily. Clara would have nothing. *Why would someone attack her?* No one on these streets had anything worth stealing. *Why?*

"It appears they hit her arm with a stick. Whether it was deliberate or if they were aiming for something else, we cannot say."

Emily pulled from him, and he put his arm through hers to lead her after the men who were carrying her to the doctor.

"They're taking her to the doctor now. Thank God it wasn't her artist's arm."

Emily, hurrying to catch up with the group, asked, to no one in particular, "could they be aiming for her painting hand?" but she received no response though all who heard it suspected it was the case.

The doctor said he could not properly see to the wound, but he injected her with morphine to dull the pain that would soon engulf her, and a cab was hailed. Emily helped calm Clara on the trip to Bellevue Hospital. Things were sleepy when they arrived. A young doctor by the name of Adam was on call and he appeared with a nurse. He declared the break of the humerus, the large bone in Clara's upper arm, was severe but that he thought she would make a complete recovery. It was fortunate that the skin was not broken.

Dr. Adam wrapped the arm in wool and then cut pasteboard and moistened it so it could take on the shape of Clara's bent arm. With the help of the nurse, he wrapped the pasteboard in bandages and then applied a starch coating which, when it dried, created a cast that immobilized the arm.

When the doctor and nurse were done, Clara sat on an examination table, and Dr. Adam pulled a chair to sit across from her. "You are lucky I am on duty. This is a trick only a few of us know. If we stabilize your arm, it will have time to heal. We must be wary of an infection, so you must come here or to a clinic to be sure that nothing is going on untoward in the arm."

He stood and took several bottles from a cabinet.

"This is laudanum. It has morphine in it, and it will dull the pain when it reappears. You may buy it at any number of stores, but do not wait until the pain is overwhelming to do so." With that, he handed the bottles to her.

"Is there someone who can mind you over the next several days?"

Clara identified Emily as her roommate, and Dr. Adam said to her, "Take care of her," and then to Clara, "It is a hard but clean break, and you should heal. You will have to exercise it when you remove the cast to get it back to full strength and mobility. Whichever doctor you see will be able to assess when the cast can be removed or whether it needs to be replaced."

He turned to the nurse. "Could you please get their information and then send them on their way?" before shaking Clara's good (right) hand and leaving.

After the nurse obtained what information needed to be obtained, including how Clara was to be contacted to take care of the bill—she directed that it be sent to her father—Clara and Emily left into the early morning air and sought for some twenty minutes on the avenue before they could find a cab that would take them to their beds.

By the next morning, Clara's world was abuzz. *Who did it?* No one doubted the motivation. From what little could be pieced together, it was a man likely solicited at a tavern. Perhaps the true villain stood with him across from Clara's studio, pointing the victim out. Several noted someone across the street in the shadows who did nothing to aid Clara as so many others did.

The police were contacted but did not arrive on the scene until Clara was being taken to the hospital. A detective appeared at Clara and Emily's place the next afternoon, while Clara was napping. Emily took him into the hallway. He said the police thought that it was not a random attack and would investigate. He promised to return the next day when he hoped Clara would be able to speak.

When her parents and sister found out what happened, they rushed down to Bleecker Street—as did others, including Ted Porter—and insisted she return to the Bowmans' to recover. But Clara and Emily thought the distractions of the Village would be best, though Clara agreed to check in periodically with William Southbridge, MD, the family physician, to monitor her status.

As for the police, after some half-hearted, unsuccessful attempts to identify the assailant, the incident was relegated to a pile of crimes deemed randomly committed and not worth further efforts.

26.

Whatever the status of the investigation, what mattered to Clara was the pain. She barely slept as her arm throbbed. She was taking laudanum for it, but it was becoming less effective each day. Emily was at a loss as to what to do. Then things took a dangerous turn.

"Do you love me?"

Emily had never seen Clara like this. It was just past dawn but there was enough light to see her, her eyes baggy and a look of insanity crossing her face. In her right hand, her good hand, she held a large knife.

"If you love me you will cut it off. Please, for God's sake, Emily. Cut it off. I cannot take the pain. It is useless to me anyway."

Emily rushed to her friend and as she reached her the knife fell to the floor and Clara was in tears.

"I cannot handle this pain." With a breath a between each word, she said, "You. Must. Help. Me."

Emily felt Clara shuddering. They were both in nightgowns, but Emily hurried to change into a morning dress and found one for Clara. While Clara was still crying, they were on Bleecker Street and signaling for a cab.

They did not have far to go. There was a doctor frequented by local artists, known for his ability to control pain, and Emily was banging on his door, demanding entry, while Clara swayed at her side. The doctor, an older man in his night clothes named Paul Frieder, opened the door and bid the pair enter. The hall was dark, but they could make out a lit room off to the right, and they followed him there.

The doctor opened a cabinet and removed a vial and opened a drawer and removed a syringe. "I can give this to her, it is morphine, and it will dull the pain. But I must have five dollars before I do so."

It was nearly all the money Emily had, but she handed it over, and when he put it into the drawer, the doctor filled the syringe and injected the drug into Clara's left arm and its effect was felt almost immediately and Clara felt liberated, thanking the doctor. She was given morphine when the arm was seen to shortly after she was attacked, and he told her to dose herself with laudanum, but she went through that quickly and had done without for over a day when, near dawn, the pain grew and grew until it crested with her plea to Emily.

Dr. Frieder warned that the morphine would slowly wear off and that in several hours the pain would likely reappear, though he thought its severity would gradually diminish as the bones in her arm healed. He advised her to purchase laudanum to control it.

It was early and the shops were still closed so they walked the half-mile or so to their flat through the noises and smells of the neighborhood awakening. Emily left when Clara fell asleep. She had to be at her restaurant at eleven but would go there and say she had to tend to a sick friend. She was of long enough standing, she hoped, that she would not be terminated since it was difficult finding such a job. But Clara was too important to her and she did, in her way, love her.

Emily was held in sufficient regard that she was granted the excuse, but she doubted her employer would be so generous in the future. For that day, her concern was Clara. Clara had enough money so Emily could buy several small bottles of laudanum and she sat on the floor, leaning against the bed on which Clara lay, though her rest was broken at moments with a cry from the artist, after which she again drifted off.

Over the next days, Clara made sure to take laudanum so the pain would not return. It did in spurts, but only slightly and often when she waited too long to take a dose. She visited Dr. Adam every two weeks to have the arm and the cast examined, and her progress was good. The cast was replaced four weeks after the attack.

Fearful of the pain, Clara continued to dose herself. She discovered that she liked how it made her feel. Before all this happened, she heard others in the community say so, but she doubted how that could be true. Then she discovered that it was.

It did more than simply ease the pain. It made her happy and, she thought, it helped with her painting. And when the cast came off and the arm was pronounced healed, subject to her doing exercises to maintain its movement, the pain was gone. Yet she enjoyed the feeling she got from the laudanum and continued to take it. When Emily expressed concern about it, since it seemed artificial to her, Clara insisted that it was only a preventative, and Emily let it drop.

It was not long, though, before Emily recognized Clara's difficulty in completing paintings, especially the commissions she needed to survive with some independence from her family. Some portraits were nearly complete, but she destroyed them simply because she became unsatisfied with one or another correctible and perhaps imagined detail.

More and more she was taking on the artist's temperament she once mocked in others, the pretentious and supposed perfection she knew prevented an artist from doing their best work. More and more she rebelled about Emily and all the other non-artists telling her what she should or should not do. They could not know her, and they did not really care about Clara Bowman.

27.

Emily shared her concerns with Grace, and in mid-November the two met with the Bowmans' family physician, Dr. William Southbridge, in his office to talk about them. Emily did not want anyone but Grace to know the depths of her worries about Clara, not even Ted, with whom she was meeting frequently. Clara was increasingly lethargic and seemed focused more on getting her dose than anything. Her appetite was gone and often she was anxious about a commission that she did not feel was going as she hoped, expected, or thought it should. She failed to complete several. With no reason, she lashed out at her roommate, of all people, and Emily learned to avoid asking Clara about her condition once it was clear that her left arm was healed.

Emily found small, fat green bottles with patent stamps everywhere. Each was empty, the laudanum it contained drunk and its cork stopper long since discarded. Even when Emily removed the bottles, more and more appeared.

The drug was widely available. One did not need a prescription, and it was ubiquitous in remedies promoted for all manner of ailments, including to help quiet children. And Dr. Frieder, the doctor in the Village, assured both Clara and Emily that there was no harm in the continued dosing. It was, he promised, an elixir that improved Clara's life.

Emily knew it was not doing that, so she spoke with Grace in an unannounced visit to the Lawfords' house and together they met with Dr. Southbridge. Emily told about Clara. The attack. The broken arm. The pain. That early morning when she pleaded to have it cut off. Grace kept silent, shocked at some of the revelations.

"I fear she is going insane, doctor," Emily concluded. "She sits most of the day and when she tries to paint, she often stops after a few strokes and ruins whatever she has done. Yet she tells me how happy she is. But she is not my Clara. She sleeps. She lies. It is not my Clara."

Dr. Southbridge looked at her.

"We see too much of it. It is even worse with women who have nothing to do all day. There are those who think it is not a problem. But as you say, she is not who she was. This is bad. This is very bad."

"I see it, too, doctor, when she comes to the house," Grace added.

He rose and began to pace as the two women watched.

Emily said, "I do not know how much is in the bottles, but she is going through each in two or three days. She has gone to her parents, which she never did before, for money."

Grace interrupted. "I did not know that."

Emily continued. "And without that, we would barely have enough for food and she is destroying canvases at a frightful rate that we cannot sustain. But it is more about her that I care."

He left the room, and Grace reached for Emily's hands. The doctor returned, holding a bottle.

"Is this the size?"

He handed it to Emily. She said she thought it was.

"And she is going through a bottle every two or three days, you say?"

"I believe so."

"Did she always take so much?"

"At first, a bottle would last over a week. Now they are empty much sooner."

He looked at Grace. "Your parents. What do they know?"

"We have not spoken about it, but I am sure they have noticed. And, obviously, the sudden requests for money, which she never did before."

The doctor sat down again, his hands gripping the arms of his chair.

"There are those who see nothing wrong with it, but they are fools. Look at what it is doing to your friend. We must...you must do something."

When Emily told the doctor about her family house in Massachusetts, Dr. Southbridge said it would be ideal. No time was to be wasted, he said. She must get away. It was her chance.

"No time to lose."

"I think what we must do, if we can, is get your friend to a place where temptations are removed. You mention Massachusetts. Can you go there with her?"

Emily said that her parents lived there and they would welcome her. At that point, they spoke of the logistics.

When they were next together, Emily had a long conversation with Ted about Clara. He often came to Bleecker Street, especially on Saturday afternoons, sometimes falling asleep on Clara's couch while the two women spoke or read. On Sundays, as often as not he accompanied them to church services—with Catholic Emily going to mass nearby and meeting up with them afterwards—and enjoyed the pleasant company at the Bowmans and the taste of George Bowman's wine.

For all the surface smiles, everyone was miserable. Clara was struggling with being civil and the rest struggled to avoid placing undue pressure on her. Emily more than anyone else.

Emily told Ted she saw the chance to use the holiday to get Clara from what was preventing her from becoming herself. At least she hoped. She and Ted agreed to shelve the plan for him to venture to Stockbridge with her.

28.

Emily and Grace decided it was best for Emily to broach the subject with Clara. On the morning after the meeting with Dr. Southbridge, Emily took her friend to a small café some blocks north on Broadway. It was not cold, but neither was it warm enough to sit outside as they often did, and they sat at a small table inside and ordered coffee and toast.

After several aborted starts, Emily said, "How would you like to come with me to my family's house in Massachusetts for Christmas?"

Clara placed the cup she held on its saucer and looked across the table. She saw Emily attempting to display nonchalance and doing a poor job of it.

"Why do you want me to go away with you?"

"It is that we think—"

"Who is 'we'?"

Emily restored her own cup to its saucer and stared back across the table and lowered her voice.

"You are in a very bad state, Clara Bowman. I see it. Grace sees it. Everyone sees it. We, and I mean we, will not allow it to continue. We will not."

"I told you I am fine. I am happy. I just wish you, and I mean the lot of you, would stop meddling."

With that, Clara pushed hard against her chair as she stood. It toppled to the floor and the entire café looked up. They saw Clara going to the door, grabbing her coat from the rack by it, and watched her head north on Broadway. Emily did not know what to do. She was off work, so she went back to their apartment to wait for Clara's eventual return.

She did not need to wait for long. About an hour after she rushed from the café, Clara entered the apartment, its door left wide open for her. She removed her gloves and put them in her coat pockets and took off her coat and hung it in the small closet near the entrance.

Emily, who was sitting on the sofa somewhat reading, stood. One glance and she knew Clara would come with her to Stockbridge.

That afternoon, she sent a wire to her mother. She was bringing a friend, though not Ted Porter as planned:

Clara is going through difficulties. We may stay a while. May we come?

Without consulting her husband, Mrs. Connor immediately responded:

You are welcome for as long as you wish. I am sorry. I would have liked to have met Mr. Porter.

On the following Sunday, as they walked home from services, Clara told her sister that she understood what she and Emily did.

"I was angry. But I think I must do it."

29.

Emily made the trip to the Berkshires several times since her family's fortune vanished almost exactly a year earlier, but none was like this, her dear friend beside her on the seat, next to the window as she watched the passing countryside.

Clara, too, had made the trip often, but those were in happier times, dating back to visiting the house the Bowmans rented in Lenox—the town to the north. Ashley and Thomas Davis often shared the ride with her. That was in spring or summer or fall. Now the trees were bare and ugly and those once-green hedges she passed were brown. Emily sat reading, though only half-reading as she tried to detect the slightest change in Clara as they headed north.

For much of the trip, though, there was little change in the artist. Her gaze locked on the passing landscape with the occasional passage of a small town or slight city. It was like one of the blurry images coming into fashion in some parts of her art world.

Clara hated who she was, unable to control herself. She knew all too well she was lying when she insisted otherwise. She knew Grace and her mother were right in sending her away with Emily. She prayed it would help her. She hated, too, imposing on all these people as she knew she was.

It had begun to get dark when the train pulled in. While the Connors' carriage was not among the more recent in town and was in need of interior refurbishment, it served its purpose and the two horses served theirs and a young man of twenty by the name of Jennings who wore many hats for the family opened the door for the ladies and lifted their trunk to and secured it on the rear of the carriage and, bundled up against a day far colder than the one the women left in town, drove them to the Connors' house.

Clara might not have had the courage to enter but Emily deprived her of any choice as she grabbed her friend's hand before the wheels stopped and pushed open the door and (the moment Jennings dropped the steps) pulled her down them to the driveway and then up the steps to the front door, which she flung open with assurances that "there will surely be a good fire to warm our hearts and our souls." As she began to unwrap herself, she added, "And our toes." Clara, stunned by the haste and brutality of her host, took a moment to collect herself and only then could she remove her scarf and remove her hat.

Mrs. Connor was watching from the drawing room and rushed down the stairs as the carriage rolled to a stop, arriving in the foyer just in time to take her daughter's and Clara's scarves and when the two arrivals were free from their hats, gloves, and coats she was introduced to Miss Clara Bowman.

Clara knew the history of the Connor family as well as anyone, except perhaps for its creditors, and was surprised at how well they appeared to be surviving in their exile.

"I will have tea and nourishment brought to you presently," Mrs. Connors promised as she turned to the kitchen while the women found a closet for their things. Emily led Clara to the promised fire, where they pulled up chairs to place their feet on the fender. Emily, first, and then Clara removed their boots to warm their toes.

The drawing room was, like the coach, worn. It was lit by only a few candles and the well-kept fire smoked everything lightly. Both women savored it as they lost themselves in the burning logs, taking in the smoke and comforted by the aroma and the crackling as they often did at the Moving Hand or some other favored spot on a cold day in Greenwich Village. It was rare for either of them, at least in their recent lives, to simply sit silently before a fire in such ease. At some point Emily reached over for Clara's hand, and it was willingly given.

They remained like that until Mrs. Connor herself carried in a tray with a teapot, cups and saucers, a cruet of milk, a bowl of sugar, and a small plate of biscuits. She placed the contents on the small mahogany table between the girls and poured the tea, told them dinner would be in an hour, and closed the door as she left.

"I like your mother very much," Clara said after each took several sips of their teas and several bites of their biscuits.

"She came through everything remarkably well. I think it helped that my father's business reputation was never such as to get he and my mother entrée into the best houses."

"You mean like mine?"

Emily paused. She did mean that but ignored it.

"They are in this house now, and my mother is doing well. There are regiments, or perhaps divisions, of bankrupted families hereabouts, and she has learned to ignore those who pretend to have airs.

"Of course there are few men here. Most women of marriageable age are back in town, doing much as I am. I assume the men are doing the same so while there may be a flurry of 'gentlemen' sniffing around when they come visiting for the holidays, we shall for the most part be safe and secure in our exile."

After a pause, Clara said, "I am so sorry to keep you from your Mr. Porter."

"He is a good man and—"

"Do you love him?"

Emily was finally ready to admit it, including to herself. "Were he the type of man who would begrudge me taking care of my friend when she is in need, I never could. But he is not that kind of man and, yes—you will be the first to know—I do love him. Very much."

"I may be the first to be told, my dear, but I have long known it." Clara had lost any jealousy she had about Emily's relationship and hated that it was once present within her. After a hand-squeeze, the pair remained silent, glancing into the fire as they absentmindedly sipped their teas.

"Emily. Do you think this will work?"

Not looking over, the other said, "We, both of us, shall do all we can to succeed."

With that they resumed their silence, each suspecting their thoughts flowed in the same direction, and the only sound coming from the crackling logs and the occasional gust of wind racing past a window.

Mrs. Connor arranged for a second bed to be brought into Emily's room. It was a little tight, but her daughter asked that the two beds be made to seem as natural as possible to Clara as they were on Bleecker Street. Jennings brought the trunk with their things up after he put the horses in the stable. The girls went to their room before dinner. They quickly unpacked and hung what needed hanging in the wardrobe.

The house was a farmhouse for most of its existence, and its central part still bore characteristics of one, with wide plank floors and low beamed ceilings. The old part of the kitchen was dominated by a large hearth that was no longer used because it was so inefficient. The wall to the rear had been knocked out by a prior owner and a serviceable kitchen installed in the extended area.

While the walls on the south and west sides of the house—the house's front looked to the south and in the winter one could see Lee Road—were kept intact, the one to the east was long gone. A large hall with a tall, molded ceiling extended out towards the woods, anchored by a porch that wrapped around. This, too, was done by a prior owner. Though the Connors did not entertain often, even when they were rich, it was largely left unchanged by them except for the placement of several large oriental rugs and tables, chairs, and sofas strewn about to create intimate spaces that were far more comfortable than would be found in the normal, underused ballroom of a house in the Berkshires.

"We are informal here for eating," Emily told Clara, and the two put on simple dresses and headed to the drawing room where they found Emily's parents.

Mr. Connor had not met Clara though he saw George Bowman in passing now and then at a function. He being with only the visitor and his wife and daughter was awkward to him. He was long a master in the art of the charm to extract money from investors and to comfort them when they expressed concern for how their investments were faring. But to be alone with this stranger, whom he agreed would be remaining in the house perhaps for months, was a novel experience for him, and that she was a tall, attractive young woman made him even more uncomfortable, not helped by her natural reticence with strangers. He did what he could to make small talk about families that the Bowmans might know until Jennings entered to advise the four that dinner was served.

Here, too, matters were simple. Mr. Connor sat at the end and Emily and Mrs. Connor to his right and left. Clara sat next to Emily. They found simple black bean soup at their places, and as Jennings pushed in Mrs. Connor's chair for her the other three were quick to seat themselves.

With the women deferring to Mr. Connor as to conversation, things began tentatively and by the end, with the entrées cleared, the substance of the talk was largely about how bare—very—the trees were on the way up and how warm—not very—the city was when they left. After which Mr. Connor returned to his library and sherry and the three ladies to the drawing room. But as Emily and Clara were spent from their journey, they did not last long and adjourned to their bedroom.

Clara was very nervous. She thought to include several laudanum bottles in her luggage, but Emily insisted they share a trunk. She took her last drops while Emily was doing her toilet shortly before they left the apartment and was reaching the point where she should normally take another. She could not recall when she had gone more than twelve hours without a dose. As they reached the bedroom it was fourteen.

Emily knew this. She knew that Clara took that final one. But she was determined that it would be her "final dose." She met with Dr. Southbridge before they left. He gave her a pamphlet on what to expect from Clara's withdrawal. But withdrawal she must go through, they agreed, and while Clara was in the toilet at the Stockbridge house earlier, Emily made sure her mother understood and that her mother would made sure her father did.

When Clara returned and climbed into her bed, Emily left to prepare. When she returned, she blew the candle out and went directly to Clara's bed and lay down next to her. She felt Clara shaking.

"I do not know if I can do this. I do—"

"We will do it, my dear. Whatever it takes, we will do it." Emily's left arm reached around to pull Clara closer to her. "We will do it together."

She kissed her friend on the side of the neck, just below her left ear, and felt Clara grasp the hand that encircled her. She was silent, but Emily felt the shudder of a low-level sob.

Both women were wide awake though they each feigned being asleep until Clara said, "I cannot do it Emily. Please let me have it. I cannot do—" and her sobbing crested into the uncontrollable as Emily tightened her grip.

"Yes, you can. I love you," and after another kiss she told her friend that she was there and would always be there and that right then all that mattered was getting the first night's sleep.

The two somehow drifted off together in the small bed but at some point, Emily removed herself to her own. She awoke first, only a little after the sun was up. It was light enough, even with the drawn curtains, to look at Clara. This is something she often did since the onset of the addiction. Watching Clara's angelic face as she slept and aware of the turmoil beneath.

Was this the longest she had been without her laudanum? Emily did not know. Thanks to Dr. Southbridge, she prepared herself for what she knew would come. It was a week before Christmas, and Emily hoped Clara would be through the worst of what was coming by then and if not by then at least by the new year.

When Emily came back from her toilet, she found Clara watching for her as she lay in her bed. When Emily approached, Clara said she hoped she was not too much trouble the night before. Emily bent down to kiss the forehead and assured her, first, that of course not and, second, that that is what they were in Stockbridge for.

She could see the sweat beading on Clara's forehead, but ignored it. Dr. Southbridge told her that it would likely be at least twenty-four hours before major symptoms of withdrawal appeared, and there were three hours to go.

Clara went to do her own toilet, and when she got back, the curtains were open and both beds were made. Emily was dressed, again in one of the simple day dresses they brought. It was very cold in the room and after Clara quickly dressed the pair went to the kitchen, where a fire had been set and there was food to eat.

For all the attempts at normalcy, Emily knew how difficult things were for Clara. In her first days in Stockbridge, Emily again sat watching her friend sleep. Clara was physically gutted as she could not get what she needed, and she was emotionally gutted as she was bored out of her skull and bristled at everyone staring at her, waiting for something, though they did not know what. She yet again wondered whether her casting Reggie away was a mistake. She wondered if she would paint again and, worse, worried that she would not care if she never lifted a brush again. Maybe she should just return to her parents' house and live her life out as a spinster.

Emily's parents were trying to be polite, but their existence did little more than emphasize the fact that Clara was sitting in a God-forsaken part of the world with no one to speak to but Emily's well-meaning parents and Emily herself, whose imagined sanctimoniousness was becoming unbearable.

These first days were horrible, as Emily warned her parents they would be. Not only was Clara manic, nausea enveloped her, and she often sat in a window seat with a book she opened but did not read, staring into the wood that defined the house's eastern border. Bags grew under her eyes from a lack of sleep. But slowly, very slowly, she was able to eat and sleep under her friend's watchful eye.

It was several days after their arrival that they ventured into town. The first of the winter's bitter cold arrived overnight so they bundled up as they took the carriage. The town was not large. The road that connected the towns in this part of Berkshire County entered from the south and then turned east, defining

Main Street before turning several blocks later to the north and continuing to Lenox.

An inn sat on the corner at the first of those turns, a squat stone church opposite it. The inn was a New England white with a large, wrap-around porch. It was the *de facto* center of town life over the quiet winter months, with large fires always burning in its several fireplaces distributed about its tavern and dining room. It was to this inn that Emily and Clara ventured, and they were given a small table not far from one of the smaller fires. It had a view to the frost-encased windows through the light smoke that filled the room, and at last Clara felt she was away. She did not know from what she was away. Just that she was.

When back at the house and two days before the holiday, Clara sat near a vigorous fire in the Connors' drawing room by a candle that gave sufficient light for her to read. Some days after her exile began, she took to devouring mystery stories and other pulp fiction she discovered in the cabinets below the leather-bound-volume filled bookshelves. She found it relaxed her immeasurably more with each passing day. Suddenly Emily invaded her space, throwing Clara's coat across her lap.

"Come on. We are going a wassailing."

"A what?"

"Whatever it is called. We are riding into town to sing carols. We leave in five minutes."

With that Emily fled the room, and Clara heard her open the door to the hall closet. After freeing herself from the coat so indelicately deposited upon her, she rushed to the hall. By the time she got there, Emily was in her coat and holding her hat and gloves. She also had boots on, and Clara's boots were in the hall waiting to be stepped into by their owner.

"I am not going out."

Emily ignored her.

"Did you not hear me? I am not going out." Clara threw her coat to the floor.

Emily ignored her. She pulled each glove on, left then right. And waited, looking at her friend. And waited.

Finally, after what seemed to both to be an extended period, Emily stepped to Clara. She ran a gloved hand across her friend's cheek.

"Please?"

Clara stepped back and went to get her boots. She sat on the third step to pull them on, right then left, promising Emily, "If you think I am singing you are horribly mistaken."

When she stood, Emily had the taller girl's coat ready, and Clara put one then the other arm through its sleeves, and Emily handed gloves and a hat to her.

"We're going, mama," and Mrs. Connor called down to them from the landing and bade them farewell.

As they approached the village in the carriage, Emily asked Clara if they could walk home.

"The walk will do us good, and we need not keep Jennings waiting for us."

Despite her objections, Clara did sing, beginning with the fourth carol—it was a rollicking one that she particularly loved and her joining in was done before she realized it—the group threw itself into as they went along Main Street, stopping here and there where folks waited with vats of warm, often spiked, cider.

By the time the two returned to the Connor house, they barely felt the cold. The walk did them good, and they remained in fine cheer the entire way. It was a crystal-clear night. It seemed that not a single sound was muffled in the near-midnight sky and they heard the eeriness of the calls of whatever creatures were up and about. As was often the case with them, they said little but their arms were intertwined, and they leaned against one another the entire way.

When they came in sight of the house, Clara said what had been bouncing in her.

"I miss the simple times, when we'd sing in the house or at services. Now look at me. All that seemed lost but, thank you, Em, for making me feel I can have some of those moments again, however briefly."

Emily kept silent but she leaned against her friend for the final yards.

From that festive night, with Christmas itself spent quietly in the house and Clara being embarrassed and pleased by the gift of a fine knitted scarf Mrs. Connor bought in a small shop in the village and the Connors *père et mère* being embarrassed and pleased by her gift of a gold pin and a gold bracelet, respectively, Clara increasingly enjoyed the cold walks to and from the village with Emily. She returned to her habit of carrying a sketchbook where she went, and the two became familiar figures, the Connor girl reading or writing letters and always mindful of the friend who drew and was known to repay kindness with a simple sketch.

Only a few in town knew Clara as the artist-who'd-been-attacked, and she was glad for it.

Back at the house, Clara drew or painted images of Stockbridge from the sketches she did of the snow-encrusted streets and bare trees. She too often bristled at Emily's watchfulness. When alone, as she was when she sat in the sunroom on the west side of the house where the afternoon light was good, there were times when she felt nauseous from the fear that hit her when she was alone. The laudanum used to help her get through such episodes. Now, with that avenue blocked, the concentration she needed to draw a simple line took its place.

She did not think the sketches of the neighborhood particularly good, but the Connors did, and Mr. Connor began to boast of the artist-in-residence at his house to the point of gaining Clara's permission to show one of her paintings to his group of cronies at a Saturday afternoon get together at their club.

These were not easy times for Clara much as she strove for some semblance of normalcy.

Emily knew her friend was bored. She hoped Clara would discover new subjects for her art, and that her boredom would find an outlet in a world completely different from the bustling one they fled. Clara mostly painted portraits, either on commission or because she liked the subject.

Shortly after the holiday, both women's spirits were lifted by a letter to Emily.

December 21, 1874

Dear Miss Connor,

I find myself very much regretting the circumstances that prevented my accompanying you at least briefly to Massachusetts although I again assure you that I understand the reasons and am very much in agreement as to them. I do hope that our dear Miss Bowman has been somewhat restored and that she is again turning to the work at which she is so gifted. I am quite pleased, you must tell her, with the small sketch that she made of you and that you gave me before your departure.

I hope that you and she and your family enjoy a most wonderful Christmas season and look forward to your return to town in the hope that you will be interested in resuming our relationship.

Your humble servant,
Theodore Porter, Esq.

The letter was a pleasant surprise. Emily meant to write to him, but the press of Clara's requirements caused her to neglect him, including in her thoughts. His letter and its final phrase had the effect of reigniting her interest.

December 28, 1874

Dear Mr. Porter,

You must forgive <u>me</u> for my neglect of <u>you</u>. It is, as you suspect, the product of my focus on our dear friend. I am pleased to report that she is making progress but the coming cold season will be the making, or unmaking, of her. Your prayers on that front would not be unappreciated.

Please write again. I ache to hear of the occurrences in town, or at least of our little part of it. The papers we eventually receive are full of stories about those either well above or well below our "station" and such gossip provides scant nourishment to us.

I look forward to your further correspondence. Be forewarned, though, that given the paucity of interesting things here, I may well show what you write to our dear friend and I have learned that she is quite observant.

Your ~~friend,~~ dear friend,
~~Miss Emily Connor~~
Emily

P.S. I must add that I mentioned your kind words about the sketch Miss Bowman made of me. It created a smile of the sort I feared I would never see again. More. She created a sketch of you, dear sir, based upon seeing you several times. I must admit that I hope that you are in reality half as handsome as she made you appear and that you think me half as pretty as she makes her model in all her drawings of me.

"You must not say that. It is far too forward of you."

"If I say nothing, he will dismiss me as having no particular interest in him. And why can't he think me forward?"

Clara could think of no reason, and so the letter was dispatched and its recipient did not find its sender forward. Not in the least, and the two—Emily Connor and Ted Porter—embarked on a regular exchange of correspondence that Emily and Clara enjoyed in the cold of winter in Berkshire County.

30.

By late January, Clara seemed to be overcoming her symptoms of withdrawal. She was nearly returned to the Clara that predated the horrible period. As both she and Emily were tired with the routine, and with fond thanks, they returned to town and the apartment. She left charcoal drawings of Mr. and Mrs. Connor and a small painting she made of Mrs. Neal of the inn that she created from several sketches done while there.

As they took the train down, Clara studied some of the sketches she did while away. Some horrified her for the anxiety evident in each stroke. Those were chiefly the early ones. She calmed over time, especially after Christmas, and her art became truer to its subject.

Clara was surprised when she returned. She did not realize the damage she inflicted in her dark days and wept when she saw some of the drawings and paintings she destroyed in her insanity. It took some time of crying on Emily's shoulder for her to return to the reality of her life. New or old, she could not say.

Emily thought it best if Clara understood where she was before they went to Berkshire County so she did not have it cleaned up while they were gone.

Clara surveyed the room. "I must draw you," she told Emily. She made many sketches of her friend from her time away. There was over a book full of Emily as well as her parents and the surrounding countryside. Several sketches of Stockbridge and a few of Lenox, the peacefulness of undisturbed snow more common than not.

It took days of cleaning, but the apartment was finally close to how it had been. The two sat. Emily had managed to get a new job, but it did not start for several days. She would be a clerk at a small bookshop. It suited her. And she would no longer have to work nights. She and Clara sat draped on either end of sofa, exhausted from the push to get things right when Emily looked at her friend.

"Oil."

"I do not understand."

"If you are to do me again, it will be in oil. You've drawn me and drawn me. Now you must paint me. I will be a commission for you, and I have already paid for it with our recent trip."

The next morning, Emily sat where Clara liked her subjects to sit. The light was good, although the sun was low in the February sky, and Clara would put a vague background in. She started by splashing a mixture of red and yellow paint liberally around the edges of the canvas to cover its raw cream color. Emily insisted on wearing nothing but a robe. She was naked underneath, and the robe was merely for some slight modesty as the two agreed the painting would be of Emily's head and naked shoulders.

Clara had done plenty of nudes, but they were studies of anatomy as part of Evans's training. She had seen Emily naked countless times. This was far more personal than anything that preceded it, and the intimacy the two women shared allowed it to be done. With the background satisfactory, Clara blocked Emily's face on the canvas. It was a face she knew perhaps better than she knew any other, and painting it came easily, especially the eyes. Those eyes long intrigued Clara, and she was forever fighting to capture their color. From moment to moment they changed, a brown that varied in intensity and seemed to swirl around the center orbs. At last, in this oil Clara thought she conquered them.

While Emily was at the bookstore a few days later, Clara went through her Stockbridge sketches and transformed some into paintings. She became more confident in doing landscapes as she sat and strolled in Massachusetts. Revisiting her sketches and humming quietly as she turned them into paintings gave her an escape from the turmoil of being back in New York.

She visited Evans, with whom she shared short correspondence while she was away. She knew he had a class and knew his routine. Bundled against the cold, she stood across the street from his building on Houston Street, getting a goodly number of greetings from those who wondered where, and in some cases were fearful that, she had gone and who were pleased to see her back.

When Clara thought all his students gone, she marched up and presented herself to her mentor. She stood, and a smile involuntarily crossed her face. He was quickly across the studio and she fell into more tears than she perhaps had since that horrible night on the sidewalk near her studio. More even than when she was with Emily.

A week or so later, she asked him to come to her studio. He walked around it slowly, a hand rubbing against his chin. Clara stood by the door. She watched for any indication of his thoughts. When he finished his lap and exploration, he turned to her. Yes, he said, you have several quite presentable landscapes of Berkshire County. "And this new *Emily*. You are well on your way back and I am very pleased for you. And proud. Very proud, my dear."

More generally, Emily was satisfied that Clara had not ventured to one or another of the places she could buy laudanum. Clara thought of it, even passing several stores that sold it, but she was able to keep from entering. The discipline of doing the formal oil painting of Emily helped steel her and though in those first days Emily nosed around the apartment to see whether any of the patent bottles were present, she found none because there were none to be found.

31.

As Clara struggled to regain herself and re-enter her world, Emily was able to consider her own situation and most particularly her feelings for Ted Porter. Each piece of correspondence while they were away seemed more flirtatious than the last and when Emily was finally back and could see him again, she was barely able to control herself. Still, propriety was maintained, and the two regularly ate out on Monday nights, continuing the tradition developed when she worked at the restaurant.

But too much it was a mere oasis in an existence that, with her job at the shop, orbited Clara.

In early March, he joined Emily for Sunday dinner at the Bowmans'. He was far more relaxed than that first time and was able to enjoy the Bowmans' hospitality. Afterward he joined Richard Lawson and Mr. Bowman in the study for some of the house's superb port and cigars.

For their part, with Mr. Porter taken, Grace and Mrs. Bowman thought it best not to push Clara too quicky and so they did not bother to even look for an unattached gentleman to join them, and Clara was glad they did not.

32.

On a Sunday several weeks after her sister came back from Massachusetts, and after the pleasant one spent with Mr. Porter, Grace learned where Emily worked. On the Monday, she ventured down to Fourth Avenue to Emily's little bookshop. It was shortly before noon. She surprised her sister's friend and offered to take her to lunch. They left the shop at about twelve fifteen for a restaurant on Fourteenth Street.

"You cannot put your life away because of my sister."

Emily knew it was true. Whenever she was out, she feared something would happen to Clara. She felt guilty that she was away. Her meetings with Ted Porter were not nearly as frequent as they both wished they were, and she hoped he understood and prayed he would not search out a more attentive companion for himself.

"She is becoming as dependent on you as she was on the laudanum. You yourself question her enthusiasm for her work."

After her initial excitement and encouragement from painting Emily, Clara spent too much of her days painting still lifes and reworking portraits she had already done. They were all quality efforts given Clara's technical skill, but her passion and enthusiasm were seeping out and at another time Clara would consider them the type of pedestrian work that she disdained when done by the likes of Kyle Smith.

"I cannot leave her. I could not live with myself if something happened," Emily said.

"You are not living now. You are too young to give up your own life. What of that Mr. Porter?"

Emily said she was seeing him. She admitted she loved him. She promised Grace that if Clara ever had any attraction to him, it had long since passed.

"I think she is much improved indeed. But do you believe she would benefit from a complete change? A visit to London perhaps?"

Grace explained that whatever good was done in Massachusetts had dwindled upon the return to town. For all Emily did and for all she sacrificed, Clara was still stuck.

"I have spoken at length with my parents and Richard. And now you. Tell me if you agree with us. That a complete change of scenery is necessary. Where this new life of hers began."

None of the others, of course, knew about Sir John, and Emily could not say anything about it. She agreed that contact with Felicity was worth the chance of reviving those memories, so she endorsed what they were doing.

Clara was surprisingly receptive. She knew the familiar territory of Greenwich Village and its assortment of artists and hangers-on and the memories of the assault that started her on her downward journey still left her in some kind of suspense. Her trip over Christmas had not been enough. She loved Emily and saw how Emily was sacrificing herself with Ted. Her guilt about that was spiraling down too. She should give Emily the freedom to develop the love they plainly had for one another.

And perhaps seeing Felicity again would help, and Felicity's letters made it seem unlikely she would need to confront the unpleasantness that was her brother. She would meet Mr. Edward Wilson and their baby. So she agreed to the trip. She was not using the laudanum, but it still cast a shadow of lethargy over her.

She hated herself for the unfairness of what she was doing to her friend.

33.

Within a week of agreeing, Clara wrote to Felicity, knowing the happiness Felicity had with the birth of her daughter, Katherine, with more light-heartedness than she felt.

March 15, 1875

My Dear Mrs. Wilson,

I must give you due warning. I fear that I, a single woman, may be unable to resist taking Mr. W away from you, if he is half as good a man as you insist he is. You see, my sister, Mrs. Grace Lawford, intends to embark from these shores and appear on yours in the early spring. On May 8 to be precise. I have consented to accompany her.

You must not go out of your way for us (though I know you will ignore this) and it will be enough for me to spend such time with you as you can afford to give to me.

I shall send you further details as the date approaches. I suggest that you arrange for Mr. W to practice his horsemanship in Derbyshire during our visit.

Your American Friend,
Clara

P.S. Do not believe this, my dear F. You shall be safe. I very much am looking forward to meeting the good man and your little Katherine.

London was far busier than when Clara arrived with her mother. Then, most fashionable families abandoned town for their country estates within weeks of the Bowmans' arrival.

Now, Felicity (after taking her friend aside to report that her brother was in Derbyshire for the next month or so) assured them, things would be as hectic as the Americans could want, and the three settled into their routine, much like the one when Clara and her mother visited. Walks and meals. The three visited Mrs. Trolley's shop on Oxford Street, where Clara's earlier visits were recalled and where Grace bought three and Clara two artistic dresses. They took in several West End shows with Mr. Wilson (with Katherine minded by his parents). The women explored galleries and what seemed like miles and miles of books in shops sprinkled around.

Once again London was much like New York with its pace and smells and dust but also different in subtle ways. Clara relished the chance to show Felicity how she had advanced from the simple watercolors she tried on that earlier trip, even with the recent interruption. That alone was a spark to her creativity.

It felt good to tell the story of that interruption, much as doing so about the Davises' death did on her first trip. Including the secret of the unpleasant incident with Reginald Turner (though this done when Grace was out of the room). And, of course, the visit to the Wilson house was a boon to Clara's spirits. It was small and one of the larger rooms on the third floor was dedicated as Felicity's studio.

Throughout the house were samples of Felicity's work, and many were beyond good. It was clear that her strength was nature, and there were numerous examples of the flowers of Regent's Park among her collection. A portrait of Edward and another of baby Katherine had pride of place in the sitting room at the front of the house, and they helped make it easily the most comfortable room. Several of Clara's drawings were framed, chiefly of Emily, hung near that sketch of Thomas Davis.

The sisters ate at the house several times, after which Felicity and Katherine in her carriage accompanied them on the walk back to the Langham. On each Sunday, they went to services at a small church in Camden Town and had dinner at Edward's parents' place, only a few doors down from his own.

Three weeks into their month-long trip, the Bowmans returned to the hotel in the late afternoon to prepare for dinner when a porter told Clara that there was a message for her at the desk. She opened it in their suite.

"I cannot believe it."

She handed it to Grace.

April 28, 1875

My dearest friend,

You will forgive me I hope, but in your absence I have become...engaged. To Theodore Porter, Esq. The ceremony will be simple and you will be a significant and loving part of it. I promise that he is the only creature I could ever love more than I love you.

I await news of your trip and, more, that you are happy for what I have done and what I hope to do after you return.

Love,
Emily

Clara looked from the note to her sister and back.

"Does it surprise you?"

"I know that it shouldn't but I think I have been so much thinking of myself that I did not realize that I was strangling her and that I kept them apart over the winter."

"Are you glad for her?"

Clara reached for the letter and looked at it again.

"I think I must be. No. I certainly am."

"I will not allow you to continue with your self-indulgence. It has always been a part of you, and I must tell you that it is not an attractive quality. I encouraged Emily to tell you to come to England for your sake, yes, but also because of what she has sacrificed for you. Do you not see that?"

The two stared at each other for a moment.

Clara was not proud of her reaction. "Do you not think that I know that? Am I so awful?"

Grace sat beside her sister on the couch.

"I am your sister and perhaps only I can tell you. You are not awful."

34.

Late on the Thursday afternoon several days after Clara received the glad news from Emily, she and Grace sat with Felicity at the Wilsons', chatting as they did with teas and biscuits after a tiring morning at Harrod's. There was a knock on the front door, which Felicity answered. Standing there was a well-liveried footman. He bowed and held out a sealed ivory-colored envelope bearing her name and address in a neat script. She took it with thanks, and he bowed again and was quickly down her steps and heading back to his employer. Felicity returned with it to her friends.

"It is from my father," she said as she looked at the envelope, and walked across the sitting room as she opened it. She read it quietly.

"It is not good. I have been summoned."

She handed the note to Clara.

Sheffield House

Felicity,

I must speak to you promptly about a matter of grave importance. I am at the house in town and await your appearance.

Arthur Adams,
Fifth Baron Sheffield

"I know it is about you," Felicity said. "I must go. I shall return when I can."

After ensuring that Katherine was being cared for by her nurse, Felicity hailed a cab and was joined by Clara and Grace. After the Americans were deposited at the Langham, it whisked her to Piccadilly. The house's door was open before she reached it, and Jones told her that her father was waiting in the drawing-room. She slowly went up the broad staircase, and her father came to the landing. He greeted her there.

"My dear Felicity. It is good of you to come," and he stepped back to allow her to enter the drawing-room first. He closed the door.

"I have received some troubling news about that American friend of yours. The one you mentioned was coming to town. If what I heard is not true, you must tell me."

The two sat, Felicity on the very edge of one armchair and her father leaning back in another.

"It has come to my attention—I will not say how—that your friend may have had...congress with your brother. He, of course, bears some blame, though I understand that he was not yet married, although he was apparently engaged."

He took a kerchief from his pocket and blew his nose into it, which he replaced in his pocket.

"So, as I say, John bears some blame. But your friend. To have done such a thing. She is, I am afraid, nothing but a harlot and I am certain that her goal was to gain some sort of financial settlement from this family."

Felicity was not surprised by the general statement but was about how her father viewed Clara and her motives. But the framing by her father would dictate his terms.

"Can this be true? Do you know anything about it?"

"Yes, father. It is true, though not your accusation about her and her intentions. She admitted to me that she did what she did voluntarily. Afterward, she wished no further contact with John and gave no indication of wanting to do anything other than try to forget that it ever happened. She had no design, if that's what you think, on seeking something for what she did that one time."

"I see she is your friend, this American. But it remains the fact, and you confirm it, that she had congress with your brother when he was engaged. And she knew he was engaged?"

"Yes, father. She did."

"It is unacceptable, and I will not have this family's name or my or your brother's reputation besmirched by any continued association with this American."

"But father—"

"No, Felicity." As he said this, he leaned forward in the chair, his hands planted on his thighs, and the movement led his daughter to sit back. "I have given you liberty, far too much I sometimes think. I tolerated that marriage of yours and am grateful for the granddaughter you have provided me. This is far too much."

He paused but just so he could sit back again. Felicity's hands were clenched in her lap and she felt her stomach turning unsettled.

"I have, however, decided to leave the decision up to you. You may continue to have something to do with this American, and I include corresponding with her, or you can elect to remain in this family."

He again paused and again leaned forward and his voice took on the hard edge he rarely used with her.

"You must know, however, that if you choose the former, you will cease to be my daughter. I know you may not care in some respects but be aware. In that case, I will have no further obligation to provide you with any financial support. Insofar as I provided money for your marriage settlement, that you may retain. But there shall be no more. Neither you nor your husband nor your child shall be welcome in this house or, I daresay, in any other reputable house.

"Your mother will cry in that case, of course, but she knows her place and will not defy what I say."

Throughout this rehearsed speech, Felicity stared ahead but saw nothing. She did not care for herself, but her own family needed her allowance. She had no choice. As the baron knew.

She stood. "Very well, father. I shall sever all ties with her."

"Immediately," he replied with a curt, triumphant nod. With that, she, still his daughter, turned and opened the door. After a "Good day, father," she went through and closed it behind her. The moment her foot hit the foyer's floor tiles, Jones had the door open and she was out in the street and did not know what to do.

For several days, Felicity sat in the sitting room after Edward went to work, telling him that she would be off shortly to visit her American friends and she really planned to but found herself unable to leave the house.

She had not told Edward about her meeting with her father or his demand. Edward would insist that she be true to her friend, "damn the consequences."

But Felicity was all too aware of those consequences and could not ask him or their child to suffer them.

Each evening when he returned from work, she told him the Bowmans were too busy that day to see her.

At the Langham, when Felicity failed to appear the morning after being summoned by her father, Clara understood. Yet not a note? Until she had news, she would not visit the Wilson house. She could not endanger Felicity if what she feared was true.

On that first morning, she did not leave the hotel, hoping that Felicity was simply delayed. She told Grace that some emergency must have taken place and that it could well be Felicity had to rush from town. That she would get a note to explain it.

On the second, Grace insisted that they walk and when they returned Clara rushed to the desk in the lobby asking if a message was left for her and learning than none had been.

They would be returning to New York in only a few days. She found it helped to wander with her sketchbook and visit some exhibitions. She even showed some of her work to those who might be interested in it, but as the time was short and she was soon to leave, nothing came of it.

Felicity told Edward that something arose that precluded getting together with the Bowmans before they left England.

35.

As Clara was preparing to leave the Langham for the train to take the Bowman sisters to Southampton, there was a knock on her door. It was only a hotel boy. He held out a silver tray on which there was a small, sealed envelope. She took it and gave the boy a coin. She sat at the chair nearest the window.

> *My Dearest Clara,*
>
> *You must understand that I cannot afford to face the rejection by my father. My own family could not survive it. I pray that you will understand that and will someday find it in your heart to forgive me.*
>
> *You are a wonderful woman and I love you with all my heart. I will never forget you.*
>
> *Always your Felicity*

There were traces of lips beside the signature. Clara gripped it hard, harder than she realized, and they—she and the note—crumbled as she stared out the window. Her understanding of the necessity of what Felicity did could not soften the blow, and she pulled out the note periodically during the crossing back to America.

She could not let her sister see it. She told Grace merely that Felicity had sent a note and regretted that urgent family business required her to journey as quickly as she could to Derbyshire, and Grace said how sorry she was that they were unable to at least say goodbye.

When the Bowmans disembarked in Manhattan, they were quickly through the immigration officers, and they hailed a cab and arranged for their trunks to be sent on to Grace's house. It was early afternoon. Grace suggested that they meet later at their parents' house and Clara agreed when she left her sister at her apartment.

Emily was waiting, and Clara told of what happened—or in truth had not happened—with Felicity.

"You know I am not abandoning you."

"I know that. I've had time to think about it and spent much of it speaking to Grace. I can never repay you for what you have done for me. I can only hope that you understand that. More than anything, I regret having deprived you of the company of the man that you love and I promise I will do everything in my power to atone for that."

It was mid-June and one of the first of the hot days that arrive with summer. Clara quickly became reaccustomed to the smells and bustling in the neighborhood, her neighborhood, as they sat at a small table on the sidewalk at a favorite café. They were frequently interrupted by acquaintances pleased to see Clara back from her trip but managed to speak about what happened.

With their coffees and pastries nearly gone, Emily asked, "Are you alright? I mean, really alright?"

"Oh, Em. I do not know that I shall ever be."

"But about the—"

"The laudanum? I was tempted in those lonely days after Felicity disappeared. Perhaps I would have dosed myself if I knew where to get it. Sometimes I think Ashley got me through. That she is looking over me, protecting me."

They spoke rarely of what happened before they met, and Emily never knew quite what Clara's thoughts were about her dead friend. She did not know if Clara somehow thought of her as a replacement.

Her voice still low, Clara said, "I am in a better place now. Accepting that she is gone and knowing that she is still with me. I do not mean to lessen my fondness for you, but I do not think you could ever be her. We went back so far."

"Clara. I never want to be anything to you but your good friend."

"I know that. It is just that sometimes …sometimes…I so miss her and conjure her up so that I am not so lonely. As I was in London. It was a great comfort, and I think it helped me more than the laudanum could have."

Emily wondered something.

"What about Thomas?"

"Tommy? That was different. I do not think of him so much I am afraid. Over time, I think of him more as being a man than a friend. Very different from his sister, though we were very close. No. He will always be a man to me, and I hope that thought will not prevent me from loving another man in my time."

Clara was dreamy-eyed when she spoke of Ashley, but her face hardened when she turned to Thomas. Even she did not know why, but she felt it as Emily saw it. While no one, not even Emily, could replace Ashley—and Emily had no desire to—Clara believed that someone could replace the man who she loved but who was forever lost to her.

"I was cast out in London, but I resisted. Instead, I spent the days, even the rainy ones, sketching in one park or another and going to exhibitions; I even brought some of my sketches to a few of them. While some expressed an interest in them and in my other work, my stay was too brief to pursue it. But I have hope.

"But the laudanum? I resisted it and my art and thoughts of Ashley and your happiness seemed to have been enough to sustain me. I must tell you, though. The loss of Felicity hurts me far more than what happened with Mr. Turner. Much more."

36.

For the next several days, Clara spent more time at her parents' with her mother than she usually did. Grace had reported on what happened with Felicity and assured Mrs. Bowman that Clara handled it as well as could be expected. Most importantly by not turning to the laudanum.

All were heartened when within a week of returning, Clara seemed to have melded into the life she led before being beaten. Often, she and Emily went for a small breakfast in one of the area's cafés or restaurants before Emily had to go to her bookshop. For the remainder of the day, Clara did exercises to steady her hand and improve her eye. She took some of the sketches and watercolors made in London and turned them into small paintings. She even took some of those random lines and shapes she made at night late in the trip and painted them, though the results she knew would never be seen.

On a cool Thursday later that month, the two shared a table outside a café on Lafayette. Their coffees were finished, and only a few bites of their pastries remained on their plates. Clara's attention was on a wagon delivering supplies to a shop down the way, trying to balance the lettering on its side in her drawing of it while Emily read the *New York Sun*.

"Do you remember Mary McNabb?" Emily looked up and interrupted Clara's sketching. Her friend, her pencil continuing its movement on the pad, answered without lifting her head, "Who can forget her? Such a horrible human being. I did a portrait of her that I rather liked but she did not. I liked her parents quite a lot."

"Yes, and to think I wasted time with her before she threw me over the side when she moved up to the Peter McNabb crowd."

"That was a while ago. Why do you ask?"

"Do you remember me telling you I met her sister when I was in exile after we lost everything. Her family did, too, but Mary McNabb avoided that fate by marrying well. Or at least rich."

"The Gehertys spoke of that. Why?" She looked up and put the pencil on the table.

Emily held the newspaper up to Clara, pointing to an article on the front page.

"The sister was Elizabeth. Read this."

Clara put her sketch pad on her lap and took the paper. The article had the headline:

SINGLE AUNT AWARDED CUSTODY OF ORPHANED NEPHEW

In what some are calling an amazing turn of events, unwed Róisín Campbell was granted custody of her nephew, Diarmaid Cassidy, by the Surrogate after at the eleventh hour the Foundling Asylum withdrew its petition seeking custody of the boy. Miss Campbell arrived in the city five years ago from a farm in Ireland.

The battle was famous among the Catholic precincts of the City. The child was left orphaned after his mother died in childbirth. Although his mother, Sophie Cassidy, was married, Mr. Cassidy filed a paper claiming that he was not the father and refusing to take any responsibility for the care of the infant.

Although rumors were rampant in the Catholic community about who the father was, he did not step forward to take responsibility.

After the Asylum reversed its position and supported Miss Campbell's petition, the Surrogate himself interviewed Miss Campbell and determined that she would be a fit "mother" for the boy, and he approved of the adoption.

Miss Campbell is a nurse at Dr. Doyle's famous clinic and is well known and admired by those who flood the Irish tenements along the lower east side. She had the support of Tammany for her application.

It is believed that the appearance of Elizabeth Geherty, also a nurse at the clinic and formerly a student at the Bellevue School of Nursing, and her commitment to fully support Miss Campbell, aided in the latter's application.

Miss Geherty is the youngest daughter in the family of Charles Geherty, which lost most of its money in the Panic of 1873 and the notorious Bolivian Railway speculation of that year. She is also the sister of the well-known socialite Mary McNabb of Twenty-Fourth Street, although Mrs. McNabb's role in the proceedings, if any, is unknown.

The two women were last seen overjoyed about the news and leaving the scene in a cab to continue to take care of the boy.

After Clara handed the paper back, Emily said, "I loved Elizabeth. Nothing like Mary. We were

Dickensian waifs hiding from creditors in the cold of Massachusetts after our fathers lost their money. When I came back, last year, I lost touch."

"I can't imagine someone like Mary McNabb would have anything to do with someone who…supports a single woman getting custody of a child."

"Nor can I."

"But, as you will recall, you happily made me aware of the cold of Massachusetts in the wintertime."

"For which you will always be in my debt."

Clara looked at the imp across from her, and just for a moment she regretted she would soon lose much of her friend's company when she became Mrs. Theodore Porter, though the date when that would occur had yet to be set.

37.

Emily decided as she walked to the bookshop after seeing the story that she would try to reconnect with Elizabeth. She let so much time pass, and very eventful times, especially for Lizzie.

Two days later, the Saturday, Emily did not have much time before she had to report to her shop. But if she reached the clinic before ten, they could speak, if only briefly. The problem was that she did not know where it was. She headed north along Second Avenue, stopping periodically to ask strangers if they knew until she at last found one who did, and with directions she repeated to herself so as not to forget them she soon found herself in front of the one-time mansion that housed the clinic. She waited, and when an older man, a laborer, stepped down the three steps to the sidewalk she approached and asked if this was the clinic where the Campbell girl worked and he assured her that indeed it was, indeed it was.

"She is very popular now, you know," he said as he placed his hat on his head and nodded as he turned east.

She stepped up and through the door to the room on the left. A sweet, Irish-looking girl sat at a desk, with three or four haggard folks waiting to be seen.

"May I help you?"

"I am an old friend of Elizabeth Geherty's. Is she here?"

The girl gave her a curious glance and told her that Elizabeth was with a patient. Emily sat with the others.

After some minutes, a striking redhead entered. She wore a nurse's uniform, accompanying and speaking in a clear brogue amiably with a young, pregnant girl. After the young girl left, the nurse turned to the desk.

Emily approached, touching the nurse's arm and asking if she was "Miss Campbell." Róisín turned, fearing it was another person responding to the recent notoriety she had not sought, and Emily hastened to add, "I am a friend of Elizabeth's."

Róisín stepped back. Emily added, "We spent time together when her family was in exile after the Panic," and Róisín gave a glimmer of recognition.

"Are you that one who disappeared on her in Massachusetts?" and Emily confessed.

"I'm sorry, I do not know your name. She told me but I forgot. She's upstairs. She tells me you made her period there survivable."

"It's Emily—"

"Emily Connor. I cannot believe it."

This latter was from the woman herself, entering the room with a patient. After tending to the man, she hugged Emily and stepped back. "I so missed you. You were my only friend in those days."

Elizabeth introduced her to Róisín, but Emily demurred.

"I am sorry, but I must leave shortly to get to work. But, please, may we arrange to meet again? The three of us?"

"Four of us," Róisín corrected, not forgetting her baby. And it was set that Emily would venture to the girls' apartment the next day after Mass to meet the baby.

When she did, she thought him a handsome boy. Emily had seen many babies, but Diarmaid Cassidy seemed special. For a moment she doubted that Róisín would let him go so she could hold him, but eventually she did. A well-nourished, and seemingly very happy child.

38.

That evening when Clara was back from spending the day with her parents and sister, Emily went on and on about her meeting with Elizabeth, Róisín, and the boy.

"It seemed that it is just dawning on them that they have him and are responsible for him. You know your sister and Richard? They are like that with one another."

The two were sitting at a table by the kitchen, with the sandwiches they ate and ales they drank late on Sundays.

"It has just happened, it being made official. It will take some time for them to realize that it is real."

"Now. When can I meet them?"

"My God. You could paint them. You'd do it for nothing, wouldn't you?"

Since her return from London, Clara was physically stable. She again supplemented her allowance with commissioned portraits, feeling better, stronger, and more confident with each. She resumed first with women in families who were in her parents' circle, but she was developing a reputation and found herself in some demand again after her many failures in her bad period. People seemed particularly excited that her portraits revealed to their subjects parts of themselves they never realized they possessed. She was particularly adept with the two or three women who recently came out in society. Each portrait showed an internal fire that Clara managed to extract from them.

On the next Sunday, Emily arranged to have Clara join her to meet her friends. Clara was at her parents' on Saturday night but received her mother's dispensation about services and dinner the next day. The four women met after Mass and walked to the river, Emily and Elizabeth ahead of Clara and Róisín. When a sufficient gap opened between the couples, Róisín spoke softly to Clara, and the two felt comfortable with each other immediately, a rarity for both.

"I couldn't have done it without her."

When Clara asked who, she said, "My Elizabeth. She is more your world than mine and she gave it up for me."

"It is not so much to give up, except for the security of knowing you will never want for anything. Anything material, at least," Clara responded. "I have never regretted it although as I understand it when Elizabeth left, she had nothing."

"I like to think she had me."

"I didn't mean to sound so cold. I just meant, well, financially. It is not easy to be a woman alone," and again Clara regretted a *faux pas*. She did not know much about Róisín Campbell but did know she came to America with nothing and had done well enough for the surrogate to award custody of her nephew to her. Not being Irish, she only knew vague details about what happened with her and her sister and the father and the husband, only what she and Emily had been able to piece together over the past days. That Elizabeth was expelled from the McNabbs' because she would not cut all ties with the Irishwoman, a choice she never regretted.

The two watched the pair ahead of them, also with their arms intertwined. They could not hear what they were saying. More than anything it was each apologizing to the other about having neglected their friendship since those cold days spent together in exile in Stockbridge.

The four found a spot along the river where Elizabeth and Róisín often stood, quietly watching the boat traffic. But Diarmaid could not be left too long with his nurse, and they had to pull away and head back to the flat.

"I very much want to paint them." Clara said when they were a block or two away after leaving.

"I thought you might."

"I have never seen two people so in love with each other."

"Do you think they realize it?"

Clara, the keen observer, said, "I doubt they care. They just are. I think I can capture that. I'd like to try."

"Do you want me to ask?"

And after Clara said she did, she asked Emily if she ever, well, thought about loving another woman. They were nearing the flat at this point.

"I've not thought about it, no."

"Nor have I. But they are so right for each other."

39.

Emily Connor occupied a strange position among the tiers of New York society. Her family was largely cast out after suffering its financial catastrophe. They fled into exile in western Massachusetts. Emily herself was labeled something of a rebel for moving to Greenwich Village and living with a member of the artistic community there (however exalted her pedigree) and herself working odd hours at a restaurant and then at a bookstore. She was several years older than most of the society girls her age when they married. And she was soon to marry the son of a middle-class lawyer who was himself a lawyer.

Emily understood the liberation of finding herself in such a strange position. It allowed her to forgo the strict regime imposed upon the more privileged brides in New York. There was never going to be reception in one of the favored hotel ballrooms. There would be no announcement in the city's more esteemed newspapers. There would be no embarking on a trip to Europe aboard a steamship.

It was destined to be a simple affair at St. Stephen's Church. Although Emily was not as observant a Catholic as her parents, her faith was important to her, and she convinced Ted to convert from Episcopalian. They were married by Fr. Parker in front of the church's marble altar on a Saturday in August when most of society was far, far away. Emily wore a simple cream dress given to her by Grace Lawford, and Ted wore his best suit. Clara served as the maid of honor and Ted's cousin was his best man. The Connors returned to town for the first time since they abandoned it (and took the opportunity to visit with those who still knew them). The couple and their guests adjourned to the Bowmans', the site of their meeting, for a wedding breakfast. It was not late when Mr. and Mrs. Theodore Porter left for their home in Ted's apartment.

Returning to the flat on Bleecker Street alone was bittersweet for Clara. Grace offered to go with her, but she would not have it. She had not lived without Emily since the day that homeless waif appeared at her door well over a year earlier with nowhere else to go. Now Emily found somewhere else—a happy somewhere else—and she was gone and Clara was again alone.

40.

On a rainy day in early September 1875, Charlotte Ogilvy took her carriage alone to Washington Square North. A week or so earlier, while she visited Mary McNabb, she saw John Evans's portrait of her host. It reminded her of something. She found the opportunity to be alone with Bradley, the butler. She asked who did his master's and mistress's portraits. Not the big ones. The smaller ones displayed only briefly, at the unveiling a year earlier, that then disappeared. Done by the woman assistant whose name she did not catch. She occasionally thought of the small one of Mary and decided to inquire about it. When she was again at the McNabb house several days later, Bradley handed her a paper as she passed him at the door, an interaction observed by no one.

Now she was in her carriage heading to Washington Square, where John Evans had his house and studio. It was a large house, and the door was answered by a maid. Bradley could only get Evans's name, so Mrs. Ogilvy was left to ask about "the girl who helped Mr. Evans when he painted the McNabbs." She was directed to the sitting room while the maid made inquiries. Soon the man himself appeared.

"I am told you are interested in the woman who did portraits of the McNabbs. I assume that you might wish her to...paint you perhaps?"

Mrs. Ogilvy nodded.

"You shall be fortunate if she does. As talented as anyone I know." He looked at the woman. She was in her late twenties and slightly plump and quite pale, but although she sat, he saw her figure was attractive beneath the layers of her dress and would be even without the pressure of a corset. It was a shame, he thought, that women of the period did so much to hide themselves beneath the intricate detail of their dresses and gowns. She had a pretty face and he imagined her hair, held up in an intricate design somewhat overdone for a morning trip to Washington Square, was long and languid. Surely Clara would insist that it be down when she painted her.

He did not doubt that she would. A commission like this would be a godsend. He motioned for his guest to sit and opened a drawer in a secretary against the wall. Evans used the pen he took from it to write Clara's name and address, including that it was at the front of the third floor.

He handed it to her. "I know you shall both be pleased by the result."

With a bow from him, she returned to her carriage for the short drive to Bleecker Street. If she was ever in this neighborhood before, she did not recall it. She hesitated before entering the building, climbing its ill-lit stairs. Two flights. She passed the first door and knocked on the second, the one that overlooked the street.

She opened the door after hearing "Please come in." She recognized Clara but was not recognized by her.

"Yes?"

"You will not recall me, but I saw you at the McNabbs' unveiling."

Clara, who was moving to the door, said, "Yes, I do recall you. You wore a maroon dress, did you not? I remember it since it is my favorite color. Please, please sit down."

She rushed to clear a space for her visitor. Clara had quickly filled at least the spatial vacuum left by Emily's departure.

"I do not often have such...pleasant company here. Is there anything that I can get for you."

Charlotte saw that there were few amenities and declined the offer. The two women sat.

"I would like you to paint me."

Seeing the artist's hesitation, Charlotte added, "I will, of course, pay you the appropriate amount for such a commission."

"That would be excellent, Mrs.—?"

"Ogilvy. Charlotte Ogilvy."

"Of course, Mrs. Ogilvy, I would be pleased to paint you. But I must warn you that I am not particularly adept. I am sure you can find someone more suitable."

"Miss Bowman. Do not talk yourself out of a commission. I saw how you painted Mary...Mrs. McNabb. Mr. Evans vouched for you not half an hour ago. I wish for you to paint me. It is as simple as that. Is that acceptable to you?"

"More than. Do you know what you will pay?"

Charlotte chuckled. "I confess, Miss Bowman, that I have no experience in such things. There is a formal portrait of me in our house, but I had nothing to do with the financial arrangements for it. I will be using my own money for this, and I will pay you what I understand is known as the 'going rate.' Is that acceptable to you? Just find out what is appropriate and when you are done send me the bill and I will take care of it."

With that Charlotte rose, and Clara quickly followed. Mrs. Ogilvy reached into her bag and removed one of her cards.

"I am here most mornings except Wednesdays and Fridays. You may come by after ten on any other morning during the week, and we can speak further about what you need from me to get started. From what I saw, I am relying on you making me look better than I really am. I shall see you again soon."

She turned to leave.

"Mrs. Ogilvy, please think about where you would like to be painted. I will oblige as much as I can, and we can talk about it."

"Thank you, Miss Bowman. I recalled you generally when I saw your name of Mr. Evans's paper. I am a bit older than you, but I am sure we must have met some time before the…well before what happened to your friends. Might I look around?"

With Clara's permission, she explored the space. Most obviously was a nearly complete oil painting of a non-fashionable couple—Mrs. Ogilvy would not know who they were—on an easel by the window.

Mrs. Ogilvy was looking through some pencil sketches stacked near the window when she stopped at a simple sketch portrait. It was of a woman, somewhat nondescript. She looked unflinchingly at the artist with auburn hair that had a wave, and she had a nose that was a little large for the face. Her skin was pale, though rouged slightly—whether by make-up or pinching was unclear—and narrow, dark eyebrows. Her eyes were some kind of brown and struck her as demanding but soft and though her broad lips pretended to be severe the hint of a smile could not be hidden. More than anything, she looked to be posing seriously but was not entirely successful in hiding some puckish notion racing through her.

Looking further, she found a painting, an oil, of the same woman. While she wore a high-collared dress in the drawing, in this one she was naked at the shoulders and her hair dangled loosely over her bare left one. Now her smile was plain, though looking to her right, the artist's left, and her eyes sparkled. It was clear she was again looking or thinking of something light-hearted, yet her seductiveness could not be denied.

Mrs. Ogilvy looked at Clara.

"I believe I know her. Emily something."

"Yes. Emily Connor. Before she recently married, she lived here. She has long been my favorite model, and this is called *Emily (Mrs. Porter)*."

Seeing Mrs. Ogilvy weigh the inescapable desire of the model in the painting done shortly after the two returned from Stockbridge earlier in the year, Clara added, "It is a wedding present to her. Though it may be more of one for her husband."

She turned to Clara. "Well, I hope you can do…justice to me as well. I have not seen her in a while, but these seem quite true to life."

She gave a final bow and a final look at *Emily*. "Until we meet again, good day, Miss Bowman."

"And to you, Mrs. Ogilvy."

Clara arrived at the Ogilvy house early on the next Tuesday. It was a pleasant fall day and she walked, so was lightly perspiring when she entered the bright foyer. Calhoun, the butler, led her to the sitting room and left to fetch his mistress. She had a slim but large package under her arm, and she cradled it until placing it on a table while she waited for her host. It was a pleasant enough room, and not as pretentious as many Clara sat in in her younger days. The wallpaper was baby blue, and the chairs and sofa were encased in the patterned upholstery that was all the rage but not so overdone as to compromise the room's lightness. The walls displayed enough pieces of art to establish the owner was wealthy but not so many crowded about to prove a want of taste. The day's heat had filtered into the room with the ubiquitous sounds and smells of a city-in-motion but Clara found it quite a comfortable place. She stood at the window to look out over the street awaiting the arrival of her host.

"Miss Bowman. How good to see you."

Unlike Mrs. McNabb's faux sincerity, Mrs. Ogilvy was truly delighted, and the artist hurried across the room to greet her.

"I have ordered some refreshments. Please sit. Sit."

Before they did, Clara lifted her bundle and handed it to Mrs. Ogilvy, who opened the paper when they sat. She found a pencil sketch, very raw, of her face, neck, and shoulders. She looked up around the room and at the formal oil portrait she mentioned in Clara's studio in her high-collared gown, and her eyes went from one to the other.

"My God, Miss Bowman. That oil of me makes me seem as dead as…George Washington compared to what you have done. I am very pleased to have commissioned you."

"It is yours. My gift."

"I cannot accept this."

"Of course you can."

Mrs. Ogilvy stood and carried the sketch to a table along a wall, where she laid it down gently.

"Thank you so much. I hope the frame will do it justice."

She came back and sat again with Clara just as Calhoun brought in a coffee tray with biscuits, which he placed on a small table between the women. After taking a sip of her coffee, into which she put a little cream and two spoonfuls of sugar, Clara asked, "Why do you want me to paint you?"

"I do not know, truly. I guess I wanted you to make me look like—well, as alive as you made Miss Connor and even Mary in her portrait."

"I have named it *A Lady in Her House*."

"Simple yet apt. Perhaps mine will be the equally simple *A Lady in Her Garden*."

The Ogilvy house was on the south side of the street and closer to Fifth Avenue than Madison. Hence, in the morning its back garden got a healthy dose of the sun. The women arranged for Clara to come by three times a week to work on the painting. She was happy with the relaxed sense she achieved with the Gehertys and hoped this garden would have a similar effect on her new subject.

One reached the garden through a French door visible from the foyer, and there was a small storage room near it, and that is where Clara kept her supplies. Mrs. Ogilvy—Charlotte—offered to have her staff handle Clara's easel and paints and canvas, but the artist preferred to do it herself. And she made all in the house promise that no one would look at the painting until she pronounced it finished.

The pair decided Charlotte would pose in a house dress, a portrait of a lady-of-leisure relaxing in her well-tended garden. Clara was familiar with the workings of a great house and accompanied Mrs. Ogilvy and her maid to the floor where the dresses and gowns were kept. In the end, they agreed to forgo a high collar in favor of something more open, more comfortable looking.

The one agreed upon was dark blue, in the current fashion, but had simple yellow pinstripes. The combination played off Mrs. Ogilvy's hair and skin. A simple blue choker was around her throat and after some reluctance she agreed to let her hair flow easily over her shoulders. Clara convinced her of its beauty and of the added texture its strands and slight curls would bring to her face. As the maid helped with her mistress's corset, Clara agreed with John Evans. Mrs. Ogilvy was the mother of two, but her lines and curves would be lost beneath the most wonderful of garments. Clara would have to use the knowledge of this body to suggest the truth about Mrs. Ogilvy's beauty.

She was a good subject, and the loosened dress, the freed hair, and the simplicity of the setting would show her at her best.

While Clara lacked Evans's easy way with his subjects, his flattery and cajoling, Clara was of Mrs. Ogilvy's world, or at least she was, and the two got on well, decidedly not mistress and servant.

Once Mrs. Ogilvy was posed, Clara went to work, and they engaged in light conversation. That talk one day reached the subject of Mary McNabb, when Mrs. Ogilvy learned of Clara's having met Elizabeth and the famous Róisín Campbell. Clara thought it strange that the two sisters were estranged, though she saw their characters were worlds apart.

"You do not know?"

"Know?"

"You must've been out of society when it happened. Lizzie's friend Róisín Campbell had some type of run-in with Mary soon after she came to America. Mary claims she tried to seduce Peter McNabb, before he became her husband. I never met the girl, but people say she, well, could get a man's attention though from what I've heard she is happy enough with Lizzie and the baby.

"Mrs. McNabb can be defensive, and I heard she tried to make the Irish girl's life difficult, but she couldn't make it difficult enough and by some coincidence, Miss Campbell met Lizzie when she was working as a nurse. They're both nurses now.

"Anyway, it took a while but apparently there was some connection the two discovered with one another—everyone thinks they are, you know—and idiot Mary cut her only sister off when Lizzie refused not to communicate with Róisín. Then there was the whole adoption thing—"

"Which is how I came to meet them, when it was in the newspaper."

"Yes, they became famous for a while, which only made Mary angrier. Apparently, she had one or two unfortunate encounters with Lizzie and then nothing since, with her poor mother making it clear whose side she is on if she had the luxury of being able to afford to take a side."

"I painted the parents. I liked them, and they talked about her. But we must return to business."

And back to business they returned as Mrs. Ogilvy stiffened her pose and Clara focused on her brush strokes and thought about the two Geherty daughters and how different they were from each other.

41.

A *Lady in Her Garden* helped make Clara's career. The large oil was unveiled in mid-October at the Ogilvy house. The process was not so formal as with the McNabbs, but more than with the Gehertys. Clara asked Evans and a number of fellow former students as well as the Porters and the Lawfords.

The guests mingled in the house's drawing room on the second floor and there was no formal entrance by the Ogilvys. Instead, when the grandfather clock that dominated one corner struck seven, Mrs. Ogilvy clapped for everyone's attention. With little ado beyond announcing that Clara Bowman, to whom she pointed, had done her the honor of painting her, she asked her husband to do the unveiling.

The husband, in the event, was the least surprised though perhaps most pleased of the guests with the result. His wife sat in a garden chair with a table to her right. It was a full image of her, with her ankles crossed and showing a pair of black boots on which inlaid stems containing four-leaf daisies swayed. The yellow pinstripes on her dress seemed to swirl around and enhance her body. Charlotte was embarrassed about the size of her bosom, but it blended in perfectly, her cleavage portrayed as both a mother's and a woman's.

Her hands were folded in her lap but her right held a single dark red rose taken, it appeared, from a vase on the table on which one could count but eleven.

She looked at the artist with the slightest edges of a smile and with passion in the eyes. Her black hair framed her pale face and dangled over her shoulders, and the face seemed to glow, the choker—Clara cheated here, swapping the original blue for a maroon that complemented the blue dress and echoed the rose—framing it perfectly. There was no hard edge between the face and the background, which was vague and mysterious, the trellis of indeterminate size, though a lily white. Vines wound through it with flowers that mimicked those in the dress.

Mrs. Ogilvy was silent. Was this her? She was short and dumpy. Everyone knew that. She had two children, and her husband was beginning to go gray with his hair thinning in the rear. The person in oil was a woman. It was the only word to describe her. Yet it accurately portrayed Charlotte Ogilvy.

The others waited for their cue from Charlotte, and as the time passed, they became nervous. Evans assured Clara that it was a magical work, and she watched for the slightest hint of Charlotte's reaction. Charlotte turned to the artist.

"Is this me?"

Her husband stepped in front of her and said, "Of course it is you. She has captured you far better than any mirror could," and as they hugged, Charlotte cried and Evans whispered to his protégé, "I did tell you, you will recall."

One guest did not join the others offering congratulations to the artist. She stood well away while they did and stepped close to the portrait when it opened up to the room.

"You must credit her, Mrs. McNabb."

The woman turned to her right. She had not noticed John Evans's approach.

"She may be among the most talented of my students, and you would do well to spend time with the portrait she did of you."

Mrs. McNabb had not deigned to take *A Lady in Her House* and at the moment she was drawn into *A Lady in Her Garden*, that early, smaller Bowman painting of her was on display in an exhibition Evans maintained in his drawing room of the better of his students' works.

Mrs. McNabb was strangely affected by the painting of her friend. Perhaps she had not been fair to this girl. Perhaps Clara Bowman did to her what she did to her friend.

> Perhaps.
> Perhaps.
> Perhaps.

She half-wished she kept it, much as she was content with Evans's more standard rendition.

With a nod, Evans backed away and told her where she could find that portrait and that she was free to visit his house on Washington Square whenever she wished.

Alone again, Mrs. McNabb stared at the painting only briefly before making her way to the other side of the room where her friends were drinking and snacking and telling Charlotte how well she was captured. By the time the evening wound down, Clara, Evans, the Porters, the Lawfords, and the fellow artists had long since returned to their homes.

42.

Mary McNabb took advantage of John Evans's suggestion and was in his drawing room several days after the Ogilvy unveiling. Evans was out, but his butler said she was free to explore the exhibition.

She liked the portrait he did of her. She studied it often above the mantel in her sitting room. It showed her in an almost classical manner, the equal of all those other society wives whose portraits needed to be complimented when she visited their homes, as proxies for the hostesses themselves.

This girl's painting was much like Evans's. They had, after all, been done at the same time and in the same place.

Yet.

Perhaps this smaller one should be hanging in her house too. Not in too public a place of course. Perhaps she would ask Evans for it.

Before she left, she wandered about the room, examining the other works. Suddenly she saw one of Róisín Campbell and her famous nephew. She had not forgiven the Irishwoman for her attempts to ensnare her husband and now realized that the harlot had her own son as Mary McNabb did not, notwithstanding numerous attempts. All the goodwill established by looking at *A Lady in Her House* evaporated in a flash when she saw *A Mother and Her Child*—she knew it was a wholly inappropriate name—and she was quickly out of the house, flinging the door open before Evans's butler could get to it and huffing in her carriage by the time it was closed.

How Clara came to paint the whore she could not know. Clara likely tracked her down for the publicity she would get for painting the infamous aunt. Only when she was in her study with a glass of sherry an hour later had Mary McNabb calmed enough to head out for a weekly engagement she had with friends. Charlotte might well be there, and from her she would find out the truth about this Clara Bowman.

43.

In fact, Charlotte was not there and Mary McNabb was not told how *A Whore and the Bastard*—its proper name in this society woman's mind—came to be. Mrs. McNabb was left to share her speculation with the friends who appeared for the engagement. All agreed with Mrs. McNabb that it reflected poorly on this Clara Bowman to debase herself to do it.

This group's opinion was of no moment to Charlotte Ogilvy ever again, though some of its members, notably not including Mary McNabb, were among the friends, acquaintances, and even strangers who took to "dropping by" the Ogilvys' to admire the painting. It hung above the mantel, and it was commented upon (thanks to Evans) in an edition of the *Illustrated News*. Given that the world considered Charlotte Ogilvy to in fact be short and dumpy, more than a few husbands were determined to have Clara Bowman paint their wives. Most did not dare admit that a portrait of their wife in the nude would not be entirely unwelcome, even if it were relegated to a discreet room in a discreet part of their house. None was brave enough to broach the prospect with his wife, let alone with Miss Bowman.

Clara did not wish to become known as the "woman's artist" and so resisted these offers, with Evans's approval. The sudden clamor for her services and the pleasure that Mr. Ogilvy had in seeing his wife's portrait left her feeling remarkably lonely. Her dearest friends were in the deepest relationships with the person they most loved.

Oddly enough, *A Lady in Her Garden* helped Clara again feel comfortable living alone. She often visited with Emily, at either of their apartments or in one park or another, and Emily often passed her days lounging in a spot familiar to her in Clara's studio, reading while her friend worked and always assessing Clara's condition. But after a time, that monitoring motive for the visits faded and it was again as it had been in the early days.

Nor did Ted or Emily object to Clara's presence on outings. Indeed, they insisted, and the three became familiar figures in various places and often were together for dinner at the Bowmans' on Sundays—even if Mrs. Bowman, and even Grace, sometimes looked at Ted and wondered what might have been had Emily not chanced to be at the house that first time Theodore Porter, Esq., came to dinner.

So matters stood as 1875 came to an end. In between paid commissions, Clara was finally able to get portraits of her sister and her mother that were acceptable. They, with a fine one of George Bowman looking even stricter than he did in life, were prominently hung along the main staircase to the second floor at the Bowmans'. And she continued her drawings and paintings of Emily.

For Christmas, such a tumultuous time twelve months before, Clara declined Emily's offer to join her family. Instead, she went to services with her own family and then enjoyed the feast at her parents'. Though it was dark when they finished eating and everyone was well sated, it was warm, and Grace asked her sister to walk with her in the neighborhood.

Between the sharing of merry wishes with those they passed, Grace told her sister how proud she was. In all the times they saw each other through the year, she never said that. Emily had continued reporting to Grace and to Dr. Southbridge about Clara's condition. Emily felt no hesitancy about doing so because there were no ill winds to report. Clara seemed well past those dark days, and even past those at the end of her stay in London.

As happened with the loss of the Davises, Clara was able to place the loss of Felicity Adams in some recess of herself. Hearing an English accent could unearth thoughts of her lost friend, but Clara had come to terms with the reality that Felicity was a mother and was acting as any mother would. That did not lessen the gap it created in Clara and it might have been far worse but for the existence of Emily Connor in her life. And though Emily was largely gone, especially with her devotion to Ted, Clara seemed to be managing. That was the verdict of all who knew her well, and into the new year she was as content as she had ever been.

44.

"We shall go to Paris. We shall go to London."

In February of 1876, with the holidays past and the time until spring stretching far into the future, Evans was at the Elk's Head with several from his first class. It was a common sight. All of the first six had flown the nest and were obtaining their own commissions and reputations. While more and more young people of varying artistic skill were coming to New York to train as artists, the imprimatur of John Evans marked these six—and the next group that Evans was mentoring—as special, and his insistence on formal training proved priceless.

Now he was suggesting Europe to his three erstwhile charges. They thought he was inspired by the whisky, but he had given thought to his scheme and had already exchanged correspondence with artists and promoters he knew in Europe. He was assured that the political turmoil in Paris eased such that a trip would be perfectly safe for him and whomever he brought with him. "*Paris est Paris. Toujours,*" he read more than once.

One of the former students at the table, Charles, said, "Where we shall surely starve, in one if not in the other." Charles Ellis was one of the middle-class students for whom Evans had provided his services *gratis*. His forte was bringing life to inanimate objects and this put him in good stead as a landscape artist. He was gaining a name for himself painting some of the more wild portions of Central Park and been invited on several trips by one of the more prominent members of the Hudson River School.

No, Charles had neither the finances nor the inclination to paint in either Paris or London. "The world does not need," he pointed out, "another mediocre painting of the Tuileries."

The fourth in their group, Gemma McCain, was from a wealthy family and could afford to go, but she was recently engaged to a fellow artist she met at an exhibition and would not leave him for a day let alone months if she could avoid it.

"It shall be only you and I, Miss Bowman."

At this point, Clara humored him, saying as she lifted her ale, "It shall be only you and I, Mister Evans."

In the following days, what she took at first as a fanciful suggestion grew into an appreciation of the unique opportunity it was. She made the crossing twice before, but then she was running from something. This would be the opposite, and everyone agreed she would be a fool not to take it.

In the end, it was just Clara and Evans, as none of the other students could make it either. The pair enjoyed the crossing in mid-March. Clara's mother would not be denied in acquiring a proper and complete wardrobe for her daughter. She and Clara's father, who gave her the cost of the trip as a present she did not refuse given the opportunities it would provide to her as an artist, saw them off in New York.

By the time they reached Paris ten days later, after disembarking at Le Havre, they were tired and anxious and happy to be on land. They settled into a hotel on the Seine's left bank.

On Clara's earlier trips to Europe, she did not reach Paris. That changed on her third. Her paintings were gaining some notoriety, often exhibited alongside portraits by John Evans. Among the most praised was *A Lady at Home*, the small portrait of Mrs. Peter McNabb.

Clara had finally and forever put Reggie Turner behind her. She sometimes thought that her liaison with Sir John was a permanent mark, a variant of Hawthorne's *Scarlet Letter* that made her forever off-limits for a respectable relationship with a respectable man. At times she was tempted to lie with someone she met but those were only brief longings. She was barely twenty-four and a spinster.

* * * *

THE AMERICAN ARTISTS brought paintings with them to be shown at exhibitions in the two cities. Evans's ten were a range of portraits of both the known, even in Europe, and the unknown, even in New York. Clara brought six: *A Lady in Her House*, *A Lady in Her Garden* (which Charlotte Ogilvy kindly agreed to part with briefly), *A Mother and Her Child* (Róisín and Diarmaid, the latter purposely labeled as "her child"), *A Couple, Emily (Mrs. Porter)*, and a side portrait of one of the bankers who was also included among Evans's work for a contrast of the styles.

The works were well received, and she and Evans spent their evenings being entertained at the more popular Parisian venues. Clara was asked by one of the leading literary lights to paint his wife, and it was the one commission of the many offered that she agreed to do while she was there, using borrowed space in the studio of a Frenchman who was in New

York at the time, a studio reeking of cigar smoke and stale wine with barely a spot on the floor that was free of paint splatter.

While Clara painted the woman, a Mme. Lacourte, her subject's friends insisted on attending and it was only with the greatest difficulty that Clara was able to have her subject sit still.

She used her slight French to chide *les amies* for interfering with the subject, the mispronunciation serving only to increase the hysterics that abounded in the studio. With her time limited, Clara warned that the work might not be as complete as she would like, but Mme. Lacourte insisted, so far as Clara could understand, that it was enough to have something from this impressive *femme americaine* that would make her the envy of her friends (who broke into a new round of hysterics when they heard Mme. Lacourte say this).

But that paled in contrast to what Clara experienced as she explored Paris. She and Evans knew who rebelled against the established order, who were being called "Impressionists" after a painting by Claude Monet. They met several in cafés and bars who were among this group and especially enjoyed the company of Marie Bashkirtseff, a Ukrainian artist about Clara's own age who had an *atelier*. She and Evans were invited to the studios of two or three. They toured the Louvre several times and copied some of the masters.

Some of what she took from those visits found itself in her portrait of Mme. Lacourte. She used the excuse of a lack of time to make rougher strokes and imprecise lines, but Evans was charmed by it and while some of *les amies* thought it undercooked and sloppy, *la femme* herself did not, and her husband paid Clara twice the agreed-upon price.

"If she is happy, *ma cherie*"—in English far better than Clara's French—"I am happy."

With that as a send-off, Evans and Clara left with two other Americans for London, and the group arrived late on a Sunday night. The hotel was not the luxurious Langham, but a somewhat downtrodden-looking place that was a favorite among artistic visitors.

As in Paris, their paintings were exhibited, this time in Piccadilly, and again received positive reviews.

One person who saw them was Mrs. Edward Wilson. She read of the exhibition in one of London's illustrated magazines and wished to attend alone. She did not go for several days after the opening, but on the first Thursday she did. She alternately hoped and feared that she would encounter her precious Clara, but she did not. Other than in the form of her paintings. They were so advanced from the early sketches of Emily, wonderful as those were. She was proud she played some small role in encouraging Clara's evident talent, that Clara's first stroke was an awkward rendering of her forehead. Felicity understood why Clara included *Emily (Mrs. Porter)*, and her recent image of her friend was flush with emotion—both of the artist and of Mrs. Porter—and proved the wonderful evolution that Clara underwent after the dark days they spoke of when she and Grace were in London, the trip that ended so horribly for them both.

She was not to know it, but while Felicity was at the exhibition, Clara sat in Regent's Park. She chose the simplicity of a watercolor. She mainly used oils and was not confident that she could control the colors of water coloring, especially as she had seen Lady F do, but felt to paint the rose bushes *in situ* she had to try.

Several passersby looked over her shoulder as she worked. She gave a quiet "thank you" after the inevitable compliment as the couple—it was usually a couple—strolled away, and after they did, she could not help watching them leaving and hoping to see someone else take their place. She sat until the sun was nearly gone and did three watercolors. She did not know what she would do with them, other than showing them to Evans, who was no expert in the medium. Most likely she would frame the best of them and hang it in her studio.

The overall reception to Clara was not quite as enthusiastic as in Paris. The preference was for the more traditional style of John Evans except among some of the younger artists who, too, had been to Paris and seen its exhibitions. On several nights, instead of attending a formal gathering, Clara sat in one tavern or another much like the ones in Greenwich Village and drank too much. She fought off more than a few male approaches, as she did in Paris, and felt sick at those who introduced themselves as "Sir This" or "Lord That." She feared Sir John Adams would make an appearance at the exhibitions or the taverns but if he did, she did not notice it.

When alone late as she tried to drift off, she wondered whether it was a mistake not to lay with at least one of these fellows, feeling the passion of an artist, the familiar smell of oil paint and the unfamiliar scent of a man everywhere. Savoring his man's body as he would hers. It would be physical, the connection, and no more. But she could not bring herself to do it. She thought of one or the other of them when she satisfied herself, and that was enough to lead her to a deep sleep.

There was one thing that troubled her during the trip. She doubted Felicity would be in Regent's Park and she, too, variously feared and hoped she would be there or would appear where her paintings were exhibited. She asked several of her hosts about Felicity Adams or Mrs. Edward Wilson, thinking she might be known, but she was not.

By the weekend following the opening, the exhibition was reviewed by several London critics, as well as several from Paris and correspondents for New York periodicals. The curator invited the American artists and their guests to a party in the back room of a popular hotel, where he distributed copies of the reviews. They were for the most part glowing, expressing some surprise at the quality of the work coming from Americans, particularly Americans who had not trained on the continent.

Clara's works were well received, although one New York critic wrote that her two *A Lady*s—which he saw in Manhattan—showed great promise but were lacking in certain aspects that were more fully realized in her more recent ones.

The highest praise came from a Parisian critic. Writing in English, he said:

> *Far and away the highlight of the entire exhibition was A Mother and Her Child. It bears an*

unavoidable resemblance to many Madonna and Childs that too often haunt the museums in Paris and Rome and Milan but only a resemblance. It does not suffer in the comparison. The Child is too old to lie helplessly on the lap of the Mother and is seen as a person in his own right, looking at his mother with a glance that is both playful and rebellious. While the mother's adoration is plain, she is seeing in the boy the makings of a man and is proud of it.

This is not some lady whose child is seen but thrice a day—and her dress is that of a working class American—and her relationship with the boy is such that her ravishing beauty is almost overlooked. Miss Bowman surely has a knowledge of her subjects that is deep and long-standing, and now displays the skill with the brush to bring that knowledge and familiarity to the canvas and to the viewer.

Though a painting should be assessed on its own merits, your correspondent learned after seeing the painting that the woman is the boy's aunt and not his mother and that she is the famous woman who obtained custody of the child a year ago when her sister died while birthing him and the aunt arrived from rural Ireland less than ten years ago and serves as a nurse. This knowledge can only deepen one's appreciation for what Miss Bowman has done.

Clara collected several copies of the review, knowing how it would please her New York friends.

After a final banquet in the back room of a club formed by artists—one of the few in London that permitted ladies to join—where promises were made of future visits to America and future visits to England, Evans and Clara were aboard a ship to take them home. Their paintings were safely stored, and Clara even had an illustrated magazine that had an image of her portrait of Mme. Lacourte, which generated some praise among the younger painters in London, notwithstanding its Parisian subject.

* * * *

THE FLUSH OF EUROPE did not last long. Clara had to return to the business of being a painter. She was not among the upper echelon of portraitists like Evans and was relegated to doing paintings of members of lesser families, even after the reviews were circulated in New York.

45.

Clara was accustomed to living alone since Emily's wedding. Not long after her return from Europe, she was awakened when one of her windows facing the street shattered. She heard people screaming from Bleecker Street and the clanging of the bells on a fire department's ladder truck and pumper getting near. She began to cough at the smoke and became oriented enough to flee the bedroom to the studio, where she saw flames begin to engulf her paintings along the wall when someone, she would never learn whom, smashed open her door and grabbed her over his shoulder and carried her the two stories to the street.

She was placed on a stoop several doors to the west. As she coughed desperately, she watched as fire companies struggled to get water on the blaze. Several neighbors from her building and the street came to her and two other people who were pulled out in time.

"Is there anyone still there?" one of the firemen asked, and Toby, who lived on the top floor, looked around the group and said, "This looks to be everyone."

There was another explosion, this time of the windows on the fourth floor, and firemen scattered to avoid the falling shards of glass. A ladder was against the building to the east, and a fireman was on it spraying water into what had been Clara's apartment. With water manually pumped from the street to him and carried up the stairs by others, the flames disappeared from sight and soon someone was at her window, calling down, "We got it. Just sparks now," and a dank smell settled over the street.

Clara was unable to speak. She stood and was restrained from going to her home. "All is lost," she said, again and again, until she felt someone's arms around her.

Another of Evans's former students lived several blocks away. He was awakened by the noise, as was most everyone anywhere nearby. It was early, a little after two. Many of the apartments were studios, and he knew nearly all the artists who lived in them. When he reached the corner of the block where Clara's place was, he was afraid it was hers as he pushed through the growing crowd watching the firemen's work.

A policeman tried to stop him, but he pointed to a now standing Clara and said, "She is my friend," and the officer let him pass. He held her closely, though she did not know it was him until he whispered that things would work out, at which she turned and buried her head in his shoulder and sobbed.

"All is lost," she was finally able to say again.

"You. You are not lost," and he took her home with him and he slept on his sofa while she was in his bed, she reeking of smoke and breaking out in coughs through the night.

Shortly after sunrise, Clara and her friend stood outside her building. It was an empty, darkened shell, with smoldering debris littering the street and sidewalk. Much of it was pushed to one side of the street so carriages, carts, and people could pass, all the latter looking up at the ruined building. The adjoining ones were unscathed except for some burn marks on their upper stories.

"What am I going to do?" she said as the reality was before her. Gone. Her *Elizabeth*s. Her Emily sketches. The others. The sketches. Oils. The watercolors from London. Her most cherished first watercolor from Felicity. It was fortunate that several of her best works were at Evans's, either on his walls or in a storage room, including those they took to Europe, except for *A Lady in Her Garden*, *A Couple*, and *Emily (Mrs. Porter)*, which were safely hanging in the homes of their subjects.

It was not long before Grace and Richard appeared, and by ten Clara sat in their house after taking a bath. With some effort, she scrubbed the soot from her face and neck. Grace was a little bigger than and not as tall as her so the clothes she wore were baggy and short, but they would have to do until she could get her own. By noon, Clara's parents were there too, and Emily arrived shortly after the Bowmans, all thankful that she was not hurt. She still coughed but not nearly so much as she had initially. She agreed to stay at the Bowmans until something else could be arranged.

A steady stream of friends came to visit, all offering encouragement, all offering to sit for her. While there were art supplies at her parents' house, she could not bring herself to do anything. Not for Emily or Elizabeth or Róisín or even little Diarmaid. She claimed that she suffered burns on her hands and could not hold a pencil or a brush as she once could and would display her hands to whoever was in the room.

This went on for three or four weeks, and those in the house were beginning to think, though they would not dare say, that Clara's petulance was becoming too much and she might be sinking back to a very dark place and that it might be best if she could move back into a home of her own. Or at least begin the process of looking for a home of her own.

Clara, though, did not care. She sat in her room or wandered the neighborhood with a head empty of inspiration or happiness. She allowed Emily or Grace to sit or walk with her on occasion but towards the end of whatever they were doing together she began to resent their inspiration and happiness and was often more miserable when they left than she was when they arrived.

46.

Charlotte Ogilvy reacted well to the minor fame that *A Lady in Her Garden* brought her. She was invited to events that would never have considered her while she remained in Mary McNabb's orbit. She broke free when assaulted by Mrs. McNabb's anger for having voluntarily sat for the traitor Clara Bowman.

On a Thursday about four weeks after the fire, Charlotte appeared at the Bowmans' unannounced and insisted she "will see Miss Bowman."

"I shall wait until she is no longer indisposed," she assured Haskins, the Bowman butler, who led her into the sitting room. She wore a simple cream-colored dress that was more utilitarian than fashionable, of the sort far more common on Bleecker Street than Fifth Avenue.

After ten minutes or so, Clara herself appeared. Her caller turned from watching the passing traffic and said, "If I could paint twice so well as you, I could not make you appear half as bad as you look." Charlotte laughed at Clara's glare.

"Get your things. We are going out. Do not bother to change."

Clara wore a light blue house dress that was even simpler than what Charlotte had on and she had put her hair up haphazardly to greet Mrs. Ogilvy.

To Clara's confusion, she said, "Clara. All I hear is poor Miss Bowman this and poor Miss Bowman that. Frankly, I am bored silly by it. I almost—I say 'almost'—would prefer to hear talk of Mary McNabb. So it must be changed and if you will not change it, it falls to me and like it or not we are leaving for the afternoon."

Seeing no alternative, Clara grabbed a shawl and pulled on walking boots and followed her visitor out, telling Haskins she did not know where she was going let alone when she would return. He could not resist a smile as the cheerful Mrs. Ogilvy led the unceasingly-sulking girl away.

Charlotte's carriage brought the pair on an increasingly rough road out of Manhattan, across a bridge to the west Bronx, an area along the Hudson known as Riverdale. They headed to the Hudson River, amid some of the mansions built as country homes by millionaires in town. There was a park at the bottom of a steep switchback hill and above railway tracks that opened to the river and, more particularly, to the palisades on the opposite, New Jersey shore.

The Hudson had a peculiarity. It was not a river, at least this far south. So its waters did not run in one way only. As a tidal estuary, it was an arm of the ocean and the salty water went up and down with the phases of the moon. For an artist, this meant that it was largely still and placid, the water's movement imperceptible.

And its geological history meant that the shore on the opposite side from the city was a craggily cliff face, offering the artist not the rolling hills and dales of the typical Hudson River style—paintings made to the north—but of intense beauty, difficult to control, let alone master.

Charlotte had an assortment of painting supplies secured to the carriage's roof with the other necessities for a civilized picnic, and when they parked and the two women took in the freshness of the air and the smells of the country, she had Austen, a footman, spread it out on the lawn with two folding chairs and a folding table, and a large, folded blanket was placed nearby. He deposited a basket with lunch on the table and prepared two place settings. Clara watched with interest, having long since forgotten the labor required to prepare the simplest thing for someone in society, but when he was done and bowed, he returned to the carriage, and Charlotte told the coachman to return in three hours.

"Three hours?" Clara had no intention of spending three hours sitting on a lawn and pretending not to notice the painting supplies off to the side.

"Go, Austen, go. Be back in three hours," and with that Austen and the coachman and the horse and the carriage and escape disappeared around a turn and the noise of their going faded until it was gone. The two women were alone, staring at the spot where the carriage was last seen before turning to the table and chairs.

"As you may have determined, my dear," said Charlotte when her napkin was across her lap, ignoring more of the glare from the woman sitting across from her, "I am here on a mission. You helped to liberate me, and it is my turn to help liberate you."

"I assure you. I do not need 'liberating.'"

"Don't you? From what I am told, you spend your days…doing nothing. Instead of improving on the wonderful work you have done and on the wonderful gift you have been given, you simply bemoan that what you have done is lost. Do you know I admire your portrait of me every time I pass it? I know I should not say so. I tell everyone I barely notice it lest they think me too vain. But I love what you made of me."

"I did not make anything of you. I just painted you."

"Which is the point. You paint people. Today, you will paint things."

"Mrs. Ogilvy. I appreciate your effort. But I cannot paint anymore. My hands were hurt in the fire."

"Oh, stuff and nonsense. I watched your hands as we came here, having been forewarned—I say not by whom—that you would use it as an excuse. Your hands are perfectly fine. Better than mine, I daresay. So, we can have our lunch and sit and bore each other for the remaining two and three quarters hours until Austen returns or you can do what God made you to do, which is paint the river and the palisades. And I assure you, as you well know, a woman of society has very little worth saying and even less worth hearing and I have become quite adept at becoming a woman of society so, my dear Miss Bowman, you are forewarned."

Charlotte continued her sickening cheerfulness throughout the (quite good) lunch, and when the food was eaten and a fair share of the lemonade was drunk, she simply smiled across the table at Clara.

"So. What shall we talk about?"

She smiled like a cherub, with her hands folded in her lap.

"You are going to make me do this, are you not?"

"Miss Bowman, I make you do nothing. How about the weather? The weather is pleasant, don't you think?"

Clara cared not a whit for the weather. She huffed dramatically—which extracted a smile from her audience—then stood and walked towards and looked across to the sheer vertical cliffs on the opposite side. Trees emerged from the river on a slight slope until they reached about halfway up.

The cliffs themselves were jagged, displaying a broad range of colors, mostly shades of brown and reds, and were capped with their own row of trees. It was fall so the trees were beginning to turn and they, too, were a range of yellows and reds and orange as well as green.

Clara was in no mood to dress properly when Charlotte took her, and it proved a blessing as her simple house dress allowed her to sit on the blanket, which she spread nearer the edge of the lawn, as she looked out. Charlotte dropped herself beside her.

She leaned her head to Clara's shoulder. She was not a good friend of Clara's. She was barely a friend at all, and they had few dealings since Clara finished *A Lady in Her Garden*. They spoke at length while the work was being done and the process led to a peculiar intimacy between the two, but other than at exhibitions where Charlotte appeared, they moved in distinct circles, insofar as Clara could be deemed to move in a circle at all.

"'Tis beautiful, isn't it?" she asked. Things were perhaps at their best, with a solid blue sky and only the occasional small cloud drifting by.

"If it will make you happy," Clara said by way of response, "I shall see what I can make of it," and she rose and walked to the supplies that were strewn about the lawn.

Charlotte spoke to someone knowledgeable about what should be taken on this trip, and it was all of the highest quality. Clara knew she overpaid for some of it, but was glad for the shopkeeper being able to fill his pockets a bit more than was necessary. Charlotte could afford it.

"Are you going to help me?" she called to the other, who remained where she sat but jumped up, and the two cleared the table off and carried it and the chairs close to where they sat.

"This will do," Clara declared.

They then carried an easel, a mid-sized canvas, a small table, a cloth bag containing brushes and oil paints, and a palette. Charlotte helped Clara position everything to her liking.

"May I watch?"

Clara looked over. She smiled against her will. "Yes, you may watch."

In fact, Clara did not have much time, and while she only started with the heart of the painting they heard the wheels of the carriage returning. She looked to Charlotte.

"Surely it is not three hours."

"My coachman is very prompt. He has a watch. It surely is."

Clara looked to the carriage and back to her new friend.

"Might I have two more?"

Charlotte waved to Austen, and the footman ran to her and after a word, he collected their lunch things and put them in the basket and carried it to the carriage, leaving two fresh bottles of ale and then he and the coachman and the carriage and the horse disappeared again around the turn.

"You have two more, but I fear it will be nearly dark by then."

And Clara was incentivized to go more quickly.

It would take time for Clara to be satisfied. Several mornings, she took the Bowmans' carriage to Riverdale and set up where she did that first day with Mrs. Ogilvy. At times someone joined her—Grace, her mother, Emily—but usually she went alone, bringing a sandwich and ale for her lunch and sending the carriage away until mid-afternoon. Once or twice, she did not make a stroke but just sat and at times strolled to savor the view for the duration.

Evans surprised her once. He often stopped by the Bowmans' house and sat with her. It was the usual you-must-resume/I-am-not-yet-ready dance she had with nearly everyone else who ventured to see her. One day he was told she was up in the Bronx so up to the Bronx he went. He left his carriage well before she could hear it and he approached her stealthily such that she was unaware of him until he spoke.

"Remarkable." He waited until her brush was off the canvas before disturbing her, and her head shot around when he said it. Before she could leap up and risk toppling the canvas, he put his arm on her shoulder to steady her. She handed him her brush and he helped her up, and neither cared about the paint stains transferring from her to him when they hugged. She did not know when she last hugged someone, as opposed to the many and well-meaning hugs she received and endured since the fire. How she loved him.

Her teacher, now mentor, pushed her away so he could again look at what she had done.

A STUDIO ON BLEECKER STREET | 241

"I think Mr. Church"—referring to the renowned Frederic Edwin Church—"would be quite jealous."

Clara's *Palisades* was not as precise as what Church and the others were doing. It owed more to the works Clara and Evans saw in Paris. For a Church, one is amazed by the detail. Were he to do a painting like Clara's, one could make out the individual trees that climbed the slight hill from the river to the stone. Perhaps even the knots in the trunks. The shadows in the crags that defined the cliffs. The clouds passing overhead could be touched or blown from the canvas with a single breath.

Clara's gave the impression of a visceral connection with the clouds and the water, trees, and cliffs below them. Evans recognized the imperfections in the work. Clara was out of practice and it showed in some of her strokes. It was perhaps a year behind where she was when her studio was burnt out, but it would not take long for her to be up to her prior standard.

As Evans stood assessing, the brush dangling between his right thumb and two of his fingers, and looking several times from the painting to the subject, she waited.

"Yes, my dear. It is remarkable. It will get better with practice, of course. But this is a first-rate job and if Church had any sense he would be jealous."

He handed the brush back to her and dropped himself to the grass as she retook her seat on her stool. (She had only the one, not expecting a visitor.)

Evans lay back on the grass and looked up as Clara turned back to the painting. Before she could resume her stroking, he said, "I think you should spend time up here before moving back to the Village. I think you should explore yourself with landscapes."

He was silent again as she resumed. It was several minutes, though for him it felt longer, before she spoke. "I have been thinking that since I began to enjoy it here. I have the luxury of my father's money, of course. Will you exhibit some of them?"

"Of course, my dear."

He sat up to watch her briefly before he rose.

"I must bid you *adieu*, as the French say, *ma cherie*." She again started to rise. "Stay where you are. I know the way."

He paused. "It is good. We both know it can be, and will be, better. You must practice."

As he walked up the hill, she called to him.

"Mr. Evans."

He turned. "John, please."

"John. May I see you in your house on Saturday?"

"I look forward to it," he said, and with a wave, he resumed his trek back to his carriage and his return to Washington Square.

And on Saturday in the late morning, Clara found Evans waiting for her. He himself answered the door. He led her through his exhibition space, where several of her pieces were displayed, before they decided to leave and walk into Washington Square itself. Soon she explained the reason for her visit, though he already knew and he assured her that, yes, she was good enough. Indeed, she was far, far better than that.

The pair continued their walk around the Square, seeming to all the world like lovers long comfortable with each other though they were far more than that.

47.

Edward Alan Nathan was one of those bankers who built his mansion in Riverdale. It stood atop a steep hill that led down to the Hudson, readily visible to anyone on the New Jersey side. It was a large, rectangular brick house with two octagonal wings and a widow's walk on the roof between two large chimneys. The northern wing was where dances were held during the season, and the southern one was a haven to the family.

By the time of year when Clara Bowman discovered Riverdale, the Nathans only came up occasionally, but on a morning during one of those visits, Agnes Nathan saw the Bowman's empty carriage—though she did not know whose carriage it was—heading away from the water. She rang her little bell, and the carriage stopped and she instructed her coachman to go where the carriage had been to investigate the unusual sighting.

When they got to the end of the path, Mrs. Nathan saw a young woman—Clara it was—sitting in front of her easel and went to investigate. Clara heard the carriage and looked to see the approaching visitor, plainly wealthy and likely from one of the nearby houses. Perhaps Clara was on her property and she would be shooed off. But then the coachman would be walking to her.

When Mrs. Nathan neared, Clara got up and stepped towards her. The older woman wore a light brown variant of a day dress that she found comfortable, and it hung loosely from her shoulders. Clara guessed she was about her mother's age and thought she was pleasant looking for a woman of her vintage. She put her hand up, palm forward, and Clara stayed where she was. Mrs. Nathan went to the painting. Although Clara was near where she was for the first of her paintings, this was a bit to the north and gave a subtle change in the angle and the way the shadows played on the stone of the Palisades.

"This is quite good, my dear. Quite good." She looked at the artist. "Do I know you?"

"I am Clara Bowman, ma'am."

"Bowman? I know the name. I am sure I must have come across your parents."

"They are George and Muriel and live on Thirty-Second Street."

"Of course. I think I must have been there. I am Agnes Nathan, and I live in a house a little bit to the north. Are you the one whose studio was destroyed in that fire?"

Clara nodded. She said much of her life was destroyed with it and that she was trying to revive herself by "painting some awful landscapes."

Mrs. Nathan shook her head. "I assure you, my dear, this is pretty and not awful. You should see some of the things that I have seen exhibited of the Palisades. Simply dreadful. This, though, when it is done, will I think be quite lovely. Perhaps you will sell it to me?"

She smiled but Clara suspected it was not entirely in jest.

While Mrs. Nathan eventually let Clara continue her work, it was not before she extracted a fair amount of information about the girl. Most important, it resulted in Clara agreeing to Mrs. Nathan's offer to have her visit for lunch at the Nathans' house in two days.

On that day, since Clara sent her parents' carriage back after she was left in Riverdale, with orders to return in mid-afternoon, Mrs. Nathan sent her own to bring Clara to lunch. As she was driven up the path to the house, she was impressed. In size, it was like many of the houses she saw in Lenox and found it similarly intimidating. A footman opened the front door, and Mrs. Nathan was on the driveway before the carriage stopped and rushed to open the door for her guest.

It was warm but not hot, so lunch was prepared on the terrace to the south, offering a wonderful view across the river of the Palisades. It benefited from being higher up than the spot where she and Mrs. Ogilvy went. A slight but not distracting wind floated across from the river. When Clara mentioned how clean and refreshing it was to be in Riverdale but felt guilty about being taken there several times a week, Mrs. Nathan spontaneously offered to allow her to stay.

"It makes no sense for you to be hauling your things up every morning and hauling them back every afternoon. So much time wasted. You must stay here. No one else is using it, and it is a shame to leave it vacant. And it would be less of a strain on your family's carriages and horses."

When Clara said she did not wish to burden the Nathans' staff, Mrs. Nathans asked if Clara could manage largely on her own. Clara, having lived alone for some time said that would not be difficult provided she could get supplies, and Mrs. Nathan said, "It is settled then. I will make sure you have enough so you will neither starve nor freeze. Someone will come up regularly as they normally do anyway to ensure that you are well. I will come up regularly to see you. It will give me an excuse to get away from the city. So, it is settled."

Unable to disagree, Clara thanked Mrs. Nathan for the offer and said she hoped neither would regret it. She was often on her own already and could arrange for the carriage to return her to town during the week and for Sundays. When lunch was over, they went back into the house and up the large staircase in the front room to the second floor. To the right was what would be Clara's room. It was little used except over the summer when a guest was at the house. Though it faced north, it had a cream-colored wallpaper with a floral pattern dancing around as well as a large bed and so was bright during the day.

Although the house was north of the spot Charlotte Ogilvy brought her, it offered a similar panoramic view of the river and the Palisades but was higher up the steep hill, with a lawn that sloped down, but not too dramatically, to a stone wall beyond which the property dropped precipitously towards the train tracks that ran along the river. It was a marvelous location.

The house also had a large terrace to the south that traced the southern and western aspects of the wing, and after lunch Clara found a chair to sit in while she lazily sketched what she saw. While her family and Emily were concerned about her being alone so far away, Clara convinced them that it gave her the chance to focus on her work without the distractions of the Bowman house or the comings-and-goings in the Village. She said they were free to visit whenever

A STUDIO ON BLEECKER STREET | 247

they wished to see her work and monitor her progress.

Within a week of having met Agnes Nathan, Grace and Mrs. Bowman accompanied Clara to Riverdale with trunks of clothing and a batch of painting supplies and when the others left, Clara spent the afternoon exploring her new home.

It was not long after Clara moved in that word of the artist-in-residence spread to other houses in the neighborhood, and ladies occasionally stopped by to see what Clara was up to. It got to the point where Clara tired of interrupting her work to answer the door—there being no staff—and simply put a note asking people to walk around to the terrace, and those who did learned to refrain from interrupting the artist as she worked.

It was not long after that that word got around that the artist-in-residence painted *A Woman in Her Garden*, and Clara was inundated with polite requests for portraits.

Fortunately, those who visited understood they were interrupting, and the visits became a trickle. She accepted two or three invitations for lunches or dinners among the otherwise sparse doings at the time of year in Riverdale. She learned that each mile from the center of town seemed to lessen the pretentiousness she grew to find so distasteful. She enjoyed herself at these meals far more than she expected.

Clara told Mrs. Nathan when she next visited that she would be happy to set aside time to meet with interested neighbors. It was a way to repay some of the kindness Mrs. Nathan extended to her.

Of course, the women in Riverdale were not the sole visitors. Mrs. Bowman and Grace made regular trips as did Emily. Charlotte did as well, once or twice with Mrs. Nathan herself. One Sunday, Elizabeth, Róisín, and Diarmaid piled out of the Lawfords' carriage with Grace, and it was the youngster's first visit to the country, enjoying the sudden freedom to ramble about the lawn under the watchful eyes of each woman there.

For her part, Clara was content to stay in the Nathans' house. She had no easy means of getting to Manhattan and was glad for it. She was charting the changing scenery from the terrace as the trees became bare and the starkness of the rocks exaggerated.

After Clara settled in, Mrs. Nathan brought her husband to visit. Edward Nathan was a short man, about his wife's height, and his roundness suggested he enjoyed more whiskies at his daily lunches at his club off Wall Street than he perhaps should. He was cheery and easy going. He gave Clara books on the geology of the Hudson, and she used the information to better understand what she painted.

When their son Joseph ventured to the Riverdale house over Christmas—she spent the holiday itself at her parents' house and desperately missed being with Emily, who was again up in Stockbridge—on a break from Yale, he began to smother her with details on the topic, but he was quickly bored and headed back into town until he could return to New Haven.

Shortly after the new year, a blizzard hit. Clara was fortunate that the Nathans kept their pantry stocked and their cords of wood stacked high. As the snow fell and mounted in the yard, she was utterly alone in some fairy-tale castle. In the fading light of the afternoon, the Palisades became invisible and the only sounds were muffled from the bracing wind and sleet crashing into the windows.

In the morning, the sky was crystal clear and the sun's reflection from the snow almost blinding. The wall at the end of the lawn was covered in white but the Palisades were back, capped in white with their colors enhanced by the sun burning into them, at times finding a reflective surface that shot bolts across the river.

Below them she could see small ice floes passing. She opened a door to the rear of the house slightly, guessing there was perhaps two feet of snow with mountainous drifts here and about, but she closed it quickly when she felt the onrush of the wind.

The southern wing had a series of French doors that looked to the west, and it was enough to give Clara a vista over her Palisades, as she began to think of them. Clara wondered how long it would be before she saw another human being. She set fires in the room by the south wing, glad of the lessons she had in Stockbridge, and these were enough to keep the wing itself tolerably warm.

And she painted. Other than eating and sleeping and tending to other necessities, it was all she did and after a week, when several warm days melted off the worst of the snow and passage to the house was again possible, she had four canvases completed in the wing overlooking the terrace, now dank from the accumulated smell of her oils. Each was different, but when placed end-to-end they created a panorama of the Palisades, the River, and the white-covered lawn of the Nathans. A bit of the terrace peeked onto the right-most work.

The canvases were not large. Clara did not anticipate doing a set. She started in the middle and then took advantage of the quiet to go to the right and to the left. The works were not precise, but they flowed from her right arm and through her right hand as nothing had before, as John Evans suggested they would. All but the one on which she worked were lined up on the floor against a wall next to one another. When the fourth and final one was finished, she arranged them carefully for the first time.

She realized that she had done something significant. It was not nearly Paris-quality, and many in Greenwich Village had done better landscapes. But as she began to feel with her portraits when she stepped back and the first time to fully take in *A Woman in Her Garden*, she felt similarly as to these landscapes.

She did not paint for several days after that beyond touching up those four and other landscapes that traced the seasons. She instead sat in the living room where it was bright, on a couch, often under a throw and with tea she brewed. She leaned one then another of the large books Mr. Nathan and Joseph showed her against her thighs and turned their pages and studied their intricately-drawn illustrations. She was not a particularly gifted student, though she enjoyed discussions about English novels in school. But she was not exposed to anything as rigorous as science and no mathematics beyond the most fundamental (since she would likely be called upon to tend to the family's books when she had a family and her family had books).

She fell into the illustrations. Meticulously drawn images of the Hudson thousands of years ago. The Rocky Mountains out west. The Great Lakes. She had often seen illustrations of Chicago and San Francisco and, of course, London and Paris where she had been, but this was all new to her. *Can I do something like this?*

The notion was folly. She had too long depended on her parents to finance her adventure. She was past the point of settling down with one of her set. Far too old and (as anyone interested would discover) too damaged. But traveling to paint landscapes would cost money and not earn any. With portraits, the expense was far less and the commissions would bring her money far more certainly than someone would like an oil of an Adirondack lake to hang above their mantel. Such commissions were reserved for the most known members of the Hudson River School, and Clara was not of that group and was unlikely to ever become one.

She knew she took advantage of the Nathans' generosity (as she had her parents') and that she would repay them with a portrait of the formidable Mrs. Nathan. It was time, though, to return to her old place and her old world. She would find a new studio, with John Evans's help, that she could afford and would resume painting portraits. Strangely, that she lost so many in the fire was an incentive to re-visit several of her subjects, to show how well or poorly they aged, and this ambition softened her loss.

When Mr. and Mrs. Nathan arrived in mid-February once the blizzard and its remnants were gone, she spoke to them about it.

"I have not done a portrait for many months," she told them, "But I would be pleased to do Mrs. Nathan's." By then, the Nathans were fully aware of Clara's reputation and struggles and insisted on paying a very handsome sum for the work, but Clara would not have it. There were those from whom she would never accept payment for a portrait, and the Nathans were now among them.

While it was still winter with only slight budding on the trees, Clara decided to begin the portrait. Agnes Nathan took Clara's suggestion that she wear only a day dress and sit in a simple chair.

Before that, though, she searched the property for where she could do justice to Mrs. Nathan. She found a stretch of lawn near an oak tree. The tree stood apart from the others, at the crest of the lawn. Thus, even with it in the background, the imposing if out-of-focus Palisades gave depth to the site.

Charlotte Ogilvy invited herself to be Clara's assistant, even if she spent more time chatting with Mrs. Nathan than she did assisting Clara. But the days were beautiful and not cold or windy and the paint flowed easily from Clara's brush, paying her guest no mind as she alternately stood and sat while she worked.

Clara did not know whether her facility with portraiture would return after her landscape sabbatical, but with some tentative drawing to outline Mrs. Nathan on the canvas, the hesitancy was gone

A STUDIO ON BLEECKER STREET | 253

and she was more pleased with it with each passing day.

The south wing of the house had long since been given over to Clara, and with the help of Charlotte, each afternoon she toted the canvas and supplies into the house. Though Charlotte stayed for dinner sometimes, usually it was only Clara and Mrs. Nathan. They would never be friends. Their worlds, and ages, were too different. Clara was Joseph's age. Joseph was their only child. But the two women enjoyed being together.

The Nathan dining room itself was an imposing place, lined in wood with a large mahogany table over which three crystal chandeliers hung. Mrs. Nathan sat in her spot, and Clara around the corner and to her left, and in this way, they learned about each other. Clara would be happy to serve herself, but Mrs. Nathan had her limits and that would have crossed them. A footman remained.

Finally, with the trees budding, Clara alternated between her portrait of a lady in her yard and her seasonal review of the Palisades themselves. The former was completed first, and there was a formal unveiling.

Mr. Nathan made something of a pest of himself before his wife's portrait was revealed, trying to steal a glance, but while in the past Clara sometimes allowed non-subjects to observe, now it felt uncomfortable, and she banned him, which he took in good grace, telling his wife that he too "must suffer in the anticipation of the final product." And so, no one else could hear, "Not unlike our wedding night," and the couple laughed at something Clara could only guess at.

It was a simple unveiling in early March. Joseph came down from Yale for the weekend and the Bowmans, the Lawfords, the Porters, and John Evans came up. Several neighbors attended and, of course, Mr. and Mrs. Nathan. A small dinner would be held afterwards, and the mood was light. Clara's stomach did its typical pre-unveiling churning, and she again wondered whether she should stop painting portraits simply to avoid the inevitable nausea.

She persevered, though, and the group assembled in the south wing. The painting, covered, was on an easel on the opposite side of the room from the door, with French doors to the (dark) terrace several feet behind it. Clara stood a bit to the side opposite Mrs. Nathan while her husband gave a little speech and then, after getting a nod from Clara, he pulled the cover over and off the painting.

Clara was best known for what she did to Charlotte Ogilvy, bringing out her inherent beauty. Now, on a far older subject, she had done the same to Agnes Nathan. The lines were blurrier and the background a swirl of the Palisades and the sky, but there was no doubt that it was a portrait of Agnes Nathan and that it was not a staid portrait of a bored society woman. She was kind, and she was sensual. Her eyes seemed somewhat closed, but not from being tired but from her being insular. Not scheming. Pensive.

Her simple dress was ill-defined, even its color uncertain, and it merged with her shoulders and her bosom as she looked slightly to her left, the artist's right. Her lips were artificially bright against her pale face but not jarringly so, and her hair was allowed to flow almost randomly down as few saw it, her widow's peak evident. Instead of Mrs. Nathan's hands being folded, her left one, with one subtle but dazzling diamond caressing her right wrist, dangled to her lap.

At evening's end, Evans convinced the Nathans to delay hanging the portrait in one of their houses. "May I exhibit it on Washington Square?" he asked. "Thirty days. Sixty at the most." And the Nathans graciously watched *A Lady in Her Yard* being carefully loaded onto a carriage and disappear to Manhattan.

48.

As spring bloomed in Riverdale, Clara was excited about her return to the Village. She first moved there to be an artist, and it was where she had to return.

John Evans found a delightful, sunny apartment for her about a block away from her burnt-out (but since repaired) place. It was superior in many details. The light was better and its separate bedroom had a window to the back.

She moved on May 1.

By mid-morning the next day, there was some order to Clara's new studio. The building was on the south side of Bleecker, and the flat was on the fourth floor to its back. The studio portion was to the left, and its windows faced south and across the yards of the brownstones along Mott and Mulberry. To the right was the kitchen with a small closet to one side, and a bedroom reached to the rear, its windows, too, looking south.

As a homecoming gift, her parents paid to furnish it, and her sense again overcame her pride in accepting the tables and chairs and bed and the other pieces throughout. Except for the studio itself. For that a group of former students joined with John Evans to buy her what she needed. Selfishly, she left a full set of easels and such at the Nathans' house in Riverdale, where she hoped to paint occasionally.

With Ted at work and herself six months pregnant, Emily sat with her friend on the floor of the studio that first morning. She offered to spend the prior night with Clara, her first back on Bleecker Street, bur Clara declined and found she had no trouble sleeping after the work of making the place habitable, and no ghosts invaded her slumber.

"Are you upset that so many of your works are gone?" Clara asked her frequent model.

"As long as you are here, you can do them again. You salvaged more than enough. I hope that I have not changed materially."

"Well, you have gotten fatter."

Emily looked over. "Paint me now."

Which is how *The Expectant* came about. Emily lying on the small sofa that Clara planned to use for posing ladies with Emily's condition free for all to see as she draped herself awkwardly and—so Clara showed—uncomfortably across it.

It was done quickly, in the ardor of the moment, and both women were pleased with it. Clara considered keeping it for her studio, but Emily convinced her that it would be far better as a part of Emily's growing house and there it hung without ceremony beginning with the summer of 1877.

In lieu of *The Expectant* being on her wall, Clara arranged for several of her landscapes to be moved from Riverdale, and they were hung so that a poser would see them and perhaps be relaxed by them. Among these was *The Blizzard*, which stood out for its brightness and how the snowbanks were given texture by Clara's hand.

John Evans often visited and even brought his newest batch of protégés to see the landscapes. Though Clara "graduated," he made a point of giving his opinion of her work but only when she asked, as she nearly always did, and this meant worlds to her.

He thought *Blizzard* in particular was worth exhibiting at a forthcoming show nearby. It was too soon for Clara to think of putting on her own exhibition where she could sell some of her non-commissioned works, but Evans said it would not be long before she could.

Blizzard was very white, and given the press of other paintings, the best Evans could do was place it partway down a hallway from the main works on display. Clara was not happy about this, and she nearly took it home where she saw where it was to be hung.

But Evans prevailed on her. It was important, he said, and it would be seen by the people who she wanted to see it.

In the end, Clara did not think it mattered. The exhibition ended after three weeks, and Evans took it to his house for safe keeping. Clara did not object and turned to making up for some of the lost works and the lost time in Riverdale and before being dragged there by Charlotte Ogilvy.

49.

Done with Yale, Joseph Nathan had to decide whether to journey off for the Grand Tour he would share with several classmates or to begin the humdrum existence he would toil at for the next forty years. It was not much of a decision, and he was set to leave town with a group of fellow graduates for Europe. Paris. Rome. Venice. Berlin. Ending it all with two weeks in London.

With time on his hands, he stopped in at the office of *Art Illustrated* where his ambitious friend Buddy Castle worked. Buddy was a year older and had done his own tour in 1876. They were to go to Buddy's club together, and Joe was anxious, pacing around the large space.

"Do you know a Clara Bowman?" Buddy asked.

Joe stopped. "Vaguely. She stayed at our house in Riverdale. Did some painting there. Why do you ask?"

Buddy handed him an advance copy of the next issue.

"Page 12."

He saw a review of the exhibition where *Blizzard* was hung in a hallway. He knew little of art and had not gone to the exhibit.

"Almost at the end."

The critic, a Mr. Thornton Isaacs, described the event in general terms and highlighted in glowing terms the specifics of several of the younger artists' works. Then:

> *Mr. Evans has been coy, though. He slipped in (almost literally as it was halfway down a hallway that one expected would lead to a kitchen) a*

landscape. Since the balance of the exhibition was of portraits, the scene of winter in Riverdale, unmistakably the place given the desolate Palisades that haunted its background, was bound to attract attention and it surely did that for this correspondent.

Inquiries of Mr. Evans established that it was, in fact, by one of his recent protégés. Clara Bowman is her name, and she displayed great promise in a series of portraits that were shown in Paris and London last year. But it is well known that she suffered horribly in the still-unsolved fire on Bleecker Street of last year. Word was that Miss Bowman had lost her ability to paint, but I am happy to report that this is far from true. Indeed, if this simple yet overwhelming landscape is any indication, her ability has been enhanced by her "brush" with death.

The painting—its official name is the turgid Winter on the Hudson, although that may be an intentional slight at the famous school—combines a perspective of, say, Mr. Church with the excitement of the denizens of Paris. It is understood that Miss Bowman, with Mr. Evans, enjoyed the hospitality of many of those Frenchmen, and their influence on her at least is palpable. While Mr. Evans has remained a staunch defender of the more realistic work that has stood him and so many others in good stead, Miss Bowman's landscape, and some of her earlier portraits, most notably A Lady in Her Garden, suggests that she is among the American artists who will prove the equal and perhaps the superior

A STUDIO ON BLEECKER STREET | 261

to those no longer granted admission to the old salons of Paris, man or woman.

"I cannot say I know anything about painting, but this chap seems to think she is talented," Joe Nathan said when he finished.

"If he likes something, it is worth liking. She is well on her way, my friend. Well on her way."

With that, Buddy grabbed his hat and led his friend to his club only a few blocks to the north but not before Joe got a copy of the new issue from him.

After their lunch, Buddy returned to work. Joe was bored. He decided to see if he could find Clara. Show her the review. She was nice and attractive enough. She came from money, though Joe did not care about that since so did he. She seemed interested in the geology books he and his father showed her. She became a great friend of his mother and did a first-rate painting of her. Maybe she would help him pass the time until he left for Paris, maybe suggest things he might do there. She was surely worth a bit of wooing.

Greenwich Village was the hub of the artists' community and that is where he went. Clara was well known given the drama surrounding her but also because she was considered one of the better of the artists flooding into the neighborhood. Joe soon had her address and climbed to the fourth floor of a large building with a mix of studios and apartments and some, as with Clara's, both.

"405." It was to the back, and Joe knocked at its black door. She recognized her benefactress's son when she opened it.

"I wanted you to see something," he said and held out the *Art Illustrated*, open to page 12, the paint fumes recalling his brief visits to the house in Riverdale while Clara worked there. She invited him in, brush in hand, and he stepped beside her at the painting.

"I just need a moment," she said.

On the easel was the most recent landscape he recognized from his house. The trees were full of green leaves, on both sides of the Hudson. The tide was running south and there was a bit of a wind, so the tiny waves had white caps, painted dots really, on the greenish blue of the Hudson. There was a small boat mid-river, heading north with its sails full and tacking into that wind with perhaps one or two yachtsmen aboard. Near the Jersey side, a far larger steamer headed south, and its wake was perilously close to the sailors and one wondered whether they were alert enough to anticipate when the wave hit and avoid catastrophe.

This time, Clara had provided more detail of the oak tree in the Nathan's yard.

She pointed her brush to it. "I did not give your oak enough attention, but I realized how wonderful it was when I painted your mother, so I hope it will forgive me for my earlier lapse."

She made several more strokes before putting her brush down and wiping her hands on a rag that was draped across the top of the painting. She took the paper out and began to read as he looked around. There was the disorderly way in which works were leaning against walls and against each other, but his glance ended up on Clara. She was in profile to him, and fingers on her left hand tapped against her lower lip while she read. Her concentration on the story allowed him to study that profile. Before his thoughts on that front advanced too inappropriately, he looked away when she said, still eying the page, "This is extraordinary."

"It is, isn't it?"

She looked at him.

"My manners. May I get you something?"

"You can say you will accompany me to dinner this evening."

It was a spontaneous utterance. Joe had arrived with no idea of what he would do or what he was doing. Now he was asking her to join him for dinner?

It turned into enjoyable evening for them both.

50.

For reasons he could not explain (perhaps chose not to explain) to his classmates, Joseph announced at their club that circumstances were such that he could no longer make the journey with them. He assured them that it had nothing whatsoever to do with his family's finances. He admitted that it was not a burning desire to begin work at his father's financial firm.

"It is a woman," was suggested by one but thought by all. "Confess it, you dog."

Joe's resistance was low. He meant nothing to her, he knew, but the thought that she meant something to him was enough to forgo being absent for an extended period.

"All I will say is that while my prospects are slight my hopes are large and should I fail, as I almost surely will, I would like you to know that I fought the battle well and warrant being taken from the field on my shield and buried in a place of honor and not pitied but celebrated by you, my band of brothers, though I dream that when you return I shall still be in her bed!"

And with that Shakespearean invocation, his mates were satisfied, and Joseph Nathan was able to watch them sail into New York Harbor two days later with his head held high.

He was a fool in what he said, but he was carried away with the thought of Miss Clara Bowman. Though it was true that it was far more likely that he would be carried off on his shield than ever lie in her bed. But he was a happy fool, and he might have detected the slightest hint of a smile when he told her during the second or third time he visited her studio after he showed her that article on page 12 that his plans were changed and he was compelled—he did not say it was because of his heart—to remain in New York while his friends sailed to Europe.

It happened that while Emily was a frequent visitor to Clara, it was not as often as it once was and with a baby ready to pop out—Emily had no difficulties but all around her remained nervous about the birth—Clara more often visited Mrs. Porter than the other way round. And on none of the visits to Bleecker Street did Emily cross paths with Joseph Nathan. It was a passing comment from Clara, that she enjoyed Joe's company, that triggered Emily's reaction. Once "Joseph Nathan" passed the artist's lips, Emily was indefatigable. They were both at the unveiling of Agnes Nathan's portrait, but Emily had only the vaguest recollection of him.

She had never seen Clara like this. With Reggie Turner, there was some deep-seated passion in her friend. Perhaps some need to prove herself a woman after what happened with Sir John. Perhaps to know what it meant to have a man make love to her, and she thought Reginald Turner was that man.

This Joseph Nathan was different. Clara liked him. It was no more and no less. It simply was. Clara was not trying to prove anything to herself or to him.

"Of course you must do it if he asks," she said. Clara was speculating that Mr. Nathan might have an interest in pursuing something with her. Emily knew how shy Clara was with men who might have a romantic interest in her, shyness manifested in a haughtiness that was not Clara. Emily considered it her duty to encourage Clara in the slightest encounter. And Mr. Joseph Nathan was far more than a slight encounter, considering the way Clara mentioned him.

"You have a sketch of him, of course."

Clara blanched a bit because she did. He had not sat for it. It was done quickly on a rainy afternoon when Clara sat alone on her sofa, glancing at some of the paintings she did at the Nathans' house in Riverdale.

Now to Emily's observation—Emily knowing her too well—she placed her brush down as she ended a stroke and walked into her bedroom and emerged with a pad, which she opened to a page that she showed to Emily.

"You have done well, my dear. And I do not mean in the drawing. He is scrumptious."

Clara hated being teased and Emily knew Clara hated being teased which was why she did it, but only rarely. For once, Clara was at a loss for a response other than the reddening of her face that Emily observed. Instead, she made her own inquiry.

"What was it like with Ted? Meeting him? Knowing…?"

"You are truly smitten, my dear," Emily said as she handed to pad back to the artist. "Good and smitten."

Her tone changed.

"Clara Bowman. Just let your heart lead you. Will he let you paint?"

Clara Bowman thought.

"If he is the type of man who deserves your love, he will let you paint."

At that moment, Clara realized she loved him.

"Yes. I do believe he will. I do believe he will."

Emily looked at her friend.

"I am increasingly uncomfortable with this one," and she patted her tummy, "and we must end the session. Walk me to the street."

After they were on Bleecker, they walked, slowly, to Broadway, where Emily hailed a cab to take her to her home, and the friends said goodbye. On the walk back, Clara was happier than she had been since...she did not recall.

He was careful when he visited. He brought *The Sun* and sat quietly while she worked. She did not understand why but she liked it and fell into the habit of asking him questions while she drew or painted and often solicited his view on what she was doing. She thought his interest was genuine, and she interspersed professional observations about how she painted in their exchanges and he seemed to be interested and he enjoyed her humming when she was concentrating particularly hard.

When she finished on mornings when he was there, they went to the Moving Hand for lunch, and soon he was greeted by name as she had long been. He would leave her when lunch was done, but she found the studio empty without him. The routine, though, was pleasant and several weeks after his friends abandoned him, she asked him to return to her studio after lunch.

She sat him down and pulled out her working stool and her ubiquitous sketchbook and asked him to be still and look to his left, her right. He deserved more than the sketch she did from memory that she showed to Emily. She only used a few strokes to shape his head and neck and to block his features. His hair was shorter than she would have liked, and she thought of how it would feel to run her fingers through it if it were longer.

"Your hair has a beautiful sheen, but I think it might be more interesting were you to let it grow somewhat."

With that, she moved on. He had a nice, long nose, well-balanced between his eyes, and his cheeks were just the right distance from his lips, with a slight mustache between them. She was not sure about the mustache. He had a nice face, and it hid it, but here she did not dare suggest an alteration, or particularly an obliteration, of something he was so proud of given how frequently he rubbed his fingers down it. It was well enough that he had no beard to obscure his solid jaw. His skin was darker than his mother's, likely from hours spent outdoors.

She turned to his eyes, sitting with her pencil in hand and the sketchbook in her lap studying him much as he studied her while she read the review he brought her. He was aware of the gaze, and it made him uncomfortable. Self-conscious. She did not care. It would take time to get the full measure of those eyes, but for now, she saw enough to quickly draw them. She took a final look at him and then at what she had put on the paper and was satisfied enough to show him, turning the pad so he could see.

He admitted some time before that he knew nothing of art but had picked up a good amount from Clara about structure and balance and perspective. But an ignorant knave would know how fine this quick sketch was, and she handed it to him. Now he was self-conscious about admiring an image of himself.

"You may have it. I would like to do a full oil of you. Might you think of that?"

He knew what she did with his mother and was flattered.

"I shall pay for it with my own funds."

"Oh, silly. It will be a gift."

"No," he said. "Don't be a fool. This is your job. This," and he lifted the sketch, "is more of a gift than I could ever deserve from you. No. I will pay you although I fear I could never pay you what it will be worth."

With that bit of bravado, it was agreed. They both stood.

"Joseph, you are the fool. But I like that."

Without thinking, she moved her body across the few feet that separated them, and her lips were on his until she pulled back, realizing the inappropriateness of the act, and turned away from him to the window.

"So, we will talk about when and where to do it...The painting I mean." She said this without looking at him, and he looked down and then at her.

"Yes, we'll talk. May I return tomorrow?"

She turned and had the slightest of smiles although whether he, a non-artist, noticed was not clear. "Yes. Of course you may come." He bowed and turned to leave.

"Joseph." This stopped him at the door. "I very much like you coming. You know that don't you?"

Now he turned. "I do now," and he was gone and Clara smiled even more as she heard him bound lightly down and down and down to Bleecker Street.

They decided that Joseph's portrait would use the river as its background. The Brooklyn Bridge was nearing completion so while it was quickly becoming common, Joseph wanted a hint of the structure behind him. The readily identifiable tower would give an identity to the work so on three mornings he walked with Clara to the promenade along the East River, with him pulling a cart on which her supplies were clustered. They found a spot and it was clear each time they arrived. The sun was behind Joseph in the morning. This allowed him to look at her without squinting.

When the work was completed *in situ*, still to be perfected by Clara (and still unseen by her subject), they returned to her studio to store her things and headed to the Moving Hand for an early dinner.

While in part it might have been the extra ales they each had, it was mostly their mutual desire and, truthfully, lust. There was an unusual but not unpleasant tension between the two. When they returned to the front of her building, Clara took Joseph's hand and led him up the three flights. Neither spoke. When they were in the studio, she turned to him and for the first time they kissed properly, and their initially hesitant arms and hands grew in confidence and each was pulling the other closer.

When they broke for breath, with his arms loosely around her waist and her hands holding his upper arms, she whispered.

"There is something you must know." She tried to push away, to tell her secret properly, but he would not release her, instead kissing her forehead.

Resigned to being forced to remain where she was, his arms holding her waist, his excitement evident against her, she said, "I have been with another man" and braced herself. It was a whisper, but each word was clear. She waited, as he was slow to speak.

"Is there another man here now?"

His confidence had soared since the moment she took his hand on the sidewalk not five minutes earlier. When she did not push him away when she surely felt him but instead pulled him, all of him, even closer. Now he did not care about "another man." Other men. *Why did they matter?* He cared nothing about her past other than the time they were together, which supplanted whatever was in his past, though there was little there, truth be told.

Clara did not know how to answer his rhetorical question. Instead, she felt his hands caress her as no hands caressed her before. Her erotic stories in the now-banned books suddenly were cruel substitutes for what was being done to her. But she wanted—likely needed—him to caress her, to again pull her even closer and she felt him and she felt unsteady on her feet.

He brought her to her small sofa. It was where he sometimes fell asleep in the afternoon on his visits. She would smile at him when she shook him awake and told him he had to get home.

Now she was only partially on the sofa as she lay awkwardly across it, her head to its right side. Joseph was on his knees and lowered his mouth to hers and she drowned into his kiss and her hands were now pulling his head to her. From that point, neither of them was in control of their senses but it was not long before they made love, a first for each of them. So different from what either had done before.

Unlike the horror of Sir John Adams, Joseph was patient and, excited as he was, he held himself in check until she felt herself shudder in ecstasy, something unknown without Joseph's presence and only then did she feel his explosion inside her. They lay there until they each could properly prepare for bed, perchance to dream.

For Joseph, this was not the first time he entered a woman. But the excitement and visceral pleasure in the release and in the too few moments of pure intimacy he shared with Clara were moments when he felt fulfilled as a man in a way he neither imagined nor understood before they lay together.

She asked him to remain with her. He was confident that if his parents noted his absence they would suspect why—they knew of his growing fondness for Clara—and would not send out a party searching for his dismembered body, at least until morning. He had nothing to wear to bed and offered to sleep in his trousers, but she said that would be nonsense, and at some point in the night he held her close to him, but in the morning, they lay quietly snoring and blissful in bed together.

Clara awoke first and was quite undone by Joseph's naked body lying beside her but not so undone to resist studying it, and she slowly got up to do so. She well knew the male form, and with John Evans she painted numerous male, and female, nudes. Yet they were always at a distance, done of clinical subjects. A sheet covered Joseph's lower half, but the rhythmic movement of his stomach and chest in his sleep struck her as the essence of a man. One arm, his right, dangled across while the other was beneath his head.

His lips, dark with a hint of maroon, were parted slightly and there was a glimmer of spittle on them. The lips themselves were surrounded by the trace of a beard. She fought the temptation to reach for his chin, to savor the stubble that crossed it like a regiment of Grant's army. He had taken her suggestion, and his hair was long enough for a woman to run her fingers through, and she took advantage of the fact in the darkness in the night and was tempted to do it again in the morning light.

Instead, she lowered herself so that her eyes were at his level, and her study of him in this place, vulnerable yet strong, made her realize how she had failed in capturing the true beauty of the man, this man, in that portrait near the bridge. She would, she hoped, do better a second time. Just as that thought hit her, she panicked. There would be no second time. He would awaken and, angry and embarrassed, he would flee from her. From his whore. Father, forgive me, for I have sinned.

The pit in her stomach stabbed her. He was so beautiful and had been so beautiful and fulfilling to her and in her and now he would leave her. She felt as though she was suddenly thrown into the abyss, the happy light receding rapidly as she fell.

She sat back on her haunches to await the inevitable.

It was not long before he roused himself, taking a moment to recognize the unfamiliar bed on which he lay. He was startled by her stare, but he melted it with a smile as he recognized his dearest Clara and held his arms out for her to rejoin him and she breathed again when they enveloped her once more.

After again making love, they dressed and walked to a café some blocks from the studio. They were less likely to be recognized and thus would be left alone. Their walk there was proper. She had her arm through his and he stood on the street-side of the sidewalk. It was still early though a steady stream of people going to their jobs passed them by and the smells and somber quiet of early morning New York hit them. There were a few empty tables. They sat, and a waiter took their breakfast orders and disappeared.

Awaiting his return, their hands clasped beneath the table, saying little and saying less while they ate. When their plates were cleared away, and Joseph paid the bill, they walked towards the water, still not having spoken of what they both wanted and needed to speak. It was only when they found an empty bench facing the river that they did.

"What shall we do? Will you leave me now?"

Joseph turned to his lover. He did not understand that she could think he would leave her. As they walked, he dreaded the opposite. She looked down into her lap, where her hands were folded but slightly shaking, and when she felt his eyes, she turned to look at them. He leaned in, the fingers of his right hand running down her cheek and then reaching for a tear that began to meander down. He turned from her lips, themselves shaking, and instead his own touched the spot where the tear had been.

His mouth was close to her ear and he moved it closer. "I will never leave you," and he pulled his head back to look at her and now her whole body shook and more, happy tears followed that first stray, far too many to be contained by his fingers or his lips so he pulled her so they dampened his shoulder.

51.

"It was late so I stayed at a friend's."

Joseph's mother seemed half-satisfied with his (literally true) explanation for why he had not come home that evening. He and Clara agreed that whatever happened between them, for the time it must be their secret. Clara loved Mrs. Nathan and knew she loved her, but that was a far different proposition than marrying her only child. Yes, Clara thought of marrying him, though neither lover dared mention it. But she was older than the women for whom he and his parents had expectations. His time at Yale done and his European tour canceled, at summer's end, he would begin working in his father's financial firm on Broad Street. Though he would have a hefty allowance.

His parents would confer with the parents of girls who recently came out in their circle and parties would be attended by men like Joseph and girls like the ones who would marry men like Joseph and after a time the former would select the latter—hopefully without too much conflict—and Joseph's would be one of a series of weddings held at Grace Church or Incarnation or any of the other prominent churches in the next year or two and there would be one or more grandchildren to eventually race around the oak tree on the lawn in Riverdale.

It was the order of their world, the natural order as Mr. Darwin would say, and likely always would be.

Clara had one chance. That Joseph would prove to be the man she believed him to be.

After Joe left the next morning, Clara went to see Emily. As they sat, news of what she did—what *they* did—sprung out and she promised her friend how different it was from Sir John Adams and how different he was from Reginald Turner. And she confessed how truly in love she was, without any reservations.

Emily well knew Clara's struggles, including regarding men, and she rose and bent down behind her friend and reached down to place her arms around her tightly and told her how truly glad she was.

"What of my family?"

Emily did not know enough of what they knew of Clara's history to do anything more than listen to Clara explain what she thought she should do, and it was clear that Clara did not want to hide her news. She felt Joe was committed to her and she knew that she was committed to him. She would first tell Grace and have Grace meet him and if that worked out, he would be introduced to the family as the one who would end her mother's determination to invite a bachelor to Sunday dinners.

Emily held Clara's face in her hands and looked her in the eyes.

"You deserve to be happy, and I hope he deserves you."

"Oh, Em, he does. I know he does."

And when Clara took her to meet him, Emily thought he just might deserve her. Since the next day was Saturday and the three agreed to introduce him to her family, they agreed to start with Grace.

Late the next morning, Clara sat in her sister's sitting room and told her about him.

"I must tell you that I am in love."

Grace stared, more than a little surprised. She was resigned that her sister would live the monastic life of an artist. Clara never spoke of love or even lust for a man as a younger sister feeling either or both would have. While there was a time when she suspected that Clara and John Evans had some sort of romantic relationship, she came to understand that it was platonic. There were men introduced at a Sunday dinner or party at their parents' house who expressed an interest in Clara, but she gave few if any of them the slightest thought. Ted Porter might have been the one, but his heart went to Emily, and Grace often regretted that Emily happened to appear on that, of all afternoons.

There was the one—Grace could not recall the name but he met Clara years earlier in Lenox—in whom Clara seemed to take an interest but he disappeared and her sister never again spoke of him. That over the years was the only glimmer.

It was a Saturday, and once she digested the information, Grace told her sister that she would need to say something about him to their parents at church but first she must meet him.

Joseph was waiting at a small park not far from the Lawfords' house, sitting in a corner with a novel. How many pages he actually read he never knew, but the plot did not advance very far while he sat. Nor could he say how many times he looked up when he heard the park's gate open, until he was finally rewarded when he saw Clara with her sister, using her free hand to wave to him and before any of them knew it he was up and greeting them on the gravel path that surrounded the green. They met at the Nathan unveiling but neither had a clear recollection of the other.

Clara, somewhat out of breath, said, "Grace, this is Joseph Nathan." She told Grace *en route* of her connection with the Nathan family so no further introduction was required.

Joseph gave a slight bow and then reached for Grace's hand, saying it was a pleasure to meet her.

Clara need not have worried. Just by the look of him, Grace saw that he was not like so many of the fools her mother brought home to match up with her sister. This was confirmed soon after they sat back on the bench, poor Joseph between the two Bowman girls.

After some awkwardness, Joseph stood. He told Grace it was his pleasure to have met her and lifted Clara's hand to give it a kiss. With that, the two pairs of eyes studied his back until he was through the gate. When he was gone, they turned to each other, each smiling. Grace said she very much approved of the choice and wondered how deeply in love with him Clara was, it being clear it was quite deep. Clara looked about, to ensure that there were no interested ears about, and she leaned to her sister.

"I have lain with him."

Grace pulled back and immediately regretted the sharp look she gave. Clara was her little sister and always would be though she had long been a woman. Her disclosure, though, was so natural, so pleasantly made that she felt joy, for want of a better word, for her sister having done what she did with the man with whom she did it.

Clara's face was frozen in fear from the initial look she received from her older sister until Grace pulled her head to her shoulder and whispered, "If you are happy for what you did with Joseph, then I am overjoyed for you."

Pushing the head back so she could look into Clara's eyes, she smiled and added, "You have grown so much and so well and I truly love you."

This time, Clara placed her head on her sister's shoulder and gripped her and was as happy with her as she had ever been in her life. Grace pushed her away, allowing her to recover her composure. After a moment, she said, "And how will we introduce him to mama and papa?"

They would do it, they agreed, the next day, before Sunday services. After they walked to Grace's door, Grace went in to change to tell her mother that Clara would not be coming the next day so she should cancel any invitations extended to a new prospect. Clara raced to tell Joe, who was waiting at a nearby café, how much she loved her older sister.

Mrs. Bowman was thus surprised when Clara came into view on Madison Avenue on the way to church and more so that she was doing it with a man on her arm.

"Who's that with Clara?" Mr. Bowman asked his wife.

"I have no idea. But I expect we will soon find out." She looked at Grace, standing with Richard.

"Yes, mother. You will soon find out."

To her mother's glare, Grace said, "I met him only yesterday so don't look so cross at me," and Mrs. Bowman's look returned to her other, unmarried daughter. As Grace had, as Joseph neared, she appreciated that Clara had an exceptionally fine eye indeed, for he was handsome, especially now that he had allowed his hair to grow a bit longer than was fashionable.

And so it went. Clara's parents approved. Róisín and Lizzie approved, and Diarmaid seemed to when Clara took Joseph to visit them on the following Sunday and the five went to a nearby playground. John Evans and most of her other artist friends liked him, the exceptions being a few harboring desires of their own for Miss Bowman.

More important, the Porters took the couple to dinner during the week, and it was not long before Ted and Joe were the greatest of friends.

The Nathans, of course, liked Clara, but she was still tense when she and her mother called on Mrs. Nathan in the middle of the following week. She need not have worried. Mrs. Nathan had long since done her research on the Bowmans. A good, respectable family. An older daughter with two daughters and a husband well-regarded in his business and from a respected family.

More to the point, she more than suspected that her son was mad about the artist. When she saw Mrs. Bowman's card on the silver plate of O'Neil, their butler, she was happy and quickly directed the two visitors into her garden where refreshments were served. Nothing was said about what they all knew circled them pleasantly, but the older women took a liking to one another, and Clara was left to wonder at the ease with which they felt free to tell the secrets of their children's mishaps, chortling as each tried to top the other's tales. Joe was relieved when Clara reported back on the visit. He realized, though, as she well knew, that he had not asked her if she wanted to marry him. Finally, two days after Mrs. Bowman and Mrs. Nathan got along so famously, while their children—Clara and Joseph—were strolling, Clara stopped abruptly and pulled Joe to the side, looking at him.

"Joseph. Do you love me?"

"You know I do."

"How do I know if you do not tell me?"

"I show you. Is that not enough?"

She shook her head. "I cannot imagine the man I intend to marry is such a fool," and then resumed walking, leaving him in her wake. He quickly caught up to her.

"What did you say?"

Again they stopped, and again she pulled him to the side.

"I said that I cannot believe that I love and intend to marry someone who is such a fool. Even for a man." This time she held her ground.

"Of course I love you," he blubbered.

"And?"

"And of course I want to marry you."

She smiled. "Now, was that so difficult?" and she resumed her walk and left him to catch her up.

52.

On the next day, Clara returned to the Porters alone. "I need your help. I think it did not happen. But I cannot get pregnant, at least not yet."

Clara knew that Emily had not lain with anyone before she was married but she suspected that Emily might be able to help her on the issue of avoiding pregnancy.

Joe was also concerned. In the past, he took precautions in the brothel adventures he and his friends periodically embarked upon. But the act, or acts, with Clara were spontaneous and while the thought of her getting pregnant appeared in his mind his will overcame it. He was afraid to speak to her about it, though it was foremost in his mind for the days following.

With his classmates in Europe, that left Buddy Castle. Joseph nonchalantly (or so he pretended) appeared at *Art Illustrated* shortly before noon on the Monday when Clara discussed it with Emily, if he could take his friend to lunch. Buddy, not being a fool, told his friend to "spit it out" after the waiter left with their orders.

"Do you remember the artist—"

"The one with the *Blizzard* painting. I do not know her, though." He leaned in. "Tell me, Nathan. How well do you know her?"

Joseph, turning shades of red not yet discovered, could not answer before Buddy resumed.

"I do not need to know details, my friend."

Just then, the waiter placed soups before them, and the pair waited until he was gone.

Turning serious, Buddy said, "I know you well enough to know you would not have done whatever it is that you have done without having feelings for her. So I am happy for you."

"It's just that I'm a little…frightened."

"About her?"

"Oddly enough, no. Not about her. About something…happening."

Buddy, fully getting Joe's drift, walked him through the care that was required. They kept their voices low enough, and were silent as their courses were deposited and removed from the table, so as not to be overheard. By the time the two left, Joe understood at least enough to be confident that he could please Clara and that there was little chance of an accident.

As Buddy returned to *Art Illustrated*, Joe went to Bleecker Street and he spoke with Clara. Their initial hesitancy dissolved as they realized they were thinking along the same lines and they spoke of how they would proceed as lovers.

And they were both relieved when a week later Clara could tell him that that first, magic, manic night did not leave her pregnant.

53.

Derrick Washington was a major on the staff of General Grant in the War. He was the second son of a prominent Boston family, but elected to move to New York after the hostilities, and was, a decade later, an Inspector with the New York Police Department. He was not much liked by his fellow officers, being neither Irish nor from New York, nor among the multitude of Tammany-connected officers. He was something of a lone wolf who was tolerated and got his promotions because of his results. He was a thin man who wore a thick beard and some thought he was a little too arrogant in his manner and confidence. That he made sure people knew he was a major on Grant's staff did not endear him to others in the department.

When he first knocked on the door of Clara's studio, there was no answer so he returned the next morning. This time the door was open as it often was, and he knocked on its frame. The artist beckoned him in, noticing his meticulous dress and his Boston accent and particularly polite manner. She was alone. Joe left about an hour earlier. One of the underappreciated aspects of Bleecker Street was the ability of a lover to leave in the morning without attracting the slightest notice.

Now the visitor spoke. "Miss Bowman?"

She rose to greet him unsure of who he was and the as-yet-unknown purpose of his visit. When he told her he was a detective she did not know what to make of it.

"May I sit?"

She nodded and she sat across from him in one of her armchairs. Although a window was open, the room had its usual deep paint smell. The Inspector wondered aloud whether he had been transported to the garrets of Paris.

She laughed. "Inspector. I have been in the garrets of Paris. They are much smaller than this."

The Inspector stood. "May I?" Clara nodded and he browsed around the various works on the floor, moving some to get a clearer look while she watched.

"Oh, these are very good, are they not?"

She joined him, forgetting for the moment her apprehension about the purpose of his visit.

"There are those who think them very good. Some days I agree with them. Some days I do not."

"Which makes you an 'artist' I think."

She laughed. "Still, I do not think this explains your visit."

He held up one of her landscape studies of the Palisades and spoke to it. "No. Much as wish it were." He replaced it and turned.

He smiled and then asked if she knew a Mr. Kyle Smith.

"Kyle Smith? It has been some time, but he was a painter here in the Village."

"Did you know him well?"

She stiffened and told him that he was an acquaintance and no more.

"We disagreed about art sometimes, as artists will. He was close for a while to a friend of mine with whom I shared a flat. Not an artist. But she was no longer with him. She has since married. Please. What is this about?"

"I have some news about Mr. Smith that you might find distressing," and he bade her sit again.

"Miss Bowman. We have reason to believe that Mr. Smith is the person behind the attack on you some years ago and that he himself set fire to your studio."

Clara had not heard or thought about Kyle Smith in quite a while. Their interactions were fleeting before then. Surely, this was nonsense.

"Miss Bowman?"

"I am sorry, Inspector. That cannot be true."

"I'm afraid it is, Miss. He has confessed."

This made no sense. He was a charming, nice enough man, and they had their disagreements and they went their separate ways. She had not heard about him recently and not seen him for even longer. Nor had the initial, somewhat lazy police investigation turned up anything.

"After he had someone break your arm—the fool was confused and broke your non-painting one and I am glad you seem to have recovered—he moved to Philadelphia where he enrolled in the art school there. Apparently, you convinced him to learn how to be an artist.

"He returned to New York about a year ago, but he lived in Brooklyn. They say he was developing a name for himself, doing portraits and such. He has family money so he did not starve. He says he went to an exhibition of Mr. John Evans and saw some of your things. You weren't there at the time, he says. It brought back feelings he'd long forgotten. About you and some woman he fancied that you convinced to abandon him. I assume the one you mentioned."

Each word was slapping across Clara as if she were on a beach facing an increasingly angry sea-wind, and she knew from the Inspector's reference to "some woman he fancied" that it was all true. She allowed Washington to complete his story.

"After the exhibition, Mr. Smith went to a tavern and drank and drank until they threw him out. He couldn't get home to Brooklyn, so he was going to sleep in an alley. Quite a comedown, I guess. He says he woke up about two and saw a pile of rags. He claims he did not know what he was doing but he went to your old building and the door to your studio was not locked and he used a match to set fire to the rags and stuffed them beneath your paintings and furniture and ran."

Clara had not moved since the Inspector began, though her head was racing.

"I must see him."

"I don't think that would be a good idea just yet."

"Inspector. I insist. Take me to him."

As they walked to the jail less than a mile away, the Inspector explained that a man was arrested for pickpocketing down on Wall Street and when they brought him in he wanted to make a deal. He said he was involved in a "terrible attack on an artist, a young lady" years before and he could finger the man who hired him. He did not know the name but remembered the bar where he was solicited, and the bartender did remember the name—Kyle Smith—and after asking around the police figured out who the victim was—Clara Bowman—and tracked Smith down with the police in Brooklyn.

When they brought him in, the Inspector took the ferry across and Smith immediately confessed to the attack and volunteered about the arson before the Inspector brought him back to the city, where he was being held until a judge could see him.

The jail, known as the "Tombs" for its pretentious exterior, was itself sinking and the cells' conditions were damp and dank, and they were a breeding ground for disease. Kyle Smith, being of a prominent family and the brother of a war hero, was relieved of having to be in a cell and was in a relatively comfortable room secured only by a single lock on its door. It was the room used for prisoners deemed superior to the common ruffians and thieves and murderers relegated to the bowels of the large building.

Clara had no feelings for Kyle beyond pity and dismay. But she would do something to help him if she could. She owed him that much.

When they reached the building, Inspector Washington opened and held the thick, ornate wooden door that was in the shadow of the large columns that helped to give the building its pretensions. The foyer had a tall ceiling with a high desk at one end, at which several police officers sat. On either side were rows of benches. They were occupied by mostly poor women waiting to bring something to their man as well as several mostly quiet infants. Some type of pastry or even several apples. Cigarettes.

Standing out among them was a well-dressed older couple, and Clara thought they must be Kyle's parents as they stood when they saw the Inspector. He warned her that they might be there. They were in the front row to the left and sat some distance from the others.

The Inspector hurried Clara forward, their steps echoing beneath the tall ceiling, so as to deny her the chance to speak to them. The guards at the desk nodded to him, and he told them he was with Miss Clara Bowman, and the fact was noted in a ledger. One of the officers led the pair through a locked door and down a long, dark corridor. At its end, they turned to the left and stopped at the third door, which the officer opened with a key.

It was a cell, however privileged, and Clara recoiled upon entering it with the Inspector. Kyle was staring at the door when he heard it being unlocked and fell to the ground when he saw who entered. She was shocked at his appearance. Like Crusoe. His hair was long and dirty. His beard unkempt and clothes torn and filthy. He smelled very bad.

The Inspector warned her that he had refused offers to bathe or get a shave. A clean change of clothing sat on a table, and a stack of drawings was beside it. The room had a window, crossed by two iron bars, and at least the air was not as fetid as it was for the less-fortunate prisoners.

The Inspector warned her that he would not see any visitors, not even his parents or sisters, and to be prepared for him to refuse to see her. Instead, he groveled. On his knees, he moved to her, and she felt the Inspector grip her hand for support. Kyle put his arms around her legs. Somehow, she maintained her calm. She then pulled from him. In a single motion she lifted the bottom of her dress and with the sole of her shoe pushed this pitiful creature away, and he lost his balance and fell to the floor, his head nearly cracking as it hit the wood.

"You are a horrible thing. You wanted to destroy me and my life. Because you were—what?—jealous? Lonely? You should die a long, slow death."

The door was still open, and she was quickly through it and then down the hall and through the lobby and out onto Centre Street, throwing up an arm to get a cab to take her from this awful place.

She told the cabbie to take her to Bleecker Street but *en route*, she changed her mind and instead went to the Nathans'. When the door was answered, she asked to see Joseph, and when he saw her and the state she was in the pair immediately left the house, with Mrs. Nathan watching them rush out and wondering, not for the first time, what sort of relationship her son had with her young friend.

It was the type of relationship that allowed Joe to calm Clara down at her studio. Yes, he knew how hurt she was. How violated she felt. But she was stronger for it. She fell asleep not long after they reached the studio, and she lay on the sofa with her head on his lap. He got up and delicately lowered her head to a cushion and placed a light blanket across her and after he kissed her forehead, he sat watching.

Yes, he might think he knew what she went through, but he knew he never could appreciate it. She was so sweet and innocent as she slept, little bubbles appearing and popping between her lips, and he vowed to protect her. His thoughts were broken when he heard a knock on the door. It was loud enough for Clara to jolt awake, and he looked at her. She nodded, and he stood and went to the door. It was Inspector Washington.

Seeing an unexpected man in the studio, the Inspector introduced himself, and Joe said, "I am Miss Bowman's fiancé, Joseph Nathan," and led the policeman inside. Clara, still a bit disheveled, was sitting up trying to get fully awake.

"I am sorry to disturb you, Miss Bowman, Mister Nathan, but it is a matter of some urgency."

She bade the two men sit and told the Inspector he could speak freely in front of her friend. With a nod to Joe, the Inspector resumed.

"I come not on behalf of Kyle Smith. I do not disagree with what you called him or how you treated him. No. I am here for his mother. When she saw you leave so expeditiously with me not far behind—you were gone before I could catch you—she left the Tombs and reached for me on its steps. I told her what happened. I did not feel to have any choice but to do so, and she was joined by her husband."

The lovers exchanged a look.

"I do not doubt that they understood what you did, Miss Bowman. It hurt them even more to see the woman he tried to destroy, even kill. His mother, I think, might have abandoned him then, but Mr. Smith would not allow it. Her only living son after the major who died in the War.

"I walked back with them inside, and we were given a quiet room. She begged me to come see you. To speak with you and try to have you at least consider forgiving him or not hate him so. She said she understood how justified you would be to refuse her.

She said, though, that she would fall to her knees before you to make her plea."

Throughout this, other than her glance at Joseph, Clara stared at her hands, but with this last description she looked up, from the Inspector to Joe.

"I love you, Clara"—which was the first public time he said it—"and will support whatever decision you take. But I think you must at least consider forgiveness. I think you must at least consider sitting with him. For your sake as much as his."

The two men sat quietly as they waited, the only sound the unavoidable noise from traffic and pedestrians on Bleecker Street even though the apartment faced the rear.

She did not know for how long she sat, silent and immobile, but finally, she agreed to again visit Kyle Smith.

"I will go, Inspector. I will go with my…fiancé. I will sit with him and listen to what he has to say. What I say in response I do not know. But I will listen to what he has to say."

54.

The day after Inspector Washington sat with Clara, and Joseph, and before Clara could return to the Tombs as she promised she would, the Inspector was back at her apartment. She was working on some details for a portrait on which the primary work was done, and after a moment she suggested they go to one of the small cafés in the area that catered to the artist crowd.

Over two coffees, Washington told her the story of Joshua M. Smith, Kyle's brother. He was in touch with some colleagues from Grant's staff, one of whom knew about Major Smith.

"He died from a Reb sniper's bullet leading a platoon of New York's eighty-third regiment in some obscure woods in western Virginia. May 1864. He was dead before he hit the ground, and he became the family's hero. Kyle was only fifteen or so when it happened, but he lived in his brother's shadow as the surviving boy."

"Why are you telling me this?"

The Inspector took more of his coffee.

"It is no excuse, but to understand Kyle Smith you must know something about his brother. I spoke to one of his colleagues at the eighty-third who works in the department. He said Major Smith was not quite what his family thought.

"I spoke to a Captain Williams. Retired after the War. He was with Smith in the nineteenth regiment. When it was disbanded in '63, most officers decided they'd done their due and went home. Smith stayed on, joining the eighty-third. This only made him more a hero to his folks. Williams said Smith did it for the glory. Nothing more. Maybe become a colonel. Even a general. He would make a name for himself in the War and use it for his climb up back in town.

"Williams made clear that Smith was no coward. Just reckless. They were both captains when they separated. Williams told me that more than anything, Smith just wanted to kill Rebs. Almost a sport to him. Maybe he thought he was immortal."

The Inspector took another sip.

"I saw my share of those and most of them got killed early in a battle. Which is what happened to Major Joshua Smith. Shot by some Virginian or Georgian who couldn't read but grew up shooting squirrels and Smith gets it between his own eyes and dead before he hits the ground near some little creek no one ever heard of."

Clara looked at the policeman as he drifted to one of his own skirmishes with Virginia or Georgia boys and finished his coffee.

"I don't know if it means anything, Miss Bowman. I thought it might help you understand more about him is all I wanted you to know."

He rose and dropped a coin on the table.

"You know where I am" were his final words as he headed down the avenue, south to police headquarters.

55.

"Now you come back to me, again so high-and-mighty. Lording it over me as you always did. Always the better painter. John Evans's creation. I was the artist. You just wanted to have something to occupy your time. Clara Bowman this. Clara Bowman that.

"But I could've accepted it if you hadn't turned my Emily against me."

This time, Kyle sat in the chair in his "cell." He was bathed and shaved and his hair was clipped. He wore new clothes, which hung loosely on him. Clara sat on the side of his bed with Washington blocking the door and a guard within earshot. Joe sat in the waiting room in front. Kyle Smith's parents set in the back of the set of benches opposite him. Clara looked at Kyle, mystified.

"I did not turn Emily against you. She never would have loved you."

"Is that what you told her? That she could never love me? And you say you didn't turn her against me? What could you possibly say that was worse than what you did say? You couldn't keep out of my affairs."

"Emily's affairs *were* my affairs."

"Even if it meant denying her the chance to find love with someone who truly adored her? Instead, she ends up with that lawyer fellow. Hollow. Empty. But, I forgot, that's what you think of me, the good Clara Bowman. Me, the empty shell of an artist. Who'd never amount to anything."

"That's not true. I never said that to Emily."

"Of course you did. Of course you did. Every time you had a bad word for my work. *My work.* Every time."

He was increasingly agitated in the chair, and his arms were beginning to flail about. The Inspector kept his eyes locked on the prisoner.

"And this justified trying to destroy me?"

"You were a dilletante. What would it matter if you could no longer paint? You'd be back in your big house with your loving family. Married and happy."

She was on her feet, her face red, pointing at him.

"How dare you? Happy? Living the life set out for me when I could chart my own. You would take that from me?"

"But you are a woman. It is not as important to you as it is to me."

Clara heard enough. More than.

"You are a horrible man. I take joy in every word I said to Emily about you. As an artist. And more as a man. You could never be the type of man that deserved her love. Never in all eternity.

"And with every word today, every move you have made since I arrived, you have proven it a thousand-fold. You tried to destroy me, and you tried to...to...to kill me when Emily left you. You are worthy of pity. No more. I will not take the excuse that you were treated badly. That you were overshadowed by your hero brother. Well, he was no hero. Inspector Washington told me. He was just a blood-thirsty, ambitious ass who got what he deserved and so you suffered for nothing. You are such a fool."

She turned and the Inspector moved to one side and before Kyle Smith knew it Clara Bowman was gone.

The Smiths were the first to see her burst through the waiting room and through the door, and they felt their last hope for their son went with her. Joe ran after her and caught her about half-a-block up Centre Street. He reached for her shoulder to stop her, but she ignored him, and he fell into step beside her. Still without speaking, she soon put her arm through his and they remained silent until they reached her studio.

She fought against crying the entire way. When the door closed behind them, the tears burst forth, and he held her tightly, feeling her tremble.

"I was horrible. He was horrible," she finally said. He kissed her forehead and then the tears that were crossing her cheeks before pulling her close to him again.

Neither knew how it happened, but soon they were naked in her bed and she allowed her anger to dissipate by making love to him. But it was different from the times before. More primal. A means for Clara to connect with the man she loved, and when they were done it was still morning and they lay with one another, naked, with their bodies intertwined until they both fell asleep.

It was Joe's turn to awaken first, and he felt her breathe easily as his right arm encircled her. In the minutes before she stirred, he decided that he would move the wedding up. They intended it to be a simple ceremony, and he saw no reason to delay it. When she began to move, she turned to face him.

"I am sorry. When I got there, he was awful and I became awful and I said awful things and raced away. I do not know what I could have done if I did not have you."

He pulled her closer so she could lay her head on his shoulder. He ran his hand along her back and said, "Let us not wait."

She recoiled.

"Wait?"

"Clara. I love you more—"

"Even though I did such a horrible thing?"

He placed his finger across her lips to quiet her.

"You did what you needed to do. He tried to destroy you. He would not accept your forgiveness and you did all you could do to offer it to him."

She turned again so she could feel him encircle her and his lips pecked at her earlobe as he waited.

"Joseph Nathan. I will gladly marry you whenever and wherever you wish." Neither saw the other's smile but she felt him tighten his grip until they lay too long and had to get up.

They had a simple lunch and thought of going to Grace Church on Broadway and Twelfth Street but decided instead to go to police headquarters to meet with Inspector Washington in a less tense environment. Police headquarters was, as it happened, one of the buildings on Mulberry Street that could be seen from Clara's building, and in no time she and Joe were up the marble stairs and inside, where they stood before a large, towering desk along a wall to the right.

The sergeant sent an officer to fetch Washington, who shook the couple's hands when he arrived before leading them out to the street. He said it would be best to speak outside.

"Miss Bowman. I assure you that I thought what you did was brave and I understand it completely. I have seen it often, victims confronting the person who hurt them. Rarely has the assault been so vindictive and personal as Mr. Smith's was on you, and I promise you that I was not surprised by what happened when he assaulted you—"

Joe had not heard the details of what happened in the Tombs and did not know she was assaulted, and he looked harshly at the Inspector.

"Mr. Nathan, I mean verbally. I was there to ensure nothing physical could pass between them."

"Thank you, Inspector," Joe said.

Clara assured him, her arm through his with the Inspector on her opposite side, "He said truly awful things to me, no more."

"You did well, my dear," Washington assured her.

"What will happen to him?" she asked.

"He has confessed. Which is in his favor. But his crimes are most serious. Assault. Arson. Even attempted murder. He will be sent for some years to the prison up in Westchester on the river. His parents will be able to visit him regularly, and he likely will receive some preferential treatment because of who they are and because of his brother. Perhaps he will become a changed man, not so…angry. Perhaps he will develop what talent he has a painter."

They were silent and continued to circle the block.

"Perhaps, Miss Bowman, he will be changed enough so you can visit him. But if not, you must not chastise yourself. You could not have done more than you have done."

As they reached police headquarters again, the Inspector shook Joe's hand, saying as he did, "You must be proud of her."

"I am, sir. I assure you."

Washington turned to Clara.

"I am always here, Miss Bowman. I am always here."

After he shook her hand, she nodded. He stopped on the steps.

"Miss Bowman, if there comes a time when you can meet with the Smiths, not now but in time, I think they would very much appreciate it." He stepped down to the sidewalk. "They do not expect you to forgive their son. They very much wish to, well, tell you how sorry they are for what he did. And perhaps in time you might forgive them."

With that and a final nod, he went inside, and Clara and Joe turned back. They needed air before returning to the apartment and continued north until they realized—neither knew whether it was intentional—that they reached Grace Church. She squeezed his hand, and together they entered the rectory.

56.

Muriel Bowman and Agnes Nathan would only admit to being "disappointed." That were at the table in the Bowmans' dining room when Joe and Clara stood and the former said, somewhat hesitatingly, that he and Clara had arranged to be married at Grace Church in just over a month. It was their secret. Not even Emily, who was at the dinner with Ted and was about to burst with her child, knew, and Joe and Clara picked the date in anticipation that the baby would be born by then.

In fact, Emily's girl—Little Emily—entered the world on August 1 and was healthy and the date of August 25 for the wedding meant Emily could carefully act as Clara's maid of honor. Buddy Castle would stand with Joe.

It was, in the end, a simple ceremony at Grace Church. At her mother's and sister's insistence, Clara wore a dress in her favorite maroon with wide vertical stripes made of thin cream-colored lines, and the sleeves merged with a similarly colored lace trim that danced across the bride's wrist. It was perfectly fitted to her slight curves, and she knew Mrs. Trolley would smile if she saw it. Clara and her mother and sister spent several days getting it to fit properly, although she was in a hurry to actually wear it. A hat in the same material adorned her head with a darker maroon ribbon that matched the wider one that danced down the back of the dress falling over her shoulders.

She held a collection of complementing roses, of course, and as she turned to the top of the aisle on the arm of Mr. George Bowman. The moment Mr. Joseph

A STUDIO ON BLEECKER STREET | 303

Nathan caught sight of her, it can fairly be said that his heart skipped several beats. Nothing could surpass her naked body, but the groom thought her ensemble came as close as humanly possible and was increasingly convinced of this with each step she took that brought her closer to him.

Few people thought Clara Bowman a particularly attractive woman with her height and gawkiness. But Joseph Nathan was among those who did, and he was in a position more than anyone to know the accuracy of his verdict. As he stood in front of the altar in Grace Church looking up the aisle with only a few others as witnesses, a chill ran over him with the thought that he would never have come to know her had it not been for Mr. Thornton Isaacs having commented on a painting done at his family's house in Riverdale that found its way to page 12 of *Art Illustrated*.

But Mr. Thornton Isaacs *had* commented and Buddy Castle *had* shown Joe an advance copy and...Clara Susan Bowman and Joseph Elliot Nathan became husband and wife, and no one was displeased or disappointed that the ring bearers, Diarmaid Campbell (whose name was legally changed from Cassidy earlier in the year) and Grace's Muriel Lawford, stole a fair share of the attention from the bride and groom.

While the Bowmans and the Nathans were not of the highest ranks, they were still high enough that an announcement trumpeting the union was in all the appropriate newspapers.

57.

The Mall in Central Park is a wide walkway between rows of trees and busts of famous men, writers mostly. Visitors often stroll there to glimpse the fashionable as they emerge from their carriages to parade. When they tire, they can recover on one of the benches set up on either side and watch the groups of twos and threes and more pass by.

Since those who must work must work for five-and-a-half days in a week, they tend to flood the place on Sundays, and society finds it more relaxing to be there on other days.

Mr. and Mrs. Edward Wilson were well aware of the customs and protocols from their native London, though they were by no means themselves fashionable. That could not be said of Mrs. Wilson's brother, Baron-to-Be John Adams, but on this afternoon Sir John and his family were at the hotel.

Edward and Felicity Wilson, with their two girls, walked in the pleasant weather but they covered a great deal of ground and came upon a comfortable bench by a statue of a seated Walter Scott on which to sit before returning to their hotel to dress for dinner. Without warning, Felicity rose and called over her shoulder, "I shall be right back" before rushing to catch up with a couple pushing a baby carriage to the north.

She tapped the woman on the shoulder.

"Pardon me. Are you Emily?"

Emily Porter turned, taken aback by the English accent that questioned her. She had no idea who this woman was.

"I am sorry. But you are?"

By this point, Emily's husband, Ted, had stopped too.

"I am Felicity Wilson, and if I am not mistaken you were the subject of drawings by a...a former friend, a Miss Clara Bowman."

It took only a moment before Emily said, "You are her Felicity? I should have known from the accent. I do know of you and of what you did to her. She is Clara Nathan now."

"May we speak?"

Ted told his wife that he would head to the menagerie with the baby, and with a nod to the stranger he turned south, pushing Little Emily.

Felicity signaled to her own husband and daughters to remain where they were.

"That is my own family."

The women started to the north.

"She must have understood why I did what I did."

"She may have understood in time. But she was far more generous to you than I would have been. It broke her heart."

"As it did mine. I promise you. But it had to be done."

Emily paused. She knew about Felicity and her father. She knew about John too but would not reveal that knowledge unless Clara permitted it.

She did not know what to say. Felicity did not wait long before breaking the silence.

"Please tell me she is happy being Mrs. Nathan. That is all I wish to know."

"She is very happy with him. But she has gone through so much to get there. I am glad for her, and she is developing something of a reputation in the art world."

"I know. I have seen articles that mention her. Even in the London magazines I see her name."

She began to turn back, and Emily turned with her.

"I have kept you too long from your family. Please. If you see Clara, tell her…Tell her that she will always have my love." Before Emily could respond, Felicity was nearly to her family, which rose to meet her. Emily rushed to catch her.

"Where are you staying?"

"I have said too much. I must…Forget I approached you."

Emily quickly reached into her bag and removed a small case, from which she removed one of her cards and gave it to Felicity, "in case you should wish to speak to me again." After a pause and a nod, Felicity joined her family and headed to where they could get a trolley back to their hotel, leaving Emily staring.

The American was shaken. She walked quickly to the menagerie and found Ted and the baby. She told him who the woman was and her connection with Clara. He knew about it in broad strokes only. They continued their talk as they left the park and then they, too, got on a trolley, taking them to their small house on Twenty-Seventh Street.

Emily saw to dinner and then left while it was still light for the Nathans'.

For their part, when Mr. and Mrs. Wilson and the girls returned to their hotel suite, only Felicity's sister-in-law Diana and her children were there, and all the young ones went in with their nurse to take a nap while the three adults spoke. Because she did not know what, if anything, would follow from her encounter with Emily, Felicity asked Edward not to say anything about seeing her at least for now, so she was not mentioned.

At the same time, Emily sat with Clara in the small sitting room in the Nathans' apartment,

"You what?"

Emily was right in telling Clara that she met Felicity, but Clara would not listen when she said she did not want to presume to invite Felicity to meet Clara. She would ask Clara first.

"But you did not get their hotel. Of course I want to see her. And her Mr. Wilson. How could you think otherwise?"

"But after she abandoned you?"

"The way you abandoned your good friend Elizabeth Geherty?"

Emily had never seen Clara so angry, and she did not understand why she did not understand.

"I did not want to have you get hurt again."

Emily dropped to the floor.

"I did not want to see you get hurt again," she repeated. "And she would not tell me the hotel. I asked."

Clara had long since moved on from the shock of her removal from England years before. She thought a great deal of Felicity when she and John Evans did their tour of London and she did some watercolors in Regent's Park. She even thought of passing by the building where her flat was when they met. When she neither saw nor heard from her during her trip, it further drifted away, their experience from a different lifetime. Thoughts of her faded until she was jolted back to them by some arbitrary object or word. A painting of the Thames or a passing remark about Sir Anyone.

Clara dropped beside Emily and placed her arm around her dearest friend.

"You know I am much stronger than then, surely."

To Emily's nod, she added, "Besides, there are only so many hotels in New York where they might be staying. It will take us no time to find them."

So the next morning, while their husbands were at work, Emily entrusted the care of the baby to Ted's mother and Clara put off doing the final touches of a woman whose portrait her husband insisted she do and made a list of potential places where the Wilsons could be.

They decided it unlikely that they would be travelling alone. They agreed to the dreadful thought that they were traveling with Sir John which, while as unwelcome the idea was, significantly limited the potential hotels where they would be. There must be only three of the highest-end hotels that catered to the European and especially the English trade.

It was not yet noon, and Clara applied her best Miss Bowman accent to inquire at the desk of the second of the three as she had without success at the first one. There they were told that the Adamses and Wilsons were guests. When Clara asked whether they had gone out, the desk clerk said, "Sir John left shortly after breakfast. The others also went out, but I believe at least the, well, simpler family has returned. They usually have lunch in the dining room at a little past noon."

In fact, all four members of the Wilson family entered the hotel's dining room at 12:17, and this was noted by the two interested observers.

"I can't do it," Clara said.

"We will leave then?"

Clara was more upset by seeing Felicity than she expected.

"No." She looked from the entrance to Emily.

"Will you come with me?"

The Wilsons sat at a round table not far from the center of the room. The dining room itself was not crowded, with perhaps half the tables taken and mostly by small families, although there was a larger family at a table in the corner.

Felicity's back was to the entrance and she did not see the approach.

"Mommy. It's the woman in the pictures. The one from yesterday."

Felicity turned, following her eldest daughter's finger to Emily and a second later she saw Clara.

Instead of rushing to her, she stood frozen.

"I never should have approached. You must go. I cannot be seen with you. Please go."

Emily looked between the two women, and realizing the panic in Felicity, she pulled Clara away, and the last they heard from Felicity was "Please go, please go," and they saw her drop into her chair grasping her napkin with Edward looking to see whether Clara was recognized by anyone in the large room.

When the Americans were gone, Edward sat beside his wife.

"I'm sure he will not know. If he sees anything, you did not invite her. It is not your fault."

"But I went to her friend. If I had not done that—"

"Just remember. You did not *invite* her."

There was little chance that John saw them. He had lunch at one or another of New York's clubs, many of which had an affiliation with one of his London clubs and offered him reciprocal privileges.

John thought of New York as an oyster, to be enjoyed to the fullest. His life in London was a bore, even when broken up for significant periods by trips to Derbyshire. He had liaisons with many of the attractive (and similarly bored) ladies he knew and a fair number he did not know, except Biblically. Before he left, a friend lent him a list of brothels that he was assured were worth his interest and money.

58.

Shortly before dinner, Sir John knocked on the door for the Wilsons' suite and when they were alone said, "I understand you saw that little American filly friend of yours, the one I...had in London."

"How did you know?"

"The one you are barred from seeing. How did I know? I didn't. Until now. The bell captain apologized when I returned for allowing 'those American women' to disrupt your lunch. I told him to pay it no mind. But since the only American woman I recall you having anything to do with was that woman from years ago, I thought it might be her. And you, my stupid sister, have now confirmed it."

"But I did not invite her. She appeared."

"Appeared. Out of the blue? I doubt father will accept that."

"I saw her friend in the park and approached her. That is all. I did not even say where we were. I promise I have had nothing to do with her, not even a letter."

"Well, she and her friend apparently discovered where you are, did they not? Oh, Felicity. What are we to do with you? I will think on it. In the meantime, when Diana asks, tell her I am doing something perfectly innocent. Can you at least do that?"

Felicity stared at him but was silent, and he did not push the issue, saying, "Now that I think on it, I should like to have her again. I very much would like to."

She knew John to be a selfish indulgent ass. Untempered by his marriage, telling their father would be of little benefit to him beyond reducing her in the view of their father and thereby enhancing his own. And perhaps eliminate her from any share of the estate's assets that would be settled on her when the baron died, as it had not been when she became Mrs. Wilson.

Felicity had long ceased disliking Diana simply for marrying her brother. She did not know her well beforehand, but they became friends when together in Derbyshire. Diana did what was expected of her and married the future baron and bore him three children, most importantly two sons. Her husband took charge of the sons and left Penelope to Diana's care. Sir John did little in terms of anything related to the actual upbringing of the boys.

Penelope, at least, was yet spared the hand of a governess, as Diana insisted on doing that for herself (with but slight help from the staff) since she had little else to keep her occupied, especially when they were in the country.

Felicity enjoyed Diana's company, and Penelope's for that matter, far more than she did her nephews. Felicity and Diana were glad to have each other for the trip, and Felicity was particularly glad to be with Diana.

So after suffering through dinner and thankful that John scurried off to one of his "clubs," she, with Edward, sat with Diana and told what happened years ago.

"I didn't know." She knew of John's pre-marital exploits and of many of his post-marital infidelities, but not of the particulars involving Clara or what happened between Felicity and the baron. "Can you afford to live without the baron's money?" Diana asked her.

Edward learned of his father-in-law's demand about Clara shortly after it was made years before, when the baron got wind of Sir John's liaison with Clara. He sat with Felicity as she wrote the note Felicity sent to Clara's hotel. He found it humiliating that he could not protect his wife and his family from the capriciousness of her father. There was no justification for the diktat, but there was no changing the baron's mind, especially when it came to his son, whom he knew was not a saint but who was his son and would inherit his title.

The issue, with the increased complication of their children, now reminded both Wilsons of what they did then and why they did it. Suddenly they needed to address it again.

The baron did not much like Felicity's independent streak and he especially did not like that she insisted on marrying someone from the middle-class who did not even know how to ride. There were so many appropriate men who expressed an interest at one time or another in his daughter, but she refused to consider any of them. No, it was Edward Wilson or no one.

While he might have purchased a leasehold for her as part of her marriage settlement, he did not. Instead, he would only pay the rent on a house not too far from his own in Piccadilly. Both the baron and Felicity understood the import of that decision, and it came to a head when she was ordered to cease all contact with her American friend who committed the unpardonable sin of knowing her brother.

Before she could answer Diana's question about whether the Wilsons could survive without the baron's largesse, Sir John returned. Silence fell over everything and the Adamses retreated to their suite and the Wilsons to theirs. Felicity immediately went to a small desk and found stationary and a pen in a drawer.

Fifth Avenue Hotel
200 Fifth Avenue
New York, New York

2 March 1878

My Dear Father,

You, some years ago, conditioned my further receipt of any consideration from you, financial <u>or otherwise</u>, on my not having any contact with an American whom I befriended. I disagreed with why you did this and still do, but I do not question your prerogative to determine how the assets of the barony are allocated.

I have decided in consultation with my husband to refuse to accept any further consideration from you, financial <u>or otherwise</u>.

I shall, of course, always remain your daughter.

Mrs Edward Wilson

She reviewed what she wrote with Edward and received his approval, though given with some hesitancy. Felicity put it in an envelope and addressed it to the house in Piccadilly. After sealing it, she rang the bell and a member of staff on the floor appeared.

"Can you have this posted for me as soon as possible? I do not know the cost to London, but please have the desk tell us what it is."

With that and a tip, the staff member took the envelope, bowed, and was gone.

In the morning that followed a restless night, Felicity confirmed with the front desk that the letter was dispatched. No turning back. She asked that they settle their bill, that they were unexpectedly required to leave. She hoped it would not be too much given the limited funds the Wilsons had and further demands that would shortly be made on them, but it would have to be borne. Edward had brought a bank draft, which allowed him to withdraw money to pay for their hotel stay.

Felicity had Emily's address and while Edward went to a nearby bank she went to the Porters'. The house was small and littered with the baby's things. After Emily tidied, she brought Felicity tea.

"I confess I did not expect to see you."

"I need your help," she said to a woman she met only days earlier but with whom she had a long-standing connection thanks to Clara's drawings.

"I have thrown it all away."

Emily looked at her in confusion.

"As you perhaps know, my father said I could have no further contact with Clara, and he made that a requirement for me to continue to receive his support. He paid the rent on a nice house not far from his own in London, but he refused to buy me one as would be normal as part of a marriage settlement because he disapproves of my Mr. Wilson. Because he is not of our class.

"It means that he made me dependent on him and thus was able to control important things in my life. Including Clara. When my brother learned that I met her, however briefly, in the hotel restaurant, he threatened to expose me to my father, which created the prospect of being cut off from the money that I need, or thought I needed, to survive. It is the same calculation I made when I abandoned Clara so heartlessly.

"Perhaps I am a fool, but I have sent a letter to my father saying I will no longer take any of his money. It cannot be stopped. I do not know what to do. I do not know where my family can stay or how we can return home or where we will live when we get there. I do not know."

It took time for her to finish as she could not control her tears.

Emily was more than shocked. She had alternatives when she decided to live on her own years ago. She had to find a job. But she did not have a husband and two children. She was not thousands of miles from her home. And she retained the support of her parents.

Felicity was far too agitated to do anything other than sip Emily's tea as she regained control of herself, with the liberal use of a handkerchief Emily handed to her.

"My husband, Edward, fully supports me, but as to these practicalities he knows no more than I do."

"But why? Why did you do this?"

"I should have stood up to him with Clara then. I did not intend to see her here in New York. I really did not, though perhaps in my mind I hoped I might, if only a passing glance. Then I saw you and I knew I could not

not see her, and when my brother found out I knew it was the only choice for me. We will survive. We will find a smaller house in a less fashionable part of town. My husband does well enough for that. It is the immediate requirements that concern me, and once I decided to move on I could not continue to take a penny of my father's money."

"But isn't it the family's money? His inheritance from your grandfather."

"That's just it. My brother is entitled to it as the oldest boy. No one else is. Had I married as I was expected to, I would be rich with the settlement. We are not one of those families with a title but no money. But it is the way of my world, or at least of my father's world. To which I do not believe I can ever be a part."

"You may be able to stay here briefly. I'm sure my husband will not object, even with my baby. We do not have much room, but we can accommodate you for at least a few days, so you need not worry about that.

"Is there a place where you can stay in London until you find a new house? Your in-laws perhaps?"

"It will be tight there, too, but I am sure we can have space with them."

"The last item, then, is getting you home. I assume you will not use the tickets because your father paid for them."

"You are right. I could view them as part of the Adams family's assets, but they are his. My husband will go to the shipping company to see what can be done and whether we can board a ship sooner so we can get on with things."

Talking it out helped calm Felicity, and she drank her now-cold tea with some relish and ate three of the biscuits that Emily had accompanied it with. The two women were quiet.

"Now we must speak of Clara," Emily said.

"Now we must speak of Clara."

* * * *

SIR JOHN DID NOT know that his sister went to Emily. He assumed his perhaps ill-advised threat was enough to keep her in her place. Nothing was said when he returned from his "club" the night before which he took to mean that the *status quo ante* was restored. Diana said nothing that suggested otherwise. He was annoyed that the Wilsons did not appear for breakfast in the hotel's dining room, and his wife claimed to know nothing. When done eating, he knocked on the door to the Wilsons' suite. Edward answered, having but recently returned from a bank with cash.

"I am sorry. We are preparing to leave."

"Leave?" After a moment's hesitation, John pushed his worthless brother-in-law aside and entered.

"Where is she?"

Edward followed him in. "She is not here. She left first thing."

Edward headed to a table in the sitting room, where a trunk was waiting to be collected, although at that point Edward did not know to where it was to go. He picked up an envelope addressed to "Sir John Adams" in his wife's artist's script.

3 March 1878

Dear John,

I have advised Father than I will no longer accept anything from him. The same is true of you.

Edward and I with the children are finding other accommodations while we are in New York and will find an alternative means to return home. We will no longer compromise your inheritance. In London, we will obtain, we also hope, accommodations that will suffice for us and allow us to survive without the charity of Father.

I remain your sister,
Mrs Edward Wilson

This was read by the addressee while Mr. Edward Wilson watched, seeing anger percolate through his brother-in-law like Mount Etna and he was prepared when it blew.

"What is the meaning of this? 'Other accommodations.' 'Charity.' This is absurd. Tell her she must stop this foolishness and not send anything to our father. This is absurd."

With that, he crumbled the note and left for his own suite.

As Diana was getting changed, her husband burst in.

"Do you know about this?" He held the note in his hand and shoved it in her direction.

"Know what?"

"That she has left, disavowed anything more to do with my father or even with me. Do you know anything about this?"

Diana stood.

"Last night I asked her whether she and her family could survive without your father's money. Apparently, she decided they can."

She neared Sir John as she said this, and he quickly closed the distance and slapped her, hard, across her face.

"Why did you meddle with your stupid question, you old cow?"

She was afraid of his anger but was long accustomed to it and so was sufficiently accustomed to being physically struck that she knew to move her head to lessen the blow. Satisfied with his violence, he quickly turned and rushed from the room, and Diana stared at the door for some time before she went to a window and cried.

* * * *

SHORTLY AFTER THESE events in New York, Baron Adams sat in his large library in the country, savoring a successful weekend. He had invited men from the City and proper gentry for the hunt, and it went off well, though few of the City men were adept on horses, which only enhanced his enjoyment. Those he invited were sufficiently deferential and sufficiently understood their place to be tolerable, and he was fortunate that unlike some of his class he was not forced to invite Rothschilds and financiers of that ilk for their money, none of whom could ride and who were even worse than the Papists about the demands made on one's kitchen. He and the baroness were to journey to town in the morning.

Drink in hand, he looked up when Rafferty, the country butler, entered with a tray on which there was a telegram. Telegrams rarely brought good news. When the baron lifted the envelope, the baroness noted this and was immediately concerned about the unusual turn of events. She watched her husband read it.

"This is extraordinary," he told her. "John writes: 'Father. Do not accept the letter that Felicity has sent to you this day. I will explain and I will get her to agree to withdraw it. John.'"

They looked at one another.

"We have no choice but to wait and find out," one of them said and the other agreed.

* * * *

AFTER HE HAD THE HOTEL send the telegram, Sir John returned to the Wilsons' suite. His sister had not returned, but his brother-in-law remained, minding the children.

"She must not do this," Sir John said.

"You do not understand. She has crossed her Rubicon. There is no turning back."

"Don't be a fool. I have wired the baron to pay no attention to whatever nonsense she sent him. The stupid cow. And you? Surely you do not countenance this lunacy."

"She would not have done it if we were not in agreement. That is all I will say to you, and I ask you to leave so we can complete our preparation for going wherever it is that we are to go."

Sir John stared at the ungrateful sod for a moment before turning and going to his own suite.

Diana was still there, waiting to learn what was happening. Her husband could only give her vague details. His sister purported to cut off all ties with his family for some reason he did not understand and that she probably did not understand either, likely to do with the artist woman.

"I have sent a telegram to my father. Fel will be alright once I have the chance to speak to her. Of that I can assure you."

59.

Sir John was increasingly unhappy as he sat in the hotel lobby. He planned on being on the way to Mrs. Brown's establishment on Twenty-Seventh Street, which was high up on his London friend's list and in his several visits so far, it, and especially Belle, who purported to be from the American South and who expressed her enjoyment of him with enthusiasm, proved entirely satisfactory. But Belle would likely be there tomorrow, if not later that afternoon so he could delay the trip until he dealt with Felicity.

Edward heard John leave his suite, and when he did, he knocked, and Diana answered. She was shaking and was fighting tears.

"I do not know what is happening," and she neared her brother-in-law so he could wrap his arms around her. He pushed back.

"Felicity asked me to give this to you. I expect her to be back later this morning, and I hope you can speak to her then."

My dearest sister,

> *I cannot tell you how much I regret what I am forced to do. I pray you will understand. I shall always be your dearest friend and sister, and my door, wherever it may be, will always be open to you and to my dear niece and nephews. And I promise that I will in no way seek to limit their contact with their cousins.*

> *Be assured of my continued love for you and your dearest children.*
>
> *F*
>
> *P.S. It might be best if you destroy this after you have read it.*
>
> *F*

When she finished, Diana looked up at Edward. "What does this mean?"

Edward explained and then returned to his suite to await his wife's return.

When Felicity entered the lobby around eleven, Sir John was on her.

"What is the meaning of this?" he said in a voice that echoed through the lobby and garnered the attention of all who were there. He flashed her crumbled note in front of her. She turned and he seemed his usual arrogant self but for the first time she detected fear.

"I have telegraphed Father and told him you will disavow what you said to him in your letter."

The pair stood, and guests and staff passed around them.

In a low voice, Felicity said, "It means exactly what it says. I will not disavow it."

"You will not survive. You are a fool. Your children will be waifs in the street, and I shall not spend a farthing to help them. You are a fool and a stupid cow married to a very stupid little man."

With that Sir John Adams turned and left his sister for the street, there still being a chance that he could have Belle before lunch.

Felicity stood in place. She shook. She dreaded this encounter, and now that it was done, she was relieved.

But also petrified about what she had done. As Edward said, she had crossed the Rubicon.

A member of the hotel staff approached her gingerly.

"Are you alright, ma'am?"

It broke her from her trance.

"Yes, thank you. I must go to my room," and she called for an elevator and was free of the stares in the lobby. She arrived at her suite. Edward and the children were waiting, as was Diana. Diana called to the nurse who accompanied them and asked that the children be kept entertained in one of the bedrooms.

When they were gone, Felicity spoke.

"I spoke to Emily Porter and confessed what I have done. She told me that she has enough room, barely, to accommodate us. We will hire a cab to take us there. I have arranged to have us leave this hotel. I do not know how we shall return to London, but we will address that when we are settled in with Mrs. Porter. She says we can remain there for at least a little time, and we must look for cheaper accommodations so we can leave as soon as possible."

Soon the Wilsons were in a cab and Diana Adams wondered when she would see let alone hug her sister again.

60.

Clara was surprised when Emily and Felicity appeared when she opened the door to her studio after the fear she saw in the Englishwoman at the hotel's restaurant. In the time between the two events, she dwelled on what happened in London when Felicity…vanished.

The Wilsons had moved their things to the Porters, and with the bags still unpacked Felicity insisted that Emily take her to see Clara. She made the commitment and could not put off the meeting. She had asked Emily not to mention her plans to Clara.

During the week, Clara usually spent afternoons at her studio while living in their apartment. Emily said she expected Clara would be there, and she and Felicity walked to Bleecker Street and up to apartment 405. Emily let Felicity knock and Clara opened the door.

She recovered quickly from the shock of seeing the pair standing in front of her and managed to ask them in. As she stepped back into her room, Clara asked if they wanted something to drink. "Tea," Emily said, more to break the tension than anything. While Clara was in her kitchen preparing the tea and putting some biscuits onto a plate, Emily and Felicity explored the art arrayed throughout the studio. Felicity had not seen where Clara worked before, and Clara was not nearly so organized as she was.

She heard good things about what Clara was doing and saw her paintings at the London exhibition with Evans's works. Now after Clara said from the kitchen that the two were free to look at the art to their hearts' content, she was slowly going through what lay in columns on the floor.

They were arrayed haphazardly, landscapes mixed in with portraits. But there was a consistent quality to each, and Felicity was unable to decide which types were more suited to Clara. The landscapes, from the Berkshires and from Riverdale, drew her into nature. But the portraits drew her into the models. Some of the portraits were flat, and Felicity suspected they were initial, rejected stabs at a commission from a member of society.

Those portraits that were repeated, particularly of the ubiquitous Emily, were far more engaging and of far greater interest. Clara knew these people, and her knowledge showed. Emily was familiar with most of the things on the floor and she lacked Felicity's expertise in matters of art, but she always enjoyed quiet moments looking at what Clara did.

Just as Felicity was admiring a relatively large landscape of the Palisades that hung on a wall, Clara said, "I think the more I paint them the more I understand them."

"And the more you understand them, the better you paint them. Like your portraits."

Clara so missed hearing what Felicity had to say about what she did, and she gave word to Clara's own thoughts with her response to Clara's collection.

"Yes," she told her friends. "Let us sit."

The peace did not last though. It was building up for too long, and Clara cut Felicity off when she tried to speak. She could not control it with Kyle Smith, and she could not control it with the far worthier Felicity Adams.

"I will not lie to you. You abandoned me thousands of miles from home, and now you want me to say all is good between us? Is that what you came for? Because if you did, it's your turn to be disappointed."

Emily intervened.

"At least hear her out. You know why she couldn't see you."

"You mean why she abandoned me?"

"Clara. I can only say I am sorry. I had no choice."

"Fine. I accept your apology. Now just abandon me again."

Emily said, "Clara, please—"

Felicity said to Emily. "Do not bother. The bridge is burned. I will go." Turning to Clara, "I can only say I am sorry." And she was gone.

The two other women watched her leave.

"I cannot believe you did that."

"Did what? Did to her what she did to me? Why is she here anyway?"

"You have no right. You sit here in your little world having your father's money to fall back on. You don't know what it's like to be worried about where you will live or when you'll eat."

"And when you ran away from your parents, I gave you a place to stay. I gave you food to eat."

"But I found a job. I worked and worked. What would you be without me? Now Felicity. Felicity had a family. She could not abandon them."

"As she abandoned me?"

"You are an idiot. Thanks to your drawings of me you sent her, she recognized me and approached me. She had to choose. You know that. But she had no choice. Right now, you have a choice. And you choose to throw her out. I did not imagine even the great Clara Nathan could be so damn selfish."

Emily was at the door when Clara said. "Wait. Why is she here?"

"Her brother found out you saw her, however briefly. He's the one you lay with in London, isn't he?"

Clara nodded.

"This 'gentleman' threatened her, but she decided to try to right the wrong she did you. She sent a letter to her father—it's already gone and cannot be stopped—saying she wanted nothing more from him. With her husband and two children—"

"She has two children?

"Yes. Two girls. Very sweet."

"They're here?"

"Yes, with her husband."

"Edward Wilson."

"Yes, Edward Wilson. We saw them at the hotel. And they don't know where they'll live and they don't even know how they'll get home. Because she sent a letter to her father telling him he can keep all his money. Clara. That's what she has done for you. Atonement? Is that not enough for you?"

Clara did not mean to go off as she did and lost control of it. Thank goodness for Emily.

"Tell me what to do, Em."

Emily returned into the studio, and they sat near one another. "You know I cannot tell you. You must decide."

"Where is she?"

"They are shoehorned into our house till they leave or find something more suitable, though they do not likely have money for it. They do not know if they have enough money to get home."

"You cannot understand how much I loved her. She became such a close friend and more the one who showed me the wonders of being able to draw and who told me I could draw. Maybe it was because she was so far away, but I could open my heart to her. Without fear of her criticizing me unfairly. More than that, she was the one I knew would help guide me to become the artist I believe myself capable of becoming. That's why losing her was such a loss. Like with Ashley. Losing her. But different."

"And now. Do you believe you are that artist?"

"I like to think I am but I so much wish that she were there to guide me and to tell me that I was, in the end, or that I am an artist. Worthy of her and worthy of her love."

Clara walked to the window, and Emily remained in her chair as her friend looked out over the yards of the houses to the south. Clara turned, sitting on the window ledge.

"Now tell me what to do." She said it loudly, to reach Emily. "I do not know what to do. Since I came home from that trip to London the wall separating me from her has gotten higher and higher and I don't know whether I can climb over it or tear it down. Emily. Tell me what to do!"

"Again, you know you must do what is in your heart. That is all that any of us can do. She is walking away from an easy life and all because of you and because of the guilt she feels for what she did to you those years ago. She cannot change what she did. She knows that but she can only be your friend and I think she wants to be your friend. If you let her."

With that, Emily rose and caressed Clara across the cheek and placed a light kiss on the forehead.

"She has brought her things, her husband, and the children to my place. You may go to her there. I know she will be happy to see you."

She went to the door and turned.

"I have said this to you many times. You must listen to your heart."

She opened the door and looked back. "I think that is all you can do."

With those words hanging, Emily was gone. And Clara was alone.

61.

Although he understood why his wife did what she did, Ted Porter was not happy about it. After leaving Clara, Emily interrupted him in his office with the news that she offered the Wilsons their house. *Could it be done?* It was a small house, but it could be. For how long was a separate question, and Emily had no answer to it.

What was done was done, and Ted did his best to maintain a supportive face as he left work with her and went to meet their guests. When things were settled, Ted took Edward to a nearby tavern to share some ales and Emily took Felicity for a walk.

"I spoke to Clara after you left."

Felicity tightened her grip on Emily's arm.

"She is understandably upset about what happened between you."

"As am I. She must know that."

"She does. But I do not know if you knew how important you were to her. She's had some bad spots and she, well, felt you abandoned her."

Felicity stopped and turned to, well, Clara's friend.

"She must know I had no choice."

"She knows but that does not change how devastated she was. She did not have many friends here at the time."

They resumed walking.

"Is there anything that can be done about it? I've risked everything for her."

Felicity had no idea where they were walking, but after Emily said, "I don't know. I have told her that," they continued in silence.

Emily tried to calm her when she got home and succeeded to a point, though Felicity did not speak much of it.

"I spoke to her. I think she will be pleased to see you again in time. She is stronger than she sometimes realizes."

After a troubled sleep, Felicity woke early in the unfamiliar surroundings next to Edward. Wide awake and using a candle, she checked in with her girls, who were asleep, and went to the strange kitchen. After turning on the gaslight, she put a kettle on the stove and prepared to make tea.

As she stood, preparing to pour the water into the pot, she heard, "Can you make some for me?"

Emily was leaning against the door, and Felicity nodded and added more tea to the pot before pouring the water in. Neither woman spoke as Emily took down a second cup and saucer and removed some milk from the icebox. After what seemed hours, the tea was steeping, and the two women were at the kitchen's small table. Little was, or could be, said.

"She knows you are here. I think she will come."

After both woman returned to their beds, they each slept, but fitfully.

Both rose only a few hours later. Together they prepared breakfast for their families. Felicity suggested that Edward accompany Ted to his office and stay away until afternoon, saying she hoped for a visitor and Ted did as was suggested, knowing who the visitor was and eager to show the London solicitor how things are done by New York lawyers.

Felicity was right. Shortly after the men left and the children were settled, she saw Clara turn to the brownstone's steps. She rushed to open the door before her lost friend reached it, and Emily watched from the foyer as the two hugged. Clara reached into her bag and removed an envelope, which she handed to Mrs. Wilson.

"I will not take 'no' for an answer. I can afford it, and you cannot. It is my gift to you. And to your family."

In the envelope were first-class tickets for a crossing to take place in one week's time.

"It is far too much," Felicity protested.

Clara looked at her. "Nothing could be too much to allow you, your Mr. Wilson, and your sweet girls to return to their homes, to whatever will be their fate after what you have so heroically done because of me. I can afford it. You cannot. It is my gift to you."

Felicity knew the battle was lost.

Clara added, "There is something that you must do for me."

Felicity was at a loss for what she could do for Clara, but she was ignored as Clara walked into the sitting room with which she was so familiar.

"You must give me the opportunity to paint you properly. That is all I ask for the tickets. I know you will not want to spend too much time here so I will first draw you. If that proves satisfactory, I shall paint you and ship you the result. Is that too much to ask of you?"

With that, Felicity sat in a chair and Clara pulled out her sketch pad and the small purse in which she kept her pencils. Emily and the children came to watch as Clara attacked the paper. She preferred to work at a more leisurely pace, but she did not have that luxury.

An hour, perhaps slightly more, and she had to send Felicity on her way to her children and husband.

She learned brevity with Mr. Evans and quickly boxed Felicity's face and shoulders and methodically placed her nose and eyes and mouth and draped her hair, initially doing it all in black but turning to colors. Before Felicity left the two agreed that Clara had a half-way decent image of her friend and would be able to make it a first-class, proper portrait.

For her part, Emily sat nearby, amused by the intimacy of the interaction she watched and once getting up to make tea for her guests.

In the days that followed, Clara went to her studio in the morning to work on the portrait and spent the afternoon with Felicity and Emily and some combinations of their families. She twice went by trolley with Felicity, carrying supplies in their laps, and they sat for hours among a group of roses bushes not far from a pond in the southern reaches of Central Park.

Joe worked, but he joined the group at the Porters' for dinner each night, and the entire group went to the Park and its Mall on Saturday and then to services (or mass for the Porters) followed by dinner at the Bowmans on Sunday.

For her portrait, it was enough that Clara had the sketch of Felicity. She found it easy to paint the outline of her oval face. Her eyebrows were like an eagle's wings and her nose was long and defined. Clara thought it an aristocratic nose above broad lips and all of it atop a long, soft neck and surrounded by chestnut brown hair that that morning had the manic disarray that was first encountered by that rose bush in Regent's Park.

She was finally satisfied by the eyes. Brown with lugubrious lids and a Puckish dazzle. Clara did not know whether that was how they were years ago or how they were that afternoon when she did the sketch.

Two days before the Wilsons were to leave America, Clara appeared at the Porters and told Felicity that her portrait was "not in such a horrible state as to prevent its model from viewing it." They agreed Emily (pushing Little Emily) and Felicity's girls could accompany them so the group walked the mile or so to Bleecker Street, Felicity's youngest being at times carried by one or another of the women, and climbed up to Clara's studio.

She moved things around to allow the easel to stand out as it would at a formal unveiling uptown except that the easel was turned. The paint was not dry, and Clara could not chance smearing it with a cloth. When the others were in position and promised to keep their eyes shut, Clara slowly rotated the easel till the painting faced them.

"You may look."

There were formal portraits of Felicity in both the Piccadilly and Derbyshire houses, though she did not know for how much longer. She never liked them. She was self-conscious about her looks, but she believed the well-known, well-regarded artists who painted those works failed to capture her as anything but the daughter of a baron and baroness. For the country one, the artist had the temerity to paint a hunting portrait as part of the background though Felicity never took to hunting, much as she loved to ride, spending an inordinate amount of her youth riding and brushing and washing a bay Irish sport horse named Rhapsody. She sat for days for those portraits and shrank each time a visitor commented on how lifelike they were.

Here, in hours, Clara had captured something. A combination of Lady Felicity and Mrs. Edward Wilson. Artist and mother. Aristocrat and commoner. Clara, with paint on her face and hands and smock, new drips joining the countless others on the wooden floor, looked at Felicity. The Englishwoman began her much rehearsed and completely inadequate speech. She stopped after a few, stuttered words.

Clara filled the silence. "I love you Mrs. Wilson. I always will. Now you must let me finish this," and she turned back to her easel and ignored her visitors.

"Feel free to look around," and Felicity regretted that she allowed her own art to lag.

There was little room in the Nathans' apartment so her parents allowed her to maintain her space on Bleecker Street as something of a wedding gift. It was her refuge, though Joe often sat with her on weekends when he was not at work at his father's firm, and it had the same feeling of comfortable intimacy that they both relished from their earliest days together.

Sketch pads were stacked near the door, and there were several places where canvases leaned against each other to a wall. At one, Felicity pulled the top one towards her to look at the next and continued the process for as long as she could. She softly placed them back humming slightly and went to the next group and repeated the process. There was one person, a woman, who kept appearing. It was not Emily.

She had a much smaller nose and reddish hair. That and her pale and round face made it clear that she was Irish, or at least of Irish descent. Her lips were large, as were Felicity's, but they did not smile quite so much in Clara's portraits of her as they did with the older ones of Emily. One painting, smaller than most of the others, showed this woman with a prettier one, also plainly Irish, and a small boy, perhaps two years old. The painting must have been made in some park in New York as the three sat on a bench—the child on the lap of the prettier woman—and the background had tree branches and bushes with the hint of an iron gate.

"Those are dear friends."

Felicity was startled at the interruption. "They were once famous for adopting the boy, who is the nephew of the woman whose lap he is in. Sad case, but the three are so happy now. They are the subjects, the aunt and the boy, of one of my best-regarded works."

"Yes. Now I recognize them. They were at your London show." Felicity did not think before mentioning London, but it created a shared connection and reminded them both of what they lost.

Clara stopped.

"You attended the London show?"

"I so hoped and feared I would see you. Just a glimpse. I cannot say what I would have done had you been there. But you were not there."

"I wonder if it was the afternoon I went to our place in Regent's Park and did, you will not believe it, watercolors of some of your roses. Sadly, they were destroyed in the fire. I hoped to see you among the passersby. But you never appeared."

Clara walked to her English friend and as Emily watched they came together and for the first time since they were reunited, they shared a cry.

After recovering her senses, Felicity resumed her wandering, studying one of the alternate *A Mother and Her Child*s more carefully.

"What do you think?"

Felicity put the group of paintings she had leaned against her leg back and turned.

"I knew you would become an artist," was the only answer she could give. "And I was right."

62.

They attended a final dinner at the Bowmans.
As the men were sequestered, the ladies spoke until Felicity said it was well time for them to leave, and the Bowman's coach took the Wilsons and the Porters to the latter's home. And the next morning, the Porters and the Nathans accompanied the Wilsons to a pier on the Hudson and the latter got aboard a fine ship that would convey them home and to what would be their own new world.

63.

Clara's *An Englishwoman of Some Independence* arrived in London not long after the Wilsons themselves did. It was followed some months later, months in which the trans-Atlantic correspondence between the friends resumed, by a letter from America.

July 16, 1878

My Dear Mrs. Wilson,

 I am sending to you a portrait I have done that I fear will fail to do its subject justice. It is of the most wonderful man in the New World, as I told you when you met him in New York. I cannot do justice to the beauty of his skin or the wonder of his...form. Much as my hands and fingers have closely examined each and every part of him, I am unable to translate what I have discovered of him to canvas though I have endeavored to do so many, many times.

 But you must give me your opinion of my image of him, however imperfect.

 I do hope in time you, too, will love him as he is the husband of someone I presume to describe as a very dear friend of yours.

 Please, my sweetest, tell me what you think. Perhaps I have prejudiced you in describing my work as imperfect. I will prejudice you further to tell you without fear of contradiction that the subject of that work is himself perfect and that I am truly in love with him as I know you are with your own Mr. Wilson.

> With the assurance that you no longer need fear my seeking to abduct your Mr. Edward Wilson and making him my own, I am
>
>> You dearest American friend,
>> (Mrs.) Joseph Nathan

Felicity spent many days wondering where this portrait was, fearing it may have sunk somewhere in the North Atlantic. Until a week later, when a crate appeared at the door of the Wilsons' modest house in Camden Town, a house Edward was pleased to be able to afford on his own earnings, not far from his parents. He was at work, but the delivery men carried it into the sitting room. Felicity found something for leverage to open its top, and carefully lowered it on its side. There was much straw, but she saw that thin wooden slats separated what were three paintings.

She carefully removed the uppermost one. It was a portrait of Felicity's little girls, done, she recognized, from a photograph of the two that went missing from her purse while she was in New York. It was no nursery image, but a full-bore one of a pair of pretty, inquisitive girls, somewhat younger than they currently were but almost prescient in their expressions.

She carried that and leaned it against a wall. The second one came out more easily. It was of her and Edward, looking suspiciously as they did in a second photograph that disappeared in New York. Felicity put it beside the first and was now ready to see Clara's husband. When she removed it, though, it was one of Clara's Riverdale landscapes. Beautiful, yes, but not Joseph Nathan.

Neglecting it on the floor, she ran her hands through the crate and lifted its bottom and with a shake tried to dislodge the missing portrait. But the crate was empty and the portrait was not there. Frustrated, Felicity lifted the third painting, which was unlike the others in being horizontal, and called for the girls to come down.

They went directly to their portrait, and Felicity was quick enough to prevent them from smashing their fingers into it. She said it was painted by one of their lady friends in America and promised it would hang in a place of honor in the house.

She stepped back and looked at the three. Each was brilliant. Clara was very, very good, and Felicity was surprised at how well she did the landscape. She would write her a letter immediately to tell her how pleased she was by the gifts. After the girls went back to their room to play, Felicity went to the secretary in the sitting room and pulled out a piece of stationery and a pen.

28 July 1878

My Dearest American Friend,

I have today received your wonderful paintings and have somehow managed to prevent my dear angels from defacing the one of them. The other two are equally wonder—

She stopped when she heard the bell and went to find who it was. She was not expecting anyone and the mail was already delivered. Standing on her stoop were her Dearest American Friend and that friend's own Mr. Edward Wilson. If she was stunned before, it was nothing compared to this.

"I told you, my dear, that I could not do him justice and I must have your opinion of him, so I brought him to you, and you must be honest and admit that he is the superior of any man you have ever seen who is not named Edward Wilson." Felicity was speechless and could do nothing save watch the two Nathans walk into her foyer, where they were soon joined by the girls thrilled by the American visitors.

While Clara felt a pang of guilt for not giving Felicity forewarning, it was washed away by the explosion in her friend's face when she saw who stood on her stoop. After some effort and not a small passage of time, she collected herself and managed to get tea and biscuits for her guests, who did well in entertaining her daughters.

Clara admitted she was pleased with herself for her little ploy, and that there was a portrait of her husband as well as several other works at their hotel. Clara was invited to participate in an exhibition with several contemporary American artists at the Linley Gallery that would run for a month. She told Felicity that the three in the crate were gifts for her but that she hoped while she and Joe were in town that she could do proper portraits of the four Wilsons.

At the event, four American artists exhibited. A second person, a man, who was among John Evans's class with Clara plus one each from Philadelphia and Boston. The gallery itself was in a Georgian house off Pall Mall and the paintings were in what was once the ballroom on its ground floor. Clara's eight paintings shared a wall with the eight of the person she knew from New York while the others' were on the walls to the left and right.

Clara brought two of her seasonal Riverdale paintings done from the Nathans'—fall and spring—and six portraits. In addition to *A New York Man*—Mr. Joseph Nathan, of course—and *A Lady in Her Garden* and *A Lady in Her House*, there were *Elizabeth Geherty*, *A Mother and Her Child*, and *Emily (Mrs. Porter)*. Lizzie asked about bringing *A Lady in Her House* since it was of her sister, but Clara told her that she wanted it seen because it offered a perspective of Mary McNabb that not even Mary understood and so was proud of it.

It took a day or so for Clara and the others to be satisfied with how their works were hung, but it was in plenty of time for the opening, which was set for the following Thursday.

The first night was formal, and Clara brought only an evening dress that was several seasons out-of-date and required some minor alterations to fit and Felicity's sole evening dress was similarly out-of-fashion for certain parts of town but not for an art exhibition.

The two couples went together. Clara was her usual nervous self until introductions were made, though she declined an offer of alcohol. She stood beside her paintings and smiled appropriately and answered the questions of the visitors.

After an hour or so, the original crowd began to thin and there was freer movement through the gallery. As Clara chatted with the artist from Philadelphia, "It's the whore" shot across the room, and Sir John Adams, clearly drunk, cut through the crowd towards her. Joe was on the other side of Clara's works with Edward and Felicity and all three were slow to react.

Before they could get to Clara, Sir John was upon her.

"I see you have made better use of your hand than you did with your—" but he did not complete the thought, insofar as it even was a thought. Clara's right arm, the instrument of her work, had flung across and struck the unsuspecting baron-in-waiting like a club, and he fell helplessly to the floor, a loud crack echoing around the room that was silenced by his initial shout across it and he sprawled on the floor with an expression of bewilderment.

His two friends stopped their laughing abruptly as they saw Clara's open hand contact Sir John's face, and they rushed to collect him. By then, Joe had pulled Clara away, preventing her from digging her shoes into the drunkard. Felicity stood over her brother, whom she had not seen since New York.

"You are a pathetic embarrassment and," she turned to her brother's fellows, both of whom she recognized from weekends in Derbyshire, "I will thank you to remove this rubbish." They stood on either side of Sir John and dragged him away through the stunned crowd. It was too much, and the foursome soon left to go to the Nathans' hotel where they sat in the Nathans' suite until the Wilsons had to collect their girls from his parents.

* * * *

SHORTLY AFTER EIGHT on the next morning, a Friday, Arthur Adams, Fifth Baron Sheffield was displeased. The source of his displeasure was on the front page of *The Times*, which he read as he was trying to eat his breakfast.

EXCITEMENT AT AN EXHIBITION

An American woman delivered a devastating blow against the British aristocracy last evening at the Linley Gallery off Pall Mall. The woman, an artist from New York named Mrs Joseph Nathan, is among four Americans displaying their oil paintings by special invitation of the Royal Academy.

Some hour and one half after the exhibition opened, Sir John Adams, presumptive Sixth Baron Sheffield, arrived with two friends. He recognized Mrs Nathan from a private encounter the two had some years ago, although they had not seen or communicated with one another since.

Sir John, who witnesses agreed was inebriated, shouted a libelous statement across the room, and then hurried to confront the American. Before he could complete whatever it was that he intended to say, Mrs Nathan's right arm shot up and her open fist made hard and loud contact with Sir John's face.

The contact was sufficient to send Sir John crashing to the floor, and he was saved from further abuse from Mrs Nathan by the quick intervention of her husband, also of New York.

It was left for Sir John's friends, whose identities remain unknown to this correspondent, to remove him from the premises, as he was unable to do so on his own.

Several witnesses observed that a second woman, who is understood to be Sir John's sister, Mrs Edward Wilson, and who has long been estranged from her brother and the rest of her family, including the current Fifth Baron and the Baroness, directed words at the prone man while standing over him.

Mrs Nathan left the exhibition with her husband and Mr and Mrs Wilson shortly after Sir John was removed.

The Times will publish an assessment of Mrs Nathan's works and those of the other Americans in the exhibition in a future edition.

In truth, the baron was not silent as he read. He sprinkled doses of harrumphs along the way and when he was done, he threw the paper on the table. Jones, the butler, rushed to pull back his chair, and after the baron's napkin joined *The Times* on the table, he headed upstairs but not before he turned back and gripped the paper.

The baroness always took her breakfast in her room. She was in bed with a tray beside her when her husband reached it. He knocked and entered without waiting for a reply. She was startled and pulled the sheet up.

"Arthur. What on earth is it?"

He stood beside the bed and held *The Times* out to her.

"Read it."

She quickly found what her husband wished her to read. Her reading was not silent either, punctuated with a series of "oh my!"s and "oh my goodness!"s.

"That boy will make us a laughingstock."

But his wife did not quite hear in light of:

Several witnesses observed that a second woman, who is understood to be Sir John's sister,

A STUDIO ON BLEECKER STREET | 349

Mrs Edward Wilson, and who has long been estranged from her brother and the rest of her family, including the current Fifth Baron and the Baroness, directed words at the prone man while standing over him.

* * * *

"AT LEAST HE CAN'T KEEP the title from you," was the best one of Sir John's friends could offer when he was in the latter's room with a copy of *The Times*. Sir John was dreadfully ill, suffering from the combination of his overindulgence in claret and the pain of having been slapped by a woman with an incredibly quick and powerful arm. His friend's appearance with the paper did not remove his physical discomfort. It merely added a mental torment on top.

He did not know why he did it. He had no idea his sister and her fool of a husband would be there. Instead, he saw "Clara Bowman"—the piece said Mrs. Joseph Nathan had previously exhibited her works in London when she was "Miss Clara Bowman"—in an article several days earlier about the exhibition, and the more he thought of it the angrier he was at the bitch. She was not even that good, he misremembered, and then he was the idiot who mentioned it when he was drunk to his father and that set off the chain of events that led to his sister disowning her own family and she no longer served as protection for when he overdid things.

In his mind, he blamed Mrs. Joseph Nathan (née Miss Clara Bowman) for destroying what was an easy existence. With the courage he got from the bottles he and his mates shared at their club in Piccadilly, he insisted on attending the opening and then, well, he could not remember what he did. Now his friend reminded him, confirming the accuracy of *The Times*'s story, with the clarification that he shouted "whore" across the room when he started towards her.

That that word would get to a correspondent for *The Times* was not considered. Nor was his sister's presence.

As he sobered up, Sir John knew he had to come up with some way to assuage the anger his father would have when he read the story. His mother he could charm and get to support him with the baron. He feared that he might have gone too far this time. The observation that he was still safe in the title provided some solace and would serve him well in the surely unlikely event that his father cut him off.

64.

The canvas was large, and the painting was done horizontally. It was not a portrait of the kind for which Clara was known. Instead, it was from across a bedroom. The bed was large and though it was clear that two people had been in it, only one remained. A woman. She slept, and a sheet covered the lower portion of her naked body. She was on her right side with her head to the left. Her right hand was beneath her head, her brown, even black, hair dangling over the frame. Her left arm crossed her stomach, beneath her breasts.

The breasts themselves—a mother's teats—were exposed and sagged slightly down, the aureoles slightly darker than the pale skin surrounding them. A lady's skin. To the left was a table on which there were two wine glasses, one half full, the other half empty, and an empty bottle lay on its side against one leg of the table.

The sheets themselves were scattered except insofar as she pulled one partially over herself, and a blanket lay in a pile, part of it visible over the frame at the bed's foot. Atop that was a collapsed day dress in a steamy maroon and bits of a woman's undergarments.

The eyes of the lover—it was clear she lay in post-coital bliss—were closed but her mouth was slightly open and could even be said to be smiling. The viewer embarrassingly was forced to consider what she was dreaming and whether it was of the one who was no longer with her.

The room was dark as if it were a cloudy late afternoon, but light enough came through the slot in the curtains to place parts of the boudoir in a haze. A vague image of a formal portrait of a man and a woman was barely visible in the upper left portion of the canvas against a light blue wall.

The woman's identity was unclear and it was possible, even likely, that were she recognized she would be banished from society. But it was clear that the model was not Felicity Wilson. Still, when it was done, Felicity and Clara agreed that wonderful as the work was, it was best not displayed in London for there were surely some who would recognize Diana Adams.

Her husband, Sir John, was convinced that Diana was having an affair in retaliation for the publicity he managed to obtain from the incident with Clara (and Felicity). In fact, each afternoon she was away from her house "visiting" was spent in Felicity's bedroom modeling for Clara. It was at Diana's insistence. Clara intended to paint Felicity, and the two were planning the details when Diana banged on Mrs. Wilson's door a few days after *The Times* piece.

In all of what happened, Felicity felt the worst for Diana. She, Diana, had gone to the exhibit the morning she later appeared at her sister-in-law's, though Clara did not recognize her. Diana wanted to see what all the bother was about. She saw the artist sitting off to one side with a pad in her lap, smiling and answering questions and nodding at compliments she received. She seemed a rather plain, thin woman who paled in comparison to the beauty of her portraits, especially of Elizabeth and Róisín.

Why was her husband so horrible to this American? She remembered that she was the one he mocked in New York. She wished to speak to Felicity about it, and so after a light lunch to help her get calm, Diana knocked on the Wilsons' door, having no idea that Clara would be in the sitting room preparing to paint Felicity, and Clara and Diana were taken aback when they set eyes on each other not three hours later.

It was Felicity's idea to have Diana model instead. "Sweet revenge," she called it. They arranged the bedroom. Diana was at first hesitant and insisted on wearing a nightgown while Clara painted her in the bed, sleeping like a cherub. Clara felt guilty about it, but she knew such a painting would be a failure. Her goal was to paint a woman in the flush of being satisfied by a lover and several days after beginning, she decided to break her rule and allowed Diana to see the progress of the work.

Clara began with the bed and the bedclothes. She allowed Diana to look at the work at the end of each session. Diana enjoyed art, but never before saw the process, and it fascinated her. She was in the bed with the sheets over her. Clara showed how even concealed one could appreciate the curves of a woman's lower body, the sensuousness of the hips flaring down to the feet.

While they stood side by side looking, Clara remained silent, almost feeling Diana's emotions. Finally, the Englishwoman asked whether Clara thought she could perhaps be…more exposed. A scarf, perhaps, draped across her breasts.

"Otherwise, it might as well be a woman sleeping after a tiring morning at Harrod's."

"I think…Yes, I think that might prove better. Thank you, Diana. We will see tomorrow."

The next afternoon, Clara asked that Felicity absent herself, fearing Diana might lose her nerve with her friend in the room, so Felicity herself went to Harrod's. Clara placed a screen in the corner so Diana could disrobe and when she came from behind it, wearing undergarments from her waist down, her arms covered her breasts. Clara simply asked her to resume her pose in the bed. When there, she pulled the sheet down to just below Diana's navel.

Diana, having come so far, lay looking at Clara. Feeling the artist's intimate gaze, she moved her arms to expose herself, displaying a smile her husband would never have recognized on her lips and in her eyes and inviting Mrs. Nathan to reveal her.

Before this session, Clara avoided painting the sheet that would cover Diana's torso because she hoped she would be allowed to paint it without the sheet and when she was given permission to do that, she quickly framed the woman.

At the end of the session, Diana, now in a robe, stood beside Clara. She caught her breath after a moment, and Clara clasped her hand but said nothing.

65.

Joe had to return to New York after being in London for a week, so after seeing him off at the train for Southampton, Clara moved her things from the hotel to the Wilsons'. It was far less luxurious, of course, but she much preferred being with her friend and the two girls, plus Edward in the evenings. Between sessions with Diana, she did drawings of each of the girls and she and Felicity carried their things to Regent's Park and the rose bushes where they met. While the girls played nearby, they did their watercolors.

Felicity had, since becoming Mrs. Wilson, too long delayed her return to her art and particularly to her watercolors, and Clara had to admit that Felicity was still far the superior with that medium. Yet how far she herself had come since the first stroke in this very spot.

Clara did not neglect the exhibition. The four American artists were present each morning to answer questions and entertain visitors, including some very prominent continental and English artists. Diana returned several times, once with Penelope, and they all enjoyed their time together.

Shortly after Joe returned to New York, a Tuesday when Clara was alone, an older woman interrupted Clara as she sat to the side, detailing a sketch of one of Felicity's girls.

"May I?" the woman asked, and Clara turned the drawing to her.

As she studied it, the older woman said, "She is such an angel."

Clara looked from the woman to the sketch and back.

"Do you know her?"

The elegant woman took a final look and then turned to the artist. "You will not know me, Mrs. Nathan, but she is my granddaughter." She was not Mrs. Wilson.

"Baroness?"

"Sometimes I am embarrassed to admit the fact, but it is true."

Clara stood and not knowing what the protocol was she half- and awkwardly curtsied and extended her free hand, which the baroness took.

"I am sorry that my family has been such trouble to you."

"Some trouble, yes, but more joy."

The two were interrupted, and the baroness asked if she might speak to Clara over lunch. Though Clara was expected for lunch at the Wilsons, she sent a note saying she had an unexpected commitment. Diana would be arriving at around two to pose, but she should be there well in time for that.

At Felicity's house shortly after the hour struck, Clara kept quiet until Diana arrived. Having crossed the line about Diana's nudity, with Diana being more confirmed in her decision each day, Felicity usually was in the house while Clara did her work. But that afternoon, Clara asked Diana and Felicity to remain in the sitting room. She explained her encounter with Felicity's mother (Diana's mother-in-law). How Clara, as the innocent (the baroness now recognized) instrument of the fissure between the baron and his daughter, might serve as a means of getting at least the baroness back in her daughter's world. Especially when she saw Clara working on her drawing of Katherine Wilson, who she had not seen properly since the Wilsons (and Sir John and Diana) took their foolish trip to New York and Felicity (understandably) severed all ties.

As it happened, while Clara spoke, Felicity's girls rushed into the sitting room to greet their aunts—Clara had long since been accorded that status—just as they were being discussed but they were soon bored by the adults and fled back up the stairs.

"What does she want?" Felicity said when she heard the girls' bedroom door slam.

Clara rubbed her right hand along her friend's left wrist. "She wants to see you and the girls. What is to happen with your father she cannot say. She fears that he might flee to Derbyshire soon considering the publicity surrounding Sir John's misadventure. She wanted to contact me to contact you before that happens. That is what she wants."

"I don't think it can hurt," Diana said.

Felicity turned on her.

"Hurt? You don't recall, dear sister, what I was forced to go through. First when I was not allowed to communicate with my friend here." She nodded towards Clara. "And then cut off in America, not knowing whether I or my family could get home, which I was only able to do thanks to the kindness and generosity of my friend here.

"My mother could have done something. For God's sakes, Diana, *you* could have done something. But you didn't. And she didn't. Suddenly John makes a fool of himself and the family is rushing to me with open arms. Hoping to make amends. Hoping I can forgive them. That I can forgive excluding my children from their lives. Fearful that something would happen to Edward and I would be left totally on my own and penniless."

At some point she stood, and her anger was somehow increasing with each word.

"Hurt, you say?"

"But why did you not let me come back to you?" This was Diana. "You could have tried to contact me without John knowing."

"And you could have done the same with me. But you didn't."

"I was just your sister-in-law."

This last statement by Diana silenced the room. Felicity went from angry to livid.

"You *were* part of my family. I welcomed you to my family. If you think you were just my 'sister-in-law,' get out and get out now." Felicity was gone from the room before either of the others could react, and they heard her rush up the stairs and then the door to her bedroom slam.

"She's right, you know," Diana was finally able to get it out. "Even when we were in New York and she left a note for me promising we would not be estranged, I could have done more. But what would I be without John? He would take the children if I crossed him in the slightest. I could not afford that. Especially against the baron's displeasure."

Clara squatted beside Diana's chair and placed an arm around her shoulders.

"She knows that. I will speak to her. But I think we cannot do anything today. None of us is capable."

Diana went home, to the house where she kept as far from her husband as was possible when he was there. She knew the incident at the exhibition would not blow over.

Clara went for a walk, taking her pad and heading up Primrose Hill to sketch the city.

When Felicity heard the others go, she went to the sitting room and thought.

After an hour, she herself went for a walk. She did not know where she would go and at times did not know where she was going but found herself near Piccadilly and near her brother's house. She stood down the block so she could not be seen from the Georgian mansion. After some time, Diana stepped on the sidewalk. She turned towards where Felicity stood. After some steps, and when she was nearly clear of the house, she recognized her sister. She quickly closed the distance and reached her arms out. They held each other tightly before separating.

"You needn't have worried," Diana told her. "John is doing penance down in Derbyshire. How the business with the baron is resolved is anyone's guess. I was coming to ask for your forgiveness."

For the first time in years, Felicity entered her brother's house and was able to see his children without fear of being assaulted. Felicity understood that Diana had done what she did to protect her family, a crime of which she, too, was guilty. She could not not forgive her sister.

The two women and the three Adams children then jumped on a trolley—the children so loved the trolley—to get to the Wilsons. Clara was not yet back, but came through to bedlam some forty minutes later, being introduced to and bowed to by the young Adamses while Felicity, the only one among them who knew anything about cooking, made dinner.

Edward arrived home in time to eat with everyone in the cramped dining room but after they ate and the children were finally exhausted and newly collapsed hither and yon and Edward retired to his study, the three women spoke. From Diana, they knew that the baroness had not accompanied her husband up north where he was having it out with his heir, and after some debate, they agreed to speak to the baroness.

* * * *

CLARA WAS NOT EXPECTING the family discord to explode on her trip and that she would be central to it. She was pleased when Felicity told her she made up with Diana and that the work could resume the next day. She agreed when Felicity said she and Diana were determined to see their mother. She was excited when they reported having done so and thus not surprised when the baroness was at the Wilsons to see her grandchildren—*all* her grandchildren, because Diana brought Penelope and the two boys over too.

But more, she was pleased to be able to get on with *A Woman in Her Bed*. It was completed several days later and shown to a select few before being crated up and included with her other paintings that returned to New York. Two of them were sold and another two were bought for the gallery's permanent collection.

Much as she enjoyed her stay, Clara was relieved to be heading home. To her Joe. There was a final dinner with the artists whose works were exhibited in the great hall in the back of the gallery the night before they and most of their works were packed off for America.

In the morning, Felicity, Diana, the baroness, and the baroness's three granddaughters saw Clara off at the Waterloo Bridge Station on the south bank of the Thames. The three adults saw *A Woman in Her Bed*, and Diana was proud of it and her courage in sitting—or lying—for it. Neither Felicity nor the baroness was the least bit scandalized by the nude form of the mother-of-three, and they were proud of Diana, too. Clara agreed that she would not display it in New York without Diana's permission, but Diana had come far and understood how alive she was made by Clara so the artist knew permission would be forthcoming. For the time, though, she agreed to limit its viewing to those who in Clara's opinion would appreciate it.

As they exchanged final goodbyes on the train platform, Felicity was the last to hug her dearest American friend. She pulled away, but her hand ran across Clara's belly before she was completely away, and Clara was glad her secret was out.

66.

October 14, 1878

Dear Baroness Never to Be,

I must first tell you that the Woman is the toast of New York. No one I think knows she is you, but I assure you that many, many—men and women—<u>wish</u> to know her.

It was the star of my recent exhibition, far more attractive than the icicle-laden (and appropriately titled) Blizzard of some dreary landscape over the Hudson River.

I will quote from one critic: "One wonders when, or if, the lover will return, but to the 'Woman' it does not matter as she is clearly in the glow of what it is like to be satiated. Her nipples it is clear have been suckled on many times, but this has not diminished her capacity for the physical connection to another. She will soon rise and perhaps finish her glass of claret before doing her toilet and dressing for the evening, knowing that she will carry the afternoon's passion with her as she dines and dances and makes small talk with the Dukes and Duchesses who have long since forgotten what it is to be alive."

Yes, she is <u>you</u>, and I promise you that she is the you I saw those many days in dear Mrs. Wilson's bedroom. I am told that you and your dear children are free of the daily burden of someone we have both known. I hope that you find it in you to find the fulfillment that I saw in you.

> With all my love,
> Your Dear American Friend,
> ~~(Mrs.) Joseph Nathan~~ Clara

And *A Woman in Her Bed* proved spectacularly popular, enough to lead to some picketing outside the gallery and murmurings about a violation of the Comstock Act in many a conservative home.

To Clara, the painting was unique. She did not fancy becoming a boudoir artist, popular as some European masters were in doing such work. She connected with Diana. It was only the intimacy that the two felt for one another before her first brushstroke and, more, in that moment when Diana smiled and opened herself and her body to the woman who was painting her that allowed Clara to portray her as she did, and with the model's involvement in the work each day she sat—or more accurately lay down—for Clara.

Clara's regular correspondence with Felicity continued, which is how Clara learned of the separation between Diana and Sir John and that Diana and her children, particularly Penelope, were taken care of. Sir John's "incident" with Clara at the exhibition and, more, the attention it received starting with the damn correspondent from *The Times* was a final insult to the baron. He realized the hypocrisy in shaming "that American woman" who had lain with his son, a woman unattached while his son was engaged, blinded to the need for his heir to have an heir lest the title go to who-knew-who.

The baron recognized his error and the error in forcing his own wife to abide by his terms as she dutifully did with the disownment. His insistence that Felicity end all contact with the American seemed to work for a time. He did not realize how it ate away at his daughter and how he risked losing her even after she showed her independence by marrying the decidedly middle-class Edward Wilson. He agreed finally to the match but gave her a settlement that was a fraction of what she would have received had she married a proper gentleman, one who, he should have known, would not be unlike his rake of a son.

He thought keeping his purse strings tight would secure Felicity to him. He was an idiot. He was not old, but he felt like a doddering fool, a Lear choosing poorly in how he divvied up his wealth and affections.

But, Felicity said in one of her letters to Clara, he showed signs of true remorse after a tongue lashing from (and she suspected a boycott by) the baroness.

Of course, the Wilsons would not move closer to Piccadilly. They took none of the baron's money except as he created a trust for his two granddaughters, although he did extract a promise from their mother that they would begin to ride the moment they saw their ponies—the baron would, of course, spoil each girl with a pony—but only after their mother extracted a promise from him that they would not be relegated to riding sidesaddle. Felicity said that even her dearest Mr. Wilson said he was willing to give riding a try.

Clara was pleased with the news from her friend in England.

And Sir John was exiled in comfort at the house in Derbyshire. Forced to be content with such game as could be found on its grounds.

Clara was more pleased by additional news. Not long after she was back in New York invitations began to appear for loans of her works for exhibitions on the continent as well as in Britain and even Ireland. The latter was particularly interesting since it asked that if the artist herself could not make the trip her *A Mother and Her Child* be sent to Dublin as even the fiercely-Protestant *Irish Times* could not refrain from praising a portrait of two Irish Catholics—Róisín and Diarmaid Campbell—in America.

Clara, though, was incapable of going anywhere. She was well along with her own child and could go to her studio daily, but travel farther afield was out of the question. She kept the studio in room 405, but little used its other rooms. She was content enough to travel up to the Nathans' house in Riverdale, where Joe converted an unused bedroom into a small studio and his mother had another converted into a nursery, though she did most of her indoor work in the southern wing and her outdoor work near her oak tree.

Clara declined offers of commissions for the time being. Instead, she revisited her friends and completed one of Elizabeth Geherty and Róisín Campbell without Diarmaid that she felt was among her best work. It was horizontal and large, with the same dimensions as Diana's portrait. It took some time to complete, because of the women's duties at the clinic, but they sat for her each Sunday afternoon on Bleecker Street. Diarmaid spent these Sunday afternoons with his benefactors, the Meades (who were his grandparents but never acknowledged the fact to the world). The two nurses posed on either end of a love seat in day dresses, each holding a favorite book—*Persuasion* for Elizabeth and *The Wild Irish Girl* for Róisín—in her outer hand while the tips of the fingers on their inner hands touched and what their legs and feet were doing was concealed by the melding of their dresses.

As she had with Diana, she allowed them to see the progress of the work each day. Several toys littered the floor behind Róisín, and a haphazard of books was stacked behind Elizabeth. The background was obscure in the maroon that Clara long favored, and it stood in sharp contrast to the blue and yellow dresses her friends wore. Their eyes were directed at pages of their books, but one doubted whether they were actually reading any of the words and wondered how long it had been since either of them turned a page and for how long only their fingertips would be touching.

Initially *Friends at Ease* was included in Evans's growing collection on Washington Square but some months later it and the others of Clara's that he had, most notably *A Mother and Her Child* and *A Woman in Her Bed*, were purchased by the Museum of American Art which prepared a large space on upper Madison Avenue for several permanent exhibits. Evans and George Bowman were board members and benefactors for the museum, although they abstained from any decisions made about Mrs. Nathan's works.

For Emily, who had the leisure to visit during the day, Clara finally was permitted to paint her nude, as if she had only recently risen from a bath. Her hair was wet and stringy and clung to her head. Her eyes were drowsy, looking down, perhaps for a towel, as a result of which one saw a slightly irregular part in her hair. Her skin was flush and translucent. A clear trail of a drop of water went from her neck and down to her right nipple, from which it was about to drop.

A window was behind her, but steam covered it, and one could just make out drips moving slowly down the white tiles. Indeed, the background was very white, which allowed the pale flesh tones of Emily and her slightly reddened nipple to jump out with the draping of her dark, wet hair and dark eyebrows and soft lips. Unlike the Diana painting, this was intended for an intimate wall in the Porters' house.

67.

May 12, 1879

My Dear (Aunt) Felicity,

It is with great pleasure that I announce to you that you are, for all intents and purposes, an aunt yet again. Your new niece is named Muriel Emily Felicity Nathan and she is fat and soft and the most beautiful creature ever created.

Please let me know when I might send her to you so that she might learn decorum as only an Englishwoman can teach decorum as this will never happen in the wilds of New York City.

My dearest Joseph is more excited than he was when he met me, but I cannot chide him as I am infinitely more excited than I was when I met him. Or you for that matter.

We shall have photographs taken as soon as we can and will send them to you, but for now, all you need do is paint the most beautiful girl you can imagine although even your exceptional gifts will, I fear, fail to do justice to my angel.

Please give my love to everyone, even the Baron—or perhaps especially the Baron—and I forgive you in advance for the jealously you are surely feeling as you read this letter.

> I am,
> The happy mother
> of your newest niece
> And shall always be,
> Your Devoted Clara

THE END

About the Author

Joseph P. Garland is a native New Yorker. He is a practicing lawyer, and lives in Westchester County, New York.

Also by Joseph P. Garland

Róisín Campbell: An Irishwoman in New York (2020) (literary fiction).

I Am Alex Locus (2022) (contemporary story of a daughter's search for the secrets in her parents' life; sent in New York and the New York suburbs)

Coming to Terms (2021) (contemporary romance of two generations of several families)

Bridget & Joseph in 1918 (2021) (a short imagined romance between the author's paternal grandparents, using bits of information obtained in geological research)

Acknowledgments

Thanks to the many who read my manuscript at various points along the way and who made constructive comments, nearly all of which are reflected in the final product, for which I alone am responsible.

My sisters Patty Garland, Clio Garland, and Liz Sauer, my brother Jimmy Garland, and my cousin Donna Vaters provided useful insights. Editor Cassandra Filice (@CassandraFilice) again took a look and provided incredibly valuable feedback. From Twitter, I obtained a regular dose of photographs of clothing from the period from incomparable @WikiVictorian (Helena DiGiusti) of Andalusia. Others who provided insights are Renée Gendron (@RenneeGendon) and Abigail Silver @SilverAbby84) (as well as others on the #LineByLineTime Twitter thread created by George Beckman (@graestonewriter)). Zunaida Moosa-Wadiwala (@zunaidamw) (a South African lawyer and Austen fan who occasionally paints) gave me suggestions as to watercolors.

Some background about the post-Civil War growth in painting by men and women, especially those in the middle class, came from *Painting Professionals* by Kirsten Swinth (Chapel Hill 2001).

An early draft had Clara and Mrs. Bowman planning on a month in London and a month in Paris, with them deciding to stay in London and cancel Paris. My friend—and best man—Gillis Heller pointed out that conditions on the ground in Paris at that time—1872—were very dicey and it was unlikely that such a trip would be done. I thus did not include Paris on their itinerary and elsewhere made note of the possibility that Americans might skip a stop there.

The references to Clara's pain after the initial attack came from my own experience with a shattered arm, albeit one broken in a running fall. My ortho Peter Rizzo, M.D., gave me helpful suggestions on the treatment of an injury back in the 1870s.

The Dermody House logo (named for one of my grandmothers) was produced by my sister-in-law, Beth Lin Garland

And, of course, I could not do this without the constant support of my wife, Bernice Garland.

Sources

I used many sources for the historic information in this novel, though I am responsible for the accuracy of what is included and do not purport to have a comprehensive understanding of these events.

Manufactured by Amazon.ca
Bolton, ON